CHRISTINA CHIU

12.5 Figure

Front Part

Beauty

Waist Line

12.5 Divided by 1
1/2 inch

Knee Line

Leg Line

2040 BOOKS

an imprint of

Ankle

Advance Praise for *Beauty*

"With sly wit and a sure hand Chiu embroiders the life of a female fashion designer whose sexuality, ambition and creative vision make the traditional roles of perfect daughter, wife, and mother, let's say, a challenging fit. Unapologetically honest and compulsively readable."

—Elissa Schappell, author of *Blueprint for Building Better Girls*, Co-founder of *Tin House*, and Contributing Editor at *Vanity Fair*

"*Beauty* immediately caught me with its propulsive force and kept me mesmerized with its lyrical writing, insight and humor as we watch the sweep of a woman's life, from young to old, through loves, lies, children, marriages, artistic promise and failure, and the changing meaning of "beauty." I couldn't put this book down, and I was so sad when such a richly described world came to an end."

—Marie Myung-Ok Lee, author of *The Evening Hero*

"In Amy Wong, the protagonist of *Beauty*, Chiu has created a rapier-sharp heroine who marches into all her messes and triumphs with a wit and bravado that is as seductive as it is astonishing. A fast-paced, sexy novel about growing up, making mistakes and learning from them, written in a defiant, witty prose that is utterly mesmerizing."

—Helen Benedict, author of *Wolf Season* and *Sand Queen*

"*Beauty* is a moving story of one woman's journey through loss, trauma, and disappointment to self-acceptance and healing. Chiu renders her protagonist, Amy Wong, with clear-eyed compassion, pulling no punches, and the reader falls in love. We cheer for Amy's successes and mourn for her losses and want to scream in frustration as she makes the wrong choice again...and again. This is an entirely absorbing, emotional novel, a deeply rewarding read."

—Cari Luna, author of *The Revolution of Every Day*

"Amy Wong, the protagonist of Chiu's captivating debut novel *Beauty*, is an undercover powerhouse. She's a person whose strength is hidden even from herself. As she navigates a life in the fashion industry, Amy struggles with expectations—expectations heaped on her by family, a string of bad-news men, and a world skewed by sexism and racism—and so, when the novel begins, Amy believes her only power is in her beauty, defined by others. But her journey is toward something deeper and more true—"Delicate. Resilient."—and we're rooting for her all the way."

—David Ebenbach, author of the novel *Miss Portland*

"As a young woman and a child of immigrants, Amy Wong discovers that she will do anything to have and to create exquisite things. But after she falls in love with the celebrated and demanding fashion mogul Jeff Jones, marriage and motherhood threaten to snuff out her radiant gifts as a designer. Only Amy's courage—her brave loyalty to her children, to her talent, and to the ex-husband who has become her dearest friend—leads her to enlightenment and back onto the path she'd pursued all along. In this mesmerizing and unflinching novel, Chiu offers a series of brilliantly curated moments, vivid examinations of the turning points in an extraordinary woman's life. Chiu fearlessly illuminates how love, integrity, and creativity can shape a world and bring wisdom."

—Lan Samantha Chang, author of *Hunger* and *Inheritance*

"I can't think of novel more unflinching in its portrayal of lust, love, and parenthood. Chiu has a unique gift as a storyteller for unflinching honesty, and the ability to see the transcendent in the details. *Beauty* is a novel of one woman's life, epic in emotional proportion. I was captured by *Beauty* and gleefully held there through to the last page."

—Mat Johnson, author of *Loving Day* and *Pym*

Praise for *Troublemaker and Other Saints*

"These are accomplished stories, with the mark of a true storyteller."

—Elizabeth Strout, Pulitzer Prize-winning author of *Olive Kitteridge*

"In sharp, witty, heartbreaking prose, Chiu communicates the Asian-American experience as adeptly and freshly as Sherman Alexie describes the Native American experience, or Junot Díaz defines Latino life in the U.S."

—*Publishers Weekly*

"A truly auspicious fiction debut."

—*Vanity Fair*

"Honest, complex...deeply satisfying."

—*Entertainment Weekly*

"Literary debuts don't come much nervier. [It] explores the generational, cultural and sexual divides with humor and compassion."

—*The Washington Post Book World*

"*Troublemaker and Other Saints* is full of intriguing situations and great conversations. In describing how Chinese immigrants deal with their American kids, Chiu reveals all our misunderstandings and hopes. I loved every page and would read anything this woman writes!"

—Alice Elliott Dark, author of *In the Gloaming*

Library of Congress Cataloging-in-Publication Data

Names: Chiu, Christina, 1969- author.
Title: Beauty / Christina Chiu.
Description: Santa Fe : Santa Fe Writers Project, 2020. | Summary: "Amy
    Wong is an up-and-coming designer in the New York fashion industry—
    she is young, beautiful, and has it all. But she finds herself at odds with
    rival designers in a world rife with chauvinism and prejudice. In her
    personal life, she struggles with marriage and motherhood, finding
    that her choices often fall short of her traditional family's expectations.
    Derailed again and again, Amy must confront her own limitations
    to succeed as the designer and person she wants to be"—
    Provided by publisher.
Identifiers: LCCN 2019022787 (print) | LCCN 2019022788 (ebook) | ISBN
    9781733777759 (trade paperback) | ISBN 9781733777766 (kindle edition)
Classification: LCC PS3603.H5743 B43 2020 (print) | LCC PS3603.H5743
    (ebook) | DDC 813/.6—dc23
LC record available at https://lccn.loc.gov/2019022787
LC ebook record available at https://lccn.loc.gov/2019022788

Published by 2040 Books, an imprint of the Santa Fe Writers Project
369 Montezuma Ave #350
Santa Fe, NM 87501
www.sfwp.com

Find the author at www.christinachiu.org

Contents

Wild Hen

"Let me give you some advice," the woman says, in Chinese.

"He's not aware you're calling, is he?" Ma says.

Phew—it's one of Ma's friends. Not Cosine Cozza calling to say I've got a C going into the Algebra II final tomorrow. Good old Georgie, my older sister, always gets straight A's, even now in medical school. Ma's on the kitchen phone. I'm in her room directly above, about to hang up, when the woman says, "Lao Tai." Oh my god. She's calling Ma "old lady".

I clamp a hand over the receiver.

"There's no need to get upset," the woman says. "We're good friends, you and I."

Ma hmphs.

"One should recognize when it's time to let things go," the woman says.

"I'm sure he won't be too pleased when he finds out," Ma replies, her voice cooler than an ice pick.

"He's given you the best years of his life," the woman continues. "He's old now. He deserves a few years of happiness."

"You Mainland girls sure are bold," Ma says.

"Old lady, why don't you do us all a favor and release him?"

"My, my, it's come to this, has it?" Ma laughs, an ugly bite in her voice. "A wild hen thinks she's taken over the coop."

My jaw drops. I've never heard Ma use that term before.

"You old, useless—"

"I tell you what," Ma says, cutting her off. "You want him so badly, go ahead, take him. Tell him I give you my permission." Ma hangs up. She doesn't even bang down the receiver.

The woman, on the other hand, curses and slams down the phone.

Shit, Ma kicked her *ass*.

Then Ma's headed upstairs. Her slippers clap over the hallway floorboards, then go silent as she climbs the carpeted steps. I race back to my room. My bed is covered with tests and quizzes. I hop into the eye at the center, switch off the TV, then hide the channel changer beneath the pillows behind me.

Ma bangs into my room. She's about to yell, but she sees me studying, and her voice catches. Her head cocks to the side. It's like she's listening to the air. She sweeps her hand over the TV. Static dances across the screen; it must be warm.

"I'm studying," I say, panicking.

She comes at me, whacks me across the face, my hair catching in her ring. Plick-plick-plick!

"Ow!" My eyes smart from the sting. I hold my cheek with one hand, rub my head with the other. "I was taking a break."

"You want a break, I'll give you a break," she says. Uneven strands of hair—my hair—stick out from the diamond. Hatred rings in my ears. I hate her.

"Where's Daddy?" I say. "I want Daddy."

Ma startles. She stumbles back, retreats from my room to hers, and shuts herself inside.

It's quiet. Too quiet.

He deserves a few years of happiness.

On the end table by my bed, there's a photo from the day I turned five. I'm sitting on Dad's lap, blowing out cake candles. Georgie's on one side of us, Ma's on the other. We're all smiling. Or at least I thought we were. When I look more closely at Dad's face, I wonder if he's grimacing instead. Is he really that miserable? I want to call him to ask if all of this is true. It can't be.

Dad has an interior design company. He goes to Hong Kong, sometimes for months at a time, and has an office there. He needs to.

Doesn't he?

I climb out of bed. The hallway has a hint of cigarette smoke. Officially, Ma quit a couple years ago, but since she never smokes in front of me, we pretend it doesn't happen. I knock. When Ma doesn't answer, I peek inside. The blinds are down. She's in bed, chain smoking Marlborough Lights, the ashtray overflowing with ash and crushed filters.

I open my mouth to apologize, but what comes out instead is: "What's for dinner?" I'm not even hungry.

Ma drags on a cigarette. The tip glows a fiery red.

I flick on the light.

"Ay!" Ma squints her red, swollen eyes. On her lap is the latest issue of *Y*, the pages warped and hardened from dried tears.

Ma blinks, seeming to notice the magazine as if she hadn't felt it there all this time. "Wah," she sniffles, tracing the object. "Now, that's beautiful."

"What?" It's an advertisement. The famous, hooked Cs embossed into leather. "Chanel," I say.

"What you see, Mei Mei, mh?"

"A purse."

Ma jerks like she got stuck by a needle. "*Handbag*, Mei Mei. How many times I have to say? Don't be such xiang wu nging." A peasant.

"Okay, okay." I describe the purse—black, quilted, rectangular-shaped.

"And?"

"I guess it's big?"

"Bigger than the typical Chanel," Ma nods. "And?"

"There's a zipper across the side."

"Yes, changing from the original look. But see the whole picture, Meme. It's not just a bag."

"There's a woman. She's got an undo. A crown. Bangs. She's like that actress from that movie—"

"Yes, breakfast at Tiffany's," Ma says.

"Yeah, what's her name again?"

"Audrey Hepburn." She scoots off the bed and digs through her DVDs until she finds the one she wants. She tosses it to me. "Look."

With the movie cover juxtaposed beside the advertisement, I see what Ma's getting at. "They're sort of alike, but different," I say.

"More modern version," Ma says, getting into bed, again. "In the movie, she wears those sunglasses, too. Sooo elegant. Sooo beautiful, mh?"

Audrey Hepburn. Her eyes. The black liner and extended lashes. The shaped, drawn-in brows. The rest of the makeup palate's neutral. "She looks like you."

Ma smiles, acknowledging the compliment.

"I'm going to be beautiful one day, too," I say.

"Ai." There's a sadness I've never seen in her before. "What's beauty, uh? Doesn't last."

"Yeah, it does." She's just trying to put me down for not being smart like Georgie.

"Getting old," Ma sighs.

Lao Tai.

"You know, when we first came here, we had nothing," Ma says. "We worked and worked. You know I was your Daddy's secretary."

"No way, you can type?"

"Way-la," she says. "I teach myself, can you imagine?"

"Actually, no. Not really."

"Back then we used typewriters. You had to punch so hard. Bang, bang, like that. So bad for your nails." She pulls on the cigarette, drawing in a long, deep breath.

"I got a C in math," I admit.

"I know." Ma crushes the butt in the ashtray. "You think I don't know? I know everything. There's nothing I don't know."

I start laughing. But then it hits me she's talking about Dad. I get a pain like I swallowed a cough drop.

Ma taps at the Chanel advertisement. "I'm not show off like your father, but I know fashion. I know advertising." For a second I think she's going to cry. "So well made this is. Such careful attention to detail."

"Where?" I ask, not seeing it.

"Ai, tomorrow, we go to Neiman Marcus. I show you."

"Tomorrow's the final."

"I take you after," she says.

"Can I have one?" I ask.

"No." She frowns like I said something crazy stupid.

"You never get me anything," I say, my shoulders slumped.

"That's not true," she says. "I just buy you the miniskirt you want."

"I mean handbags."

Ma watches me a moment. "You get A on the math final, mommy buy you this handbag," she says, tapping the page.

"That's not fair."

Ma gets up from the bed and pops the DVD into the player. "Go back to study."

"Can I watch a little with you?" I ask.

"No."

"Please? I've been studying for two whole weeks."

"Half hour," she says. "Then you go study and I make dinner. Understand?"

I slip under the summer blanket, grab the remote, and press play.

Ma falls asleep. I watch *Breakfast at Tiffany's* to the end. I leave without waking her, then nuke leftover beef and broccoli for dinner. Ma appears when I'm done eating. She's got major bedhead. "You study already?" she asks.

"Yeah, lots."

"Good," she says. She returns to her bedroom to sleep. I rush the last couple of math tests and quizzes. Run through the questions I got wrong. When I'm done, I watch TV until I fall asleep.

The next day, I realize while taking the final that maybe it wasn't such a good idea to watch the whole movie and stay up so late. Maybe I should have gone over *all* the tests and quiz questions. It would have helped to read through my notes, too. When I hand in the final, Cosine Cozza takes one look at it, and sighs with disappointment. Georgie was only fifteen when she took Algebra II; she skipped a grade. I'm sixteen and still fucked up. I'm a fuck up. Cozza said it before, so he may as well say it now. *Georgie was such a good student. She worked so hard. She did so well.*

Exactly three days and two finals later, Ma busts into my room again. I'm not shocked. Actually, I'm so not shocked that I've hidden my Chanel under the living room sofa.

"What is this?" Ma yells, shoving her computer in my face. "You tell me! What is this?"

There it is on the screen:

Algebra II: Amy Wong.

Final: C.

Year: B-.

"A B's a B," I say.

"Not true," she says. "Tenth grade!" Meaning, of course: This year, unlike the rest of high school prison camp, possibly counts more.

Does she really think I can get every question right, including the two bonus questions at the end? Only Georgie can do that.

Ma's mouth twitches. Oh, god. She *does.*

"I'm sorry," I say.

"Give me back the Chanel."

"That's not fair."

"Life's not fair." She leaves. No yelling. No crying. No throwing. It's downright scary.

From my room, I can hear her manicured nails clicking angrily against the computer keys. Then, the squeak of the attic ladder and Ma climbing to the top of it.

"What are you doing?" I ask, going into the hall.

She appears with a large red suitcase. "Take it."

"What for?"

"Pack," she tells me.

"Where are we going?" A guy named Moongazer is having an open-house party tonight. His parents manage Reefer and The Happies; they're away this weekend.

Ma leaves without answering.

"Ma," I call.

She returns to the attic for another suitcase, which she wheels to her room. The computer is on, and when I sit on the bed, it jostles awake to the United Airlines website. Hong Kong.

Are you for real? I want to say.

Ma opens one cabinet drawer after another, taking out a shirt here, a skirt there. Her garment bag contains three dresses, including a Givenchy. As angry as I am with her, I can't help but watch her pack. She's thoughtful and methodical. Reverent. From the way she handles her clothes, it seems they're precious. She has a lot of couture, but Ma isn't so much into labels as she's into design and quality. Every ensemble is a balancing act, depending on what she wants people to notice. An elegant black dress won't draw attention; the eye will automatically be drawn to the Chanel.

Job complete, Ma lights up a fresh cigarette and steps back to assess the combinations she's laid out, each with a matching purse. Once she's satisfied, she packs. It's a snug fit with all the clothes, handbags and toiletry bags, one specifically for makeup.

Ma turns to me, her lips pinched tight. "You packed?"

"I don't want to go," I complain, crossing my arms over my chest. "I'm not going."

"Oh, yeah?" She pushes past me, and in my room, kicks the suitcase on its side. She unzips it, then starts going through my dresser.

"Stop," I say.

She throws the things she's gathered into the suitcase and goes back for more.

"Ma!" I yell, blocking her with my body. "Stop!"

She freezes. "When Mommy say, 'pack,' you go to 'pack.' Ting da dong ma?" Understand?

"Okay, all right? I got it."

"Good." She storms off. I dump in shirts and skirts, a pair of blue jeans and a pair of white ones. I add underwear and bras. Shoes and sandals. It's overstuffed. I can barely zip the thing.

"Take it downstairs," Ma says.

I lug the suitcase to the car. Ma trails me so closely, the tips of her Pradas nip at my heels.

I shove the suitcase into the back seat. Ma stuffs hers into the trunk. "Get in the car," she says.

"But—"

"*Now.*" We get into the car. She chain-smokes and takes the Bronx River Parkway like it's the Indie 500. She starts and stops. My head whips forward and back. The highway's like a rattlesnake. Narrow and winding. Sometimes deadly.

"Ma!" I brace a hand against the dashboard. "Stop it."

Ma stares at me so hard and long, I'm positive we're going to swing into the next lane. Our car and the one next to ours sway closer, then drift apart. She wants to scare me.

Heat rushes to my eyes. A part of me hopes we'll crash; hopes we'll die. I turn away so she can't see me cry. The river opens into a pond-like area. There are both brown ducks and white ducks. One day, I'm going to come back and run them the fuck over. The brown ones because they stick around during winter. The white ones because they're clipped, pathetic losers.

Ma gets off the West Side Highway.

"Why are we going to Georgie's?" I ask, wondering if she's going to make Georgie come, too.

She flicks the butt out the window, then shuts it to keep the heat out. She exhales from the corner of her mouth. Smoke curls and rises.

At Georgie's building on 165th street, across from the Children's Hospital, Ma double parks and flashes the emergency lights. "Out," she says.

"Here?" Usually she circles until we find parking.

"Out!" She reaches across and shoves the passenger side door open. "Take the suitcase."

I climb out and drag the luggage from the backseat. Sweat beads across my face and body. Ma brings down the passenger side window.

"Does Georgie know we're coming?" I lean into the car, not expecting Georgie's keys to be suddenly flying at my face. I block with a hand, and they clap against my palm, dropping to the pavement. *Cachink!* A sound that's tinny and flat.

Ma screeches away. The car turns the corner. Disappears.

Bootman

Black boots. There in the window. Could they really be lace? Wow. Floral and paisley-drops. Open-toed, trimmed with leather, knee high. They'd go perfect with my strapless. Sexy, yet delicate. A smidgen of the masculine. Dolce and Gabbana? No, judging from the pencil-thin heels, Jimmy Choo. Yes. No. Maybe.

Heat rises off the pavement. The sidewalk rumbles, steam rising through the grill. Bodies rush up from the subway. I press against the glass as people brush past. Could they be Chloe? Hard to say. Everything's in the details, and it's already a little too dark to tell.

Is Ma gone for good? I wonder. When I was little, we used to go to Chinatown to watch the Chinese double feature. It was always packed; hot, full of cigarette smoke, and with the cracking sound of people snacking on watermelon seeds. One time, Georgie and I got into a fight. Ma shushed us, then passed me over to Dad. His lap was soft and squishy. I leaned against him. It was hot, but in a good way. "Go to sleep," Dad said, pressing my head to his chest.

"But I'm not tired!"

Dad tried to give me back to Ma. "Doesn't she need a nap?"

"You're welcome to tell her that," Ma said. "You take her."

"No, you take her." Back and forth I went.

Neither wanted me then, neither wants me now.

Suddenly, I feel something. Someone's watching. I look past the display. The sales guy. He comes toward me, his gaze like a magnet. His eyes are pale, pale blue, his hair dark, dark brown and spiked at the top. "Try them?" he mouths, and I get a rush like the boots are already mine.

The store has the delicious smell of new leather and shoe polish. Also a spicy, sweet fragrance. The walls are the kind of lavender you want to wrap around you and sleep inside. At the register, a saleswoman rings up a customer with a shivering Chihuahua in her purse.

"They're either Jimmy Choos or Dolce," I say, about the boots. "Or maybe Chloe."

"Impressive. You know your shoes," my salesman chuckles. "But, you're wrong."

"Ouch."

"Don't take it to heart, beautiful." He tells me it's a new Italian designer. He eyeballs my gladiator sandals. "Six?" he asks.

"Wow, you're good."

"That, I am. And not just about shoes." He points me to an oversized-squooshy sofa in the far corner of the store. I sink into the soft, velvety chair. It sighs under my weight. Feels like lying on a bed of clouds. He disappears to the back, and when the red velvet curtain pushes aside, I make out the floor-to-ceiling shelves stocked with Prada boot boxes. I picture myself in the middle of the room, surrounded by pretty shoes. Wisps of cool air sweep over my skin. Goose bumps.

The woman with the Chihuahua leaves. Her salesperson withdraws a purse from a cabinet. She peeks behind the curtain and tells my guy she's taking off. He mutters something I can't hear, but she okays him and heads out the door. On the way out, she draws the gate a third of the way down so people know the shop's closed. The track light dims.

My guy returns with an oversized silver box. He extends a hand and helps me out of the deep chair. He lifts the lid of the box, revealing tissue paper with my boots tucked like the perfect gift inside, then carefully removes the soft cardboard. I slip off my sandals and reach an arm into the smooth, almost silky bootleg. It gives me a dull heartache.

Bootman kneels. Slips the boot on. Then he leans in. One hand cups my calf, clasping the upper sides of the boot together. The other hand zips. The lace mesh makes it feel snug and sturdy while the lining reminds me of a silk slip. I hand him the other boot and he sets me up. He smoothes his hands up and down the backs of the boots, then slides them to the bare insides of my knees. I rock onto the soles, the front of my skirt brushing the spikes of his gelled hair. He squeezes the sides of my foot and presses a thumb at my big toes. He moves so close I feel the warmth of his breath at my thighs. "What a good fit."

I check the mirror. "You think?"

"Oh, yeah." He pats my ass. "Now, walk for me."

I swish my way to the mirror, lean right, then left. The boots make me taller and thinner. They're magic.

"God, you really are beautiful," he says, leaning his weight onto his heels. "You do know that don't you?"

Heat rushes to my cheeks. Beautiful. No one has ever called me that. People sometimes say "pretty" or "fashionable." Sometimes, they even say I'm like Ma. "Na li, Na li," Not at all, not at all, Ma always insists.

"How much?" I ask.

"Twelve fifty," he says, "not including tax."

"Ugh." I have a credit card for emergencies, but it's capped at a thousand. I sink into the chair. Air squeaks from its seams. "Oh well."

"You mean to tell me you're going to let these go?"

"Guess so," I shrug.

"Oh, beautiful," he says, running his hands up my legs and resting his palms over my knees. "Don't pout. Please don't pout."

"I can't help it."

"You're killing me." He glances at his watch. "I must be crazy, but…"

"Yeah," I yelp, hugging him so tightly he nearly falls on me.

"Hold on, there. I can't give it free. It's still going to cost you."

"I know," I say. "I know."

He hovers for a moment. His breath smells like Scope. "What's your name?"

"Georgie," I lie.

"Tell me, Georgie—" His hands slide upward, his thumbs nestling in the crook of my hips. "What're you, fifteen?"

"No, I'm, like, twenty?" Georgie's age.

"Twenty?"

"Yeah, like, I'm a med student? Every day, it's like, study, study. You know?"

"You Asian girls sure do look young," he laughs. He tucks the box lid under his arm. "This is torn. I'll find another. Just give me a couple minutes."

I relax into the chair. The velvet fabric feels cool against my skin. As cars and trucks drive past in the street outside, shadows shift and change over the ceiling. Georgie will be off her shift at the hospital soon. With my suitcase in the middle of her apartment, she's going to need an explanation I'm not sure how to give. Yeah, Ma dumped me here. Why? Well, uh, Dad sort of hooked up with a Chinese woman in Hong Kong, and now Ma's on a plane—to what?—drag him back?

He's old. He deserves a few years of happiness.

Maybe it's my fault; maybe none of this would be happening if only I was smart like Georgie.

The store suddenly seems too quiet.

"Hello?" I call.

I peek in the stockroom. What a shocker. It's not much larger than mom's walk-in closet. The floor's cement mouse grey. Aside from the shelves in the line of sight behind the curtain, no other shelves exist. Just boxes stacked seven-feet high. In the middle of the ceiling, there's a single bare bulb. Bootman's hunched over on a step stool, elbows to knees. Next to him on the floor is a sneaker-sized box. In his hands, a half empty bottle of soda.

"Oh, beautiful," he says. He seems surprised to see me.

"I've been, like, waiting?"

"I'm sorry." He scoots to the floor and indicates with a wave of the hand to take a seat. "I got caught up in my thoughts. That ever happen to you?"

Why don't you do us all a favor and release him?

I nod. Feel myself start to cry.

"My, my. What's so dark and heavy inside this pretty little head of yours?" he asks, brushing the tears away with his thumbs. "Go ahead, you can tell me."

It's like a hand squeezes my heart and a knot of pain jumps to the back of my throat. "Who are you?" I ask.

"My name?" he asks. "Call me 'in love'."

"No, really."

He gulps his soda as if it were beer, even swallows as if it burns going down. "Who do you think I am?"

"You're Bootman."

"I like that." He hands me the box. "Here. Open it."

A matching bag. "For me?"

"All for you, beautiful," he says. "Now, I'm your everything man."

I start to sob. He kisses me. With his hand at the back of my neck, he holds me there. When I pull away, I see the bulge inside his pants. He unbuttons his shirt. He does it steadily, no rush. Gray hairs and a pot belly. He drapes his shirt over the floor and helps me onto it. He creeps up, kissing my shin, knee, thigh. He bunches my skirt to my hips. My fingernails dig into his shirt and the cement floor. I stare up at the bulb until my eyes hurt. When I shut my eyes, it's like the sun in the sky, only no warmth. Cold moves up from the floor, but his tongue runs along the seam of my underwear, and my body flashes hot, making me shiver.

"Yes, beautiful. Oh, yes."

I'm thinking it's lucky I'm wearing my favorite bikini underwear when his tongue sneaks into my panties. He bunches my skirt up and tugs my panties off. I tense up, lift my head. There's a clear line where skin has never seen day. A pale triangle of straggly black hair.

"Relax," he says. He tugs me forward, cups his hands beneath my ass. His tongue laps, first slowly, then almost greedily. It's like I'm totally naked, even with most of my clothes on. He makes sounds like he's eating, and he likes what he tastes. "You're wet, oh, so wet." That guy Moongazer pops into my head. "She's hot," he said, about his girlfriend, "but what a dead fish."

"Taste how good you are," Bootman says, sticking a finger inside me, then bringing it to my lips.

"No, th—"

He pushes his fingers into my mouth. The taste is a little sour, which is surprising, but, definitely not like dead fish. I feel myself relax. He moves his tongue. It's like waves from the ocean. There's a warm, yummy itch. A tingling that expands, stretches to my fingers and toes. The more I feel, the more I want. In Sex Ed, we learned about the clitoris. But the teacher never mentioned the buzz; craving for more.

He unzips his pants and his penis is as hard as a broom. There were penises in *Your Body and You*. None of the penises looked like this. The tip of Bootman's penis is so brown, it's almost purple. And it's round, orb-like.

Then it's like a shovel digging inside me. The feeling is sharp and jagged like a sword up my spine. The waves disappear. "Ow—"

He grabs my head with his hands and pulls me down, smothering my face in his chest. He bangs. The back of my head knocks the cement. My shoulders scrape. The lightbulb makes my eyes tear.

Fang soong, don't resist. I give in to the pain. Think about Ma. Put myself there with her on the plane. See her crying. Just crying.

Bootman's throat catches. He stiffens and gasps. He releases my hair, his weight pinning me to the floor. The agony in his face gives way to an ecstatic smile.

Then I'm sticky and wet.

"Wow," he says, pushing to his knees.

Between my legs, there's a raw burning sensation, but it doesn't stop the hungry itch that's still there. How can something suck so bad, yet leave you wanting more?

"That was incredible," he says, his eyes brimming with tears. "You're incredible."

I try to cover myself. That's when I see it. The splotch on his shirt. It's the size of my palm. Dark, ruddy brown like day old blood. In European History, everyone laughed when the teacher said men welded locks onto their virgin brides. They wanted to be certain the women stayed "pure" while they were away at war; their hymens intact. We laughed even harder when the sex ed teacher told us women weren't educated about menstruation. Some thought blood meant they were dying.

But I'm informed, and I can say for a fact that it means exactly that: I'm dying. A part of me is lost forever. And while my virginity didn't mean anything while I had it, now it means everything because it's gone.

He buries his face in the shirt and inhales the smell. "Come back some time, okay?"

I want to grab it and run. But it's too late. That spot. He'll take me home, keep that part of me there forever, and wherever I go, another part will always be here on the cement floor with the light burning through my eyelids, horrified yet hungry for more.

Shadow

The mutt leaps up. Its nails catch on my skirt. I feel a warm spritz at my knee. Did she actually piddle on my *Louboutins*? They're suede for God sake! I've just come from the dinner shift at the restaurant; all I've got is the moonlight behind me. It's impossible to see.

"Down, Shadow!" Rick snaps, with a slight southern drawl. He jerks her by the collar. Shadow's a black lab mix from the ASPCA.

"Yes, *down*," I tell her. You fucking beast. I endured three months of pb&j to save up for these boots. You come at them again and I'll roundhouse these heels right through your goddamn head.

"She didn't mean it." Rick smiles apologetically, tugging her out of the doorway.

"Of course not," I say, smiling. The fluorescent light from his apartment reveals the dark stain zig zagging over the suede. My stomach shrivels.

"Come in." Rick drags Shadow back by the collar. He's 29, a transplant from Tennessee. Like most of us, he's a wannabee. A playwright. Five years ago, he won a "New Voices" contest, and since then, he's been trying to finish the play. To earn a living, he manages at the restaurant, and for fun, he plays drums in a band. At work he wears a yuppy button-up, khakis, and a tie. I'm relieved to see in real life he's about a grey T, camouflage gym pants, soccer shoes.

I step into Rick's ground floor tenement. It's like a long, narrow bowling alley. There's a dim fluorescent light on the ceiling. To the left side of the room is a wood loft. To the right, a desk and a small armoire missing a handle. Against the far wall a sink, a mini fridge, and a hot plate. He's lit a cranberry-smelling candle, probably to mask the mix of dampness, urine, and dog.

"Here." He hands me a paper towel, then unravels a bunch around his hand. He drops the bundle to the tiled floor to soak up the piddle. With his shoe, he follows the trail to the doorway. I brush the dampness from my knee. But my boots …. Should I pat them dry and risk ruining the suede? Or should I leave them for the cobbler tomorrow and chance a permanent stain?

"You seem stressed," Rick says. When things ramp up at work, he can always tell which waitresses are off their game. Shadow nuzzles Rick's knee until he pats her head.

"It's just a long night," I say. "It was crazy busy."

"Tonight?" His brows shoot up with surprise.

"I know," I say. It's Tuesday. In the restaurant industry, Mondays and Tuesdays are typically slow nights. "And get this—a woman on the way to her table? She knocked right into some grandpa. Guacamole went flying *everywhere*. Got all over his arm candy wife."

"Oooh. That couldn't 'a gone over well. You comp them?"

"Round of drinks and dessert." I rub my sore eyes.

"How late were you at your studio?" He knows I went straight from work last night.

"Pulled an all-nighter." My latest dress designs were due today for Fashion Design Workshop; I'm getting my masters at FIT. Next week my mood boards get critiqued. They include my illustrations, a juxtaposition of voile and velvety fabrics, a mind map with all my initial ideas, and a collage of Pinterest photos of doors and archways.

"I'm wiped," I say.

"I figured you'd be," Rick says. "I took her for a good long run at the basketball courts. Got out some energy. Now, I'm all yours."

It's the way he looks at me. Heat rushes to my face.

Shadow whines.

"What's the matter?" Rick coos, kneeling and patting her neck. She licks his face, jumps up and nearly knocks him over.

"Oh, yes, I forgot your treat, didn't I?"

Shadow whines.

"Shhh! We don't want the neighbors complaining again." From a medicine bottle beside the kitchen sink, he pours two pills onto his palm. Rick told me Shadow's on Prozac, and now I'm wondering if we're on the same dosage.

He opens his fridge and I see that it's empty except for a couple bottles of beer, a Ziplock of cheese from the supermarket deli counter, and a white Styrofoam take-home container from the restaurant. Rick molds American cheese around the pills.

Shadow lopes happily around his legs, then rises on her hind legs.

"Down," he orders.

For a moment, she obeys. Then she jumps and jumps again.

"No," he yells. "Down."

"R-r-reh-r," she replies.

"I said quiet," he says, shoving her with his leg. "Here."

Shadow swallows the cheese in a satisfied gulp. Rick licks his fingers clean. He trains his pale blue eyes on me. His Adam's apple bobs in his throat.

"I like your loft," I say, feeling myself flush again. "You make it yourself?"

"It's technically the second time around," he says. Shadow nuzzles against his leg. "I rebuilt it from scratch."

"What happened to the first?" I ask.

"Shadow ate it."

"She *ate* it?"

"Yeah, the Friday before last, I get home after work and the legs are gnawed through."

"Wow," I say.

Shadow barks. He pets her. "Quiet," he says.

"How many weeks did you say you've had her?" I ask. "Three?"

"Too long," he jokes. He commands her to lie down in her bed directly beneath the loft. Shadow obeys and curls up, her nose angled down submissively.

"May I use your bathroom?" I ask.

He tugs open a door adjacent to the kitchen sink, revealing a small porcelain sink, a toilet, and a bath. He switches the light on. I move past, but a magnetic charge between us draws me back to him. He smirks, his eyes catching the light like a night animal. "You've been thinking about this, haven't you?" I say.

"All night. Just kissing, of course."

"Just kissing?" My weight shifts to my toes. I lean toward him.

Shadow leaps from the dark, hurtling toward us.

I duck and shut myself inside the bathroom. Her nails nick and scrape the door.

"No, Shadow!" Rick pulls her away. "Bed. Now. Go!"

I sit at the rim of the tub. Dogs can't be jealous, can they?

Rick taps the door. "Amy? You okay in there?"

"Yes." If this were any other guy, I'd be making a B-line for Houston and hailing a cab home. Then again, if this were any other guy, I wouldn't have had three orgasms in a row back at my place the other night. I'm 24; until I met Rick, I thought multiple orgasms were a myth.

"She's calm now, I promise," he says through the door. "She gets overwhelmed when I have visitors, that's all."

"Great." In this too-bright fluorescent light, it's clear that my boots may be unsalvageable. The urine has soaked into the suede. Patting isn't going to work. Rinsing water over it won't help, either. Seltzer water, on the other hand, might work. I know it gets stains out of fabric. But does it work for suede also? I smooth my fingers over the supple leather, its even stitching, and pencil-thin shape of the heel. There's the smooth red underbelly; the Louboutin signature sole that made him famous. No, this one is out of my league. I could call Ma. She knows of a place in Port Chester. Then again, when she sold the house and moved into the city with Georgie, she also sold the car, so I wouldn't have any way of getting there.

Rick taps at the door again. This time I open it to his gorgeous smile. It's enough for me to almost forget, almost forgive anything. Rick embraces me. Glancing at himself in the mirror over the sink, he combs his fingers through his tussled hair. We stare at our reflection. This is what we would look like if we were a couple. Me, with my Asian features, dark brown eyes and black hair. Him, with his tar beach tan, pale blue eyes, and head full of highlights. He's muscular, thick and squat in all the right places; I'm small and thin, some say too thin.

Shadow barges into the bathroom, bulldozing into the backs of Rick's knees, nearly toppling us into the tub.

"Woah, out, girl, let's go." Rick pushes Shadow with one hand and leads me out with the other. He tells Shadow to lie down in her bed, and this time, he adds, "Stay."

He kicks off his shoes.

"I'll keep mine on for now," I say, afraid they'll get trampled or chewed.

"Now that's an idea worth pursuing."

Climbing loft steps in three-inch heels turns out to be pretty difficult, but Rick supports me from behind. At the second rung, his hands slide beneath my skirt, up and to the front of my thighs. My legs automatically clamp shut, his fingers like a wedge between them. He presses me against the ladder, and his heat moves right through me.

Shadow grumbles.

"It's okay, girl," Rick says, tempering his voice. He shifts away. "It's okay."

I ascend another rung, using strength from my arms to haul myself up. Rick runs his thumbs down the back zippers. I'm not sure if I make a sound or he does; maybe neither of us do. Shadow sniffs. Maybe she smells the invisible pheromones. She lunges at me from the other side of the ladder. I scream, jump a rung and dive onto the mattress. My right foot catches and my knee scrapes the wood edge. "Shit!"

"Down, Shadow," Rick commands, catching hold of me. "Bad girl! Down! Bad girl."

Shadow bares her teeth.

"Back!" Rick orders. "Get back."

Shadow reluctantly retreats. Her paws click against the tile as she circles beneath me.

"Down," he insists. "I said, down!"

She pants. The clicking stops. My heart bangs inside my chest.

"That's right," Rick says. "Good girl, Shadow."

The sheets are silky and cool. I just want to crawl between them. I rub my knee. Rick ascends the ladder in five steady steps.

"I've got you, baby," Rick whispers, spooning me from behind. "It's okay."

"She's really like this with everyone?" I ask.

"No, just women, I guess."

Women?

"Just you," he says, reading my thoughts. "There's no other girl right now."

"Then go ahead, unzip me," I say, lifting my foot.

"Not just yet," he mutters. "I want them on."

"I can't sleep like this silly."

"Who says you're going to sleep?"

"It's not happening," I laugh. "Not here. No way."

"She'll be asleep in a minute. You'll see." Rick switches off the light. I stare at the flame of the purplish-red candle on the stovetop. The cranberry smell is suffocatingly sweet, fake like cheap perfume.

Pavlos, the cobbler on 86th, I decide. He's good with suede. That's where I'll take them.

Rick and I keep still until the dog starts snoring. He moves to the foot of the bed. The loft creaks, and he freezes. When he sees that

Shadow doesn't rouse, he unzips my right boot. An inch, two. The teeth part, the leather sides peel away. It's like my entire body sighs. My legs can breathe again. "More," I whisper, reaching for the latch.

"Wait." He slides the zipper down, kissing the indentions from the zipper, like tracks, over my calves.

"Oh, my god." Goosebumps rush over my skin. My body hums. The nape of my neck and shoulders have always been my erogenous zones. But the back of my legs?

Shadow yelps. Neither of us moves. "She's having a nightmare," he whispers.

"Poor thing," I say.

"The vet thinks she might have been abused."

"How awful."

"She definitely suffered neglect."

Dogs are like people, I realize. Fucked up.

Rick liberates me from the second boot. When the zippers are at my ankles, I turn onto my backside to face him. He cups the heel of one boot, then the other, in his palm and gently tugs them off. He kisses the arch of my foot, ankle, then shin. At my knee, he bunches my skirt to my waist, his mouth caressing my inner thighs. That familiar tingling sensation. It extends to my fingers and toes.

I tug his pants down. His penis stands at attention like a soldier with a helmet. I take him in my hand. Guide him between my legs. He finds me. Hovers a moment before sinking inside. The fullness leaves me breathless. He rocks and burrows deeper, the pace of his breath quickening. His odor fills my nostrils.

Shadow whimpers. Rick stiffens.

"Don't stop," I say. It's like he's touching me perfectly, just right, like a spark before a fire.

Shadow howls. It's so sudden and foreign, it takes me a moment to comprehend what's happening. Her voice is desperate, heartbroken, full of rage. The sound is piercing and loud, murky and dark, like getting doused by cold pond water. A chill races over my body, my face.

Rick pulls out. He leans over the side of the loft. "Quiet, Shadow!"

She scratches and claws at the wood post.

"This is not the way I planned for things to go," Rick says, his penis flaccid and shriveling

"It's fine." I feel for his hand and lace my fingers between his.

Shadow shakes her head, her whole body, as if she's just come in from the rain.

She stands on her hind legs, nose sniffing the air. She jumps, trying to get onto the loft with us. She can't possibly reach, and yet it seems as if her desperation and sheer determination might catapult her onto the mattress. I can feel her breath, the damp heat of it, even though I'm on the inside of the loft. The cumulative stench of frustration between all of us makes me queasy. As aroused as I was a few minutes ago, my body has now petrified.

"We can go to your place if you want," Rick offers.

"Let's just get some rest, okay?" I locate my panties and pull them back on. "I have class early tomorrow."

"Fuck." He lies on his back, rigid with anger, and glares at the ceiling.

"Roooohhhr…" Shadow bellows. "Roooohhhr."

"Stop, the neighbors," Rick says, slamming his fist against the beam to get her attention. "You're gonna wake every last one of them."

Shadow laments louder, deeper, and from a place that calls up her wolf ancestry.

"Shadow! I said stop!"

"Rooooohhhr…"

"That's it, you fucking dog," Rick leaps from the loft into the dark below. I hear the dog tags jangle like maybe he's wrestling her to the floor. She yelps, her voice sharp and octaves higher.

I feel a sudden, terrifying dip. "Rick!"

"She's fine," he snaps, his accent thickening. He muzzles her with his fist. "She doesn't want to be quiet. I'm showing her how to be quiet."

Shadow's voice pinches again. Her paws scratch and scrape desperately over the floor. She finally wriggles free and scurries away, darting for cover beneath the desk. She whimpers. Licks her wounds.

"That's right, you better hide," he says, kicking the desk chair.

A part of me retreats into myself; another drifts out. I hug my boots. Stroke the fuzzy texture beneath my hands. It's here; I'm here.

"Let's go to your place," Rick says, pulling a pair of jeans on.

I hear myself say okay, but it's like I'm a body, a shell; no one's home. My fingers search the suede like a blind man decodes braille.

"Come on," he orders.

Shadow wails. Her voice reverberates, deep and guttural, filled with longing and loss. If I didn't know better, I might have confused it for human. I might have confused it for myself.

There's something primal about it. Maybe it's that thing people call a soul. She's just a dog, but she's got something that goes beyond the physical body, something that's indestructible and eternal.

Even as I fix my clothes. Even as I step down the ladder, boots in hand, and force my legs back inside. Even as we ride the cab to my apartment and then fuck on my bedroom floor until I come and come and come. I'm still there, trapped in the dungeon of a tenement on Avenue C.

I know I should walk away. I also know I can't. It's too late.

Why, Amy? Why is it too late?

Through the rest of the day, or weeks, or maybe lifetime, it's that soothing, tactile feeling of suede beneath my fingers, the one tenuous thing, that keeps me from drifting away.

A Kiss

"**D**'you hear? Versace's in town," Ben says. "He might stop by with his entourage."

"I heard Naomi Campbell is going to make an appearance," someone adds.

"That's right," Ben says, fist bumping everyone. "It's *the* party of the year and *we* got invited." Designer and fashion icon Jeff Jones, also the Publisher and Editor-in-Chief of *Y* Magazine, is celebrating the Designer of the Year Award for women's apparel. It's being presented to Helena Putterman-Stewart, our workshop instructor at FIT.

"Helena said Gong Li's flying here from Cannes before heading back to Asia," I say.

"Who's that?" someone asks. They stare at me blankly.

"Never mind," I say. "It was nice of Helena to invite us."

"Pinch me," Ben says. Jeff Jones has appeared in several fashion documentaries. He's had cameos in dramatic comedies, one time actually playing himself. A reporter once asked for advice for younger designers, and he revealed patience and tenacity were his best attributes. If something didn't go his way, he'd say to himself: "Not immediately; eventually."

"I know exactly what I'm going to wear," Ben says. "Meet, later?"

"No, I don't know." After today's critique in Fashion Design Thesis Workshop, I don't feel up for a party.

"Oh, darling, you've got to shake it off," Ben says, giving me an awkward hug. He's one of the smartest people I've ever met. He's older

than most of us, in his 40s, and while he loves design, he's actually interested in fashion writing. He's confident and one of the most elegant
designers in the program. There's a car wreck inside me, and while
some people smell blood and are going in for a kill, he's here being my
friend.

"Tacky," I say. "She said 'lacking originality'."

"That's just Katrina."

Katrina's a star in the program. Each year, Jeff Jones takes two
interns from thesis workshop students; this year, Katrina's one of them.

"She went to the *Dean*," I say. Katrina complained about the cal-
iber of the students. She believed some were in the program simply
due to quotas and affirmative action; not because of talent. "Everyone
thinks I suck," I say.

Ben exaggeratedly clears his throat.

"You don't count," I say.

"I take offense to that," he says. "No *man* has ever said that to me,
I don't see why I should be hearing it from you."

"You're my friend. Of course you're going to say nice things."

"That is so not true," Ben says. "When you came up with that jean
fringy thing, I was the first person to tell you it should be contained in
the zoo, wasn't I?"

"I guess."

"She's jealous," Ben says. "She's just trying to spook you and any
other competition she can scoop into her net. And you're basically
stupid enough to take the bait. Look, who are you going to listen
to—Katrina? Or *me*?"

Ben is as much a star as Katrina. He's already been asked to write a
column during Fashion Week, and when it comes to design, not only
does he have a unique aesthetic, often incorporating recyclables into
his work, his ideas are shockingly different and yet stunningly beautiful. "You," I concede. Tears well up in my eyes. Without my designs
propping me up, I've got nothing.

"That's right," Ben says, using his 6-foot bulk to shield me from our peers. "Now, go see your shrink, get beautiful, and I'll meet you at 8:30 for a quick bite."

"Zach is going to be there." Zach is a guy I'm fucking. He's the other Jeff Jones intern.

"You like him, he likes you. That's a good thing, right?" Ben fakes a smile. He doesn't actually like Zach because I told him about the first date. Zach and I walked back to his place after dinner. I hung back, waiting to see if he would slow down and pace accordingly, and sized him up. He had a lean, muscular body. I was imagining my hands on his tight ass when he turned to me and said, "Why are you walking behind me? I would have thought a woman like you would have overcome such old world customs." I let it go, figuring it would be one of those things we'd laugh about once we got to know one another better. "Remember that butthead comment you made," I'd say.

"Zach could have asked me to come with him tonight, but he didn't," I say.

"You don't know the politics around that, girl. Maybe it's like, not the thing interns do there, you know?" Ben nudges me. "Surprise him. Show up gorgeous. It's a done deal."

I pick at the callous on my finger. It's from pressing sequins by hand to give them a distressed quality, then sewing them to leather. "I just—" Tears drain from my eyes. "I can't," I gasp.

Ben takes my hand, draws me into the women's bathroom and locks the door. "Keep crying, girl, and you're going to be puffy like a goldfish."

"I don't care."

"You're really going to let Katrina win this?" he says. "She spoke first so everyone followed her lead. You know how it goes in workshop."

"Well, maybe she's right," I say.

"If you believe that, you're wasting your time in this program," he says sternly.

A part of me knows Ben's right; another part wants to give up. "I miss Rick."

"Girl, you better remember what you told me."

"What's that?"

"Repeat after me," he says. "I'm independent."

"I'm independent."

"I see who I want, when I want."

"I see who I want, when I want."

"I'm beautiful."

"I'm beautiful," I sigh.

"Say it like you feel it."

"But I don't."

"Fake it, girl."

I think about Zach; how he looks at me sometimes. "I'm beautiful," I say.

"Good." He nods. "Now, onto more important things—I'm hungry."

"Well I'm definitely not," I say.

"Matzo ball soup and french fries? Really, girl?" He unlocks the door. "8:30, sharp."

My shrink is located on the upper west side. I pause at the gate outside her office. It's on the ground level of a red brick townhouse. The bay window is shuttered as always, but usually light shines through the slats. This afternoon, it's dark inside. Dark and vacant. My mind drifts to Rick.

"I need to write a screenplay," he said, during brunch at his favorite restaurant. He was miserable going on thirty without having gotten a single play produced; even if he did, he'd still be broke. If he sold a screenplay, on the other hand, he'd at least have some money.

"Okay," I said, enjoying a bowl of chicken soup. I was used to his pronouncements. Last year, he booked gigs with his band every single weekend.

Rick stared at me, his blue eyes bulging with seriousness.

"Uh…Is this…" I set the spoon down. "Are we, like, breaking up or something?"

"It's just something I need to do," he said.

"Apart?"

"Yes."

"How long does it take to write a screenplay?" I asked. "Couple weeks? Months?"

"I can't honestly say for sure, but yes, two months."

"Two months?" I thought about all his band's gigs, many of which were out in Jersey and Long Island. I went to all but one due to the flu. I also walked his dog Monday and Thursday afternoons when he had double shifts at the restaurant. I didn't even like the mutt.

"Yes," he replied.

Fuck this, I thought. I don't need this shit. I pushed the soup away from me. From now on, everything was going to be about me. I wasn't going to waste my energy on men. It would go toward school. Design would come first. And I would see who I wanted, when I wanted. "You do realize I'm not exactly going to be sitting around waiting for you, right?" I said.

"I take full responsibility," he said.

"Hello? Where are you?" Iggy, my psychiatrist, asks, appearing beside me on the sidewalk.

"Just thinking," I say, following her back to the office. My stomach aches. It's like I can still taste matzo ball soup from that stupid day with Rick.

The room has two facing leather chairs with footrests, a sofa against the wall, and a desk by the window. Iggy knows about Rick. She's also heard about the string of men, some way older than me, but who fuck like they're twenty. It's all the same shit. I should just stop. Why can't I stop?

"Amy?" Iggy leans toward me in her chair. "Hello?"

My eyes refocus on her big, brown eyes. I feel myself come back to the room. Her office may be on 86th between Columbus and Amsterdam but it's like I'm drifting in space. "We were together for almost two years," I say.

"How does that make you feel?"

"Stupid. I mean, I went to all his gigs. Walked his fucking dog. It's so damn humiliating."

"What is?"

"I basically bent over backwards to support him—I mean, I molded my whole life around his—and here he is treating me like I'm the one who stands between him and his work."

"It sounds like you don't feel appreciated." She offers a compassionate smile.

"I don't," I say. "I mean, maybe he should try doing what the rest of us do."

"What would that be?"

"Work."

Iggy laughs, then in a more sober voice, says, "I'm wondering… you poured so much of yourself into Rick. Have you ever done that for yourself?"

"No."

"Why is that?"

"I don't know," I say.

Almost two months to the day, a 400-page screenplay from Rick arrived in my email.

"Dear Amy, I wrote this for you," Ben read aloud. "Love always, Rick."

"What should I do?" I asked.

Ben trashed the email, then cleared the bin. "All done."

"Think he wrote it for me?"

"Sweetheart, if he truly loved you, he would have edited that thing down to 120 pages before giving it to you."

"Hello?" Iggy calls. "Come back, Amy."

"Huh?" I blink. The room comes into focus.

"Where'd you go again?" Iggy asks.

"I just don't get it, you know?"

"Get what?"

"Anything. I mean, why?"

"Why?"

"I thought we were good together," I gaze at my lap, unable to bear the weight of her wide-eyed stare. "I loved him. Love him."

She nods.

"Do you think he's right? I mean, if I truly love him, I'd give him the space he needs to do his work, right?"

"I don't know," she says, her voice softening. "Do *you* think he's right?"

I shake my head. "Why can't I stop thinking about him?"

She sighs.

"It's all so pointless," I say, a dagger of self-loathing sticking me in the heart.

"You seem unusually fragile," she says. "You look like you've lost more weight. Have you lost more weight?"

I shrug. "Ben's all over me about it. He makes like I'm turning into his anorexic sister."

"Have you lost your appetite?" she asks.

"I try to eat, but I can't. I just can't."

"Have you experienced any sleep issues? Sleeping too much—"

"No, I can't sleep. Every night I go to bed and it just won't stop."

"What won't stop?"

"This," I say, pointing at my temple. "Everything just goes over and over inside my head. I read the songs he wrote me. His voice is stuck inside my head. It's exhausting."

"What's exhausting?"

"I don't know. Being alive?"

"Well, we talked last week about taking SSRIs again, and I know I told you I'd like to hold off and see what happens—" She scribbles a prescription. "But I think I'd like for you to get started."

I take the paper. Zoloft. 25 mg.

"One pill today, and if all goes well, we'll increase tomorrow," she says. "No alcohol."

"But I've got the party tonight. I'm seeing Zach, remember?"

Iggy blinks. She knows I'm not into bars or partying. Unlike most people in the program, I have little design background; I don't have time to waste. Iggy points the back end of the pen at me. "If you know you are going to drink, wait until tomorrow. Otherwise, start tonight."

"Will it work right away?" I ask.

"Everyone reacts differently. Usually it needs to build up in someone's system. But, yes, some people feel some relief almost immediately."

Relief? Oh, my god. There's hope.

A dress. I hop the train to Georgie's apartment where I'll borrow a dress of Ma's. I fixate on Zach whenever I find myself thinking about Rick. The last time I was at Zach's place, he asked me to fit model for him since he'd finished cutting the patterns for a new dress.

"Sure." I pulled the T-shirt over my head and stepped out of the skirt. Matching bra and thongs. Lizard skin sandals. "How's this?" I asked. He was holding the front torso of the dress. "Fuck," he rasped through a mouth of pins. I unhooked my bra and tossed it aside. He worked in a methodical, controlled manner, being careful to pin everything perfectly while not sticking me. Occasionally he stopped, stood back, and checked his work from different angles. He was intense, striving for perfection, and willing to accept redo's for as long as it took. And yet, as I modeled in a thong, I could feel his heat, drawing me closer. His warm breath and the brush of his magic hands over the muslin made my nipples hard. They poked out from the white gauzelike fabric.

"I hope my dress turns on every girl like this," he whispered. I could barely move. The pins scratched at my skin, warning me not to shift too suddenly or swiftly. He ran the back end of the pin between my breasts and down my abdomen. He lifted the hem of the dress, ran the blue ball over the thong, his middle and forth fingers reaching down between my legs. He dropped the hem and moved behind me, unzipping his jeans and squeezing my buttocks with both hands, the sharp tip of a pin accidentally sticking me on the right side. I jerked forward, and he grabbed my hips, slipping all the way inside, the force of him shifting me several feet forward to the work table against the front window, where I braced myself on tip toes. He fucked with blind desperation. I was terrified of the pins, and yet, maybe because of them, I felt intensely aroused. "Yes," I sighed because I was sure this was exactly what I wanted—*who* I wanted—and Zach came so hard, yelling so loudly that people in the street actually looked up and stared.

The train arrives at 165th Street. I exit, climb the steps, and take a packed elevator to street level. Georgie lives a block away, directly across from the children's hospital ER. Ma has lived with her ever since she sold the house. She would never admit it, but part of the reason she moved in, I believe, was to thwart any chance of Georgie getting back together with her boyfriend Mark. Ma thought it was bad enough that my college boyfriend at the time was white and Jewish. Mark was black.

Luckily, tonight, neither Ma nor Georgie will be at the apartment. Georgie usually remains late at the hospital in order to check on patients, and Ma's on a Caribbean cruise with her new boyfriend. Ma would flip if she knew I was raiding her closet, but I figure what Ma doesn't know can't hurt her.

On the way, I drop off the prescription at the closest pharmacy. The pharmacist says it'll take a couple of hours to fill, so I walk three blocks south on Broadway to get a manicure and pedicure, then go around the corner to have my hair blown. The entire time I'm getting beautified, I find myself thinking about workshop and my stupid sequined dress design, and then Rick's there in my head, again. I'm a failure; a total fuck up. Always have been, always will be.

Zach, I think, Zach. We'll go back to his place. It's time to move on.

I work my way through Ma's walk in closet. Each dress is in its own plastic sleeve. Psychedelic Pucci prints—a pinkish brown shift dress, matching bluish top and bell bottom pants. There's a red bohemian gown. The upper body's a simple bikini-strapped tank with a flowerlike motif and organza appliques, the lower is a mix-and-match assortment of transparent devorees layered softly like waves.

I drape the dress on Ma's bed and continue looking. Yves Saint Laurent shifts, Pierre Cardin dresses, one of which is a cream-colored car wash mini worth god knows how much. And oh—the Givenchy. It's Ma's go-to little black dress, one she's had forever. It's hard to believe it's not traveling with her to the Caribbean. The first time Dad left, I was sixteen and in high school. Ma packed a suitcase with only three dresses, and this was one of them. I set it carefully beside the red Pucci and go back for more.

Herve Leger. Dior. Chanel.

Oh my god. Another Givenchy. This one a gown. Ma's last boyfriend must have invited her to a black tie ball. Deep V neck. Sleeveless. Halter-like and with a fitted waist. Silk sheer-paneled netting, a floral macramé design elegantly hiding the breasts, and yet drawing the eye straight to it. There's a rear central vent, cut from the same sheer panel netting as the front, embroidered with dots like a bride's veil.

Gaultier. Fendi. Miu Miu.

Then, I see it. Tibetan floral brocade pattern recreated in a thin red lace layered over a silk, black mini dress. It's a Jeff Jones, one of his earlier '60s styles, which broke him into the industry. He is one of the first major designers to successfully incorporate East Asian patterns into Western women's apparel; it became his signature. Ma's kept it well. There's only a touch of discoloration at the inner neckline.

I try it on. The dress fits perfectly. It would be cheesy to wear a Jeff Jones to a Jeff Jones party, but it's so unique, so perfect, so rare. I match it with Louboutins to give it a contemporary twist, but next to the dress, the red soles are like a loud, gaudy stepmother. That's how I picture Dad's new wife, though I've never actually met her. When Dad finally left, he left. No calls. No cards. No visits. He got a son, and that's all that mattered. He gave Ma the settlement she wanted, and it was like he clapped the dust from his hands and pronounced, "Done."

Didn't he love me anymore? I wondered. Had he ever loved me? I felt like the loneliest person in the world. In the mirror, an ordinary Chinese girl stares back at me. She may be my reflection but it's as if the real me is stuck on the other side of the glass.

My energy drains. I sit at the edge of the bed and hold my head in my hands. What the hell am I doing? I can't go to the party, yet I can't stay here alone, either. Somewhere out there, Rick is moving on. Why can't I? I've got Zach; it makes no sense.

That person in the mirror. She's everything and nothing; I'm here and yet not here. Is this what it feels like to be dead? Maybe I'd be better off that way. Ma has sleeping pills in the bathroom cabinet. It's easy. It wouldn't hurt. All of this could stop. Make it stop.

Don't. My body shakes. The Zoloft. I grope for it in my purse, tap a pill from the bottle, swallow it. There. No alcohol, tonight. I grab my purse and escape out the door.

Ben and I arrive fashionably late at 10 PM, but not nearly late enough. Other than the catering staff, there are more students from Helena's class than anyone else. The apartment's a duplex. The living area is a large open space with a gold seated Buddha set into the wall. Beneath, an antique red opium bed. What's strange is that it matches the one Dad had down to the floral, ruddy red pillows. There's also a velvet sectional arranged in an open square configuration, a round glass table in the middle with purplish-white orchids and oversized coffee-table books. East meets West. The decor makes sense.

"My dad had an opium bed exactly like that," I say. "My mom hacked it to bits with a cleaver."

"No way," Ben says. He's wearing black jeans and a black leather bomber jacket he designed and embossed by hand. It's interesting, yet casual, and more important, subtle.

"Yep, grilled it up with the rest of his antiques in the back yard."

"Drama."

"Major when your husband takes a lover who gives him the boy he always wanted." Outside of therapy, I try not to think too much about the divorce or Dad, but for a split second, I can see the dreamy look on his face and the longing in his voice when he recounted stories about his own dad. "My father," he always said. Before they ran from the Communists, my grandfather was a scholar and a shipping tycoon, transporting peanut and soybean oil to the West. He had a Western advisor with whom he spoke English as well as some French. When they lost everything except for a briefcase containing US $200, Grandfather cashed in an old favor and took over a friend's Hong Kong furniture business.

Back in college, there were people who yammered on and on about cultural heritage and pride, throwing around terms like "cultural misappropriation," "Imperialism," and "exploitation." I found them tiring and boarish, especially since I hated both my parents, and figured I'd hate the grandparents, too, if they were around, but, I have to admit now, seeing that bed at the heart of this room, I am proud to be Chinese, and I'm proud to be the granddaughter of the man who created it.

A tuxedo-decked server offers red wine from a tray. Ben takes a glass, but slaps the back of my hand when I reach for one also. "None for you, darling, remember?"

"Oh, right."

The room is being cleared of the table, chairs, and carpet in order to set up a bar, and the pool table is being transformed into a mammoth, table-sized charcuterie board. Lots of food, which tells me it won't just be industry people. The spread may as well be a beautifully roasted, fat hog with an apple protruding from its snout.

"I don't think I've ever gone to a party and not had a drink," I say.

"Frankly, that would be my definition of torture," Ben says. "Especially now that I've quit smoking? I wouldn't know what to do with my hands."

"Exactly." I cross my arms genie-like over my chest, then recross them the other way. When another server goes by, I give in and pluck a glass of white. "Just for show," I explain.

"Beer before liquor never sicker," he says.

"Yeah, and this would be wine." I swirl the glass.

"Not liquor, darling. Licka, as in, you know, a lick 'a food?!"

"I ate an entire poached egg. I guess you forgot?"

"Yeah, and I bet that would be all you've had the entire day."

"That's so not true." I shake my head.

"Don't lie to me, bitch."

"I'm not anorexic, okay?"

"Prove it."

"Oh yeah?" I cross my arms over my chest and tip my nose up at him. "Challenge accepted." I hand him the glass and help myself to a plate. Sopressata, Gruyere, and a cracker. I add an olive and almonds. I bite into the cheese. "Satisfied?"

"Getting there." He hesitates, but hands the glass back.

"Relax, I'm not going to drink, okay? Besides, the pill was only 20 mg."

"That may not be a lot for a 180-pound guy like me, but on a 90-pound frame—"

"A hundred and two."

"A hundred and two," he says. "Whatever."

"A sip won't hurt." I can feel people staring at the dress. "Shit, I knew I should have worn the Givenchy. It's, like, so tacky to wear a Jeff Jones to a Jeff Jones party."

"Oh stop. You look fabulous."

Zach. I glance around, trying not to be too obvious that I'm looking for him.

"Not every girl has a vintage Jeff Jones, honey, and even if she does, she doesn't always look this good in it," Ben says.

Katrina enters the room. She's wearing a bamboo green lace dress with gold chain straps.

"As I was saying," Ben says, into his drink.

"You're the best," I laugh.

Ben grins, tapping my glass with his. We drink. The wine is refreshingly cool and dry.

More classmates funnel into the apartment. I hope to see Zach, but no luck. From the corner of my eye, I see Katrina whispering with one of the guys in workshop. I pretend not to notice even as they continue to stare.

"Ignore it," Ben says, smiling majestically. "Their cattiness can't touch you here. Not tonight. It's all about Zach, right?"

"Right," I say through a smile.

One of the guys from workshop crosses his arms over his chest and mimics Jones' deep, Darth Vader voice: "The worst you can be is oblivious, and the best you can be is fabulous."

"That was dead on," I laugh.

The guy's girlfriend rolls her eyes. "Please don't encourage him."

"Come on, it's good, right?" he argues. "Admit it."

"Yeah, that movie was epic," Ben says.

"Take the DVD," the girlfriend says. "He'll bring it to school tomorrow."

"I will not."

The couple share a silent, hostile exchange.

"Toppers, anyone?" Ben asks. He counts hands. I still have more than half a glass, but I disappear to the bar with him. There are only two bartenders and people several rows deep, vying for their attention. The light's dim. Despite the real glassware—wine glasses and beer jugs instead of plastic cups—there's the indelible feel of a college frat party. "Don't go anywhere," Ben says, maneuvering into the crowd. "I'm going to need the extra pair of hands."

I lose Ben almost instantly in what has suddenly become a swarm of bodies. Alone, I feel exposed. Like Katrina, everyone can see through me. They think I'm substandard; an imposter. My face pricks with shame. I down the rest of the wine. I'm about to elbow my way to the front of the bar when I hear Zach's familiar laugh. Far right, ten feet ahead, his arm couched around a woman. She's blonde and blue eyed, which shouldn't bother me. So, why does it? J Crew skirt. Cardigan. She's around my height, but wider in the hips. She's got a b-cup bust, the kind of skin that burns before it tans, and is otherwise absolutely and totally unremarkable. I creep forward, and nearly startle when Zach throws his head back, guffawing at something she's just whispered in his ear.

"These are pour toi," Ben says, passing me two glasses of wine. "You all right?"

I steel myself. "Where's the beer?"

"I'm on it." Ben soldiers back through the veil of people.

Zach's laughter fills me with dread. We were never exclusive. I have no right to be upset. I'm seeing other guys. Jewelry and clothes. Flowers. Fun restaurants and underground parties. One of them took me to London for the weekend. The other to his ski house in Jackson Hole. But, Rick. My body trembles, yearning to be with him. Yes, that's what I need. Some dark, hot sex to get my mind off things. I'll call him after the party. I can make things right.

No. I close my eyes. Feel the gauzy muslin and the scratch of pins against my skin.

What the fuck is wrong with me?

Men. Sex. Love. Why does everything have to be hot-wired?

"Woh." Ben's back; three beers in one hand, three in the other. "Girl, you need to sit."

The buzz dims. People clap. Ben and I return to the living area. It's Helena with Jeff Jones. The entire party leans toward them. He's what would be described as "distinguished." Silvering brown, wavy hair, thick brows, and a large, beaklike nose. It's slightly bent; he must have broken it at some point. Jeff Jones has deep inset eyes and wrinkles spanning his forehead. He's wearing an Armani jacket over a T-shirt and jeans. It's simple, classy; sexy. Helena's wearing a royal blue Lanvin gown that drapes to the floor. It's satin with a round neckline, long dolman sleeves, and an A-line skirt. I wave to Helena and she smiles.

"Let's go say hi," I say, draining the rest of my glass.

Katrina exchanges a glance with someone that intimates something along the lines of "We don't do that here." I am about to break the golden rule. Which is what? To mind one's place in the strata of things? Uh, hello, I want to say, I'm Chinese. If anyone gets order and invisibility, it's a girl raised in a traditional Shanghainese family, and especially, as my shrink points out, one with a narcissist for a father.

The party swims like heat over the summer pavement. Then, out of nowhere, Zach appears with the blonde. They're holding hands. It's obvious she's the girlfriend. He seems surprised to see other students from the program. Me.

A shadow crosses his face. His arm moves robotically up and away from his girlfriend's shoulders. "You didn't tell me you were going to be here," he says through gritted teeth.

"I'm sorry," I say. "Just because I fuck you, doesn't mean I report to you."

Katrina chokes on the wine. The girlfriend flushes. I turn to go, and *bang!*—right into Jeff Jones.

"Oops, sorry," I stutter. "It's, like, nice to meet you."

He notices the dress, his dress, and smiles.

"Jeff." He's drinking whisky on the rocks. "And you are?"

I introduce myself, explaining that I'm one of Helena's students, glancing quickly at Zach to reveal a practiced but sexy pout that could drive even the dullest of knives in. "I love the opium bed," I say.

"You know about opium beds, now do you?"

"Her dad had one," Ben says, squeezing into the conversation.

"Had?" Jeff Jones asks, leaning so close I can smell the whisky on his breathe.

Ben and I exchange a glance. "Has," Ben says.

"Down to the pillows," I add, swapping my empty wine glass for a full one.

"Is that so?" he says. "I bought that bed from a Chinese carpenter in Hong Kong more than forty years ago. A real local, you know? Could hardly speak English. Practically wearing one of those straw sampan hats." He laughs, and I stare into my wine. "Then, one day, his idiot son changes the business to some mediocre interior design business. That was it. Next time I visit, the store's gone."

"Huh," I utter, wondering how it is that white people can get so much wrong about others while having the arrogance to always think they are right. Resentment I never knew existed boils up. I hate every white person along with their ignorance, determination to believe that everything is equal when everything has been skewed by the colonialist lens and labels, and I *especially* hate the fact that, right now I'm turning into one of those crazy, blathering idiots whining to myself about colonialism and appropriation. He moves closer like he's trying to hear something I've just said, which I haven't said yet: You can all take your J. Fucking Crew lack of originality and plainness, which gets passed off as classical American elegance, and shove it up your asses. Maybe Jones sees something cross my face, because he quickly adds, "But his work, ah, it was impeccable. In fact, I have a matching red desk and chair upstairs. Would you like to see it?"

"Yes, we'd *love* to!" Ben says.

Jones moves swiftly across the room to the spiral staircase, waving people off as he goes. Ben tows me along. On the way, I switch my empty glass for a full one. The steps leading to the next floor are narrow and triangular-shaped. I grip the rail and hoist myself up and around, up, around. Upstairs, to one side of the staircase is a massive desk overflowing with paperwork and fabric samples. It's decorated along its edges and drawers with the quintessential oriental "bamboo" design. The tabletop, however, is covered with smooth red leather and framed with copper trim. The walls are floor-to-ceiling bookcases jammed with magazines and swatches. There are stacks crowding the floor that come up to my waist.

"This is where I *really* work," he says, taking us to the other side of the stairs. This side of the room contains an open area with a large work station and computer, story boards, a wall containing rows of hooks with different rings of fabrics, an industrial-sized supply cabinet, shelves overflowing with spools of thread and wire and other supplies, and two industrial sewing machines. There's a thick velvet curtain draped across the room.

"Wow," Ben says.

However much I dislike Jones, I've slipped back into "awe" mode. This is my dream home. He's a goddamn genius.

"There's more," he says, pulling the drape aside. Behind, the layout is similar to the one downstairs, only there's a leather Stickley chair and another opium bed, this one lacquered with porcelain inlay.

"Ming Dynasty," he says, sitting in the big chair and inviting us to take a seat on the bed.

"Is it comfortable?" I ask, sitting on it beside Ben.

"Oh, it is," he says. "Trust me."

Between us sits a large leather ottoman with a large tray containing a decanter filled with rusty, dark whisky and a crystal bucket of melting ice. He offers us a glass, and while Ben jumps on it, I wave it off. Jones adds ice to a glass and pours, handing it to Ben, then tops off his own.

"Cheers," he says. When he sees my wine glass is empty, he moves the tray of whiskey to the floor. He lifts off the top of the ottoman, which doubles as a storage space. There are bottles of red and white wines clustered in the corner, but most of the stuff is baby toys: a play mat, rattles, teething toys, bottles, baby blankets, light-up musical toys, stuffed animals.

"I didn't know you have grandkids," I say.

Ben jabs me with an elbow. "Is your family here tonight, Mr. Jones?"

"No, my wife and daughters are staying at the W." He hands me the wine.

I drop the toy back into the ottoman and take my glass. *Wife?* I could swear he just got divorced. I saw it in a tabloid magazine at the grocery store. When did he remarry and have a kid, and how did I miss it? I try to recall how old he is. Late sixties? No, probably 50s. White people skin. It's hard to tell.

"How *old* are you?" I ask.

"She means your daughters, sir," Ben asks. "A year, aren't they?"

"Six months," Jones replies, refilling Ben's whisky.

"This is amazing," Ben says, swooshing it in his mouth. "Really complex."

"Bushmills 16," Jones says, tasting it off his lips. "Peach, a hint of vanilla, dried fruits—"

"Honey," Ben adds.

"It makes it so smooth," Jones says.

I dig out a rainbow xylophone. Knock out twinkle, twinkle.

"It must be a challenge to balance work with family," Ben says.

"Not too much. My wife handles it so I can work. But this helps—" With a miniature stainless steel spoon—it looks like a Chinese ear pick—Jones scoops white powder from a small folded piece of paper. I know exactly what it is. Rich kids in high school used; it always made me nervous.

I dump the toy back. It crashes on a D note.

Jones sniffs. The coke vanishes from the spoon. He offers the bag to Ben, who goes through the same motions. There's a familiarity to his movements that surprises me.

"You?" Jones says, offering it to me now.

I shake my head. "No, thanks."

"Oh, come, come," Jones says. "Have you ever tried it?"

"I'm good," I say, showing my empty glass. "Too much to drink already."

Jones turns to Ben. "Is she always this uptight?"

Ben cracks up, laughing. "Yes. She's a work-a-holic."

"Not because I want to be," I say.

"She's playing catch up," Ben sighs. "She's from the liberal arts."

"You want to be a good designer?" Jones says. "Don't be so uptight."

"I'm not uptight." I stare at the smirk on his face.

Downstairs, music pulses. Laughter erupts. Zach's in the mix. Zach and his girlfriend.

"You look angry," Jones says. "Are you always this beautiful when you're angry?"

"I'm...not...angry," I say, enunciating each syllable for affect.

"There seem to be a lot of things you are not," he says. "So what *are* you?"

Nothing. Nobody. For a fraction of a second, the girl on both sides of the mirror fuses together. Pain overwhelms the body; numbness callouses the soul. Why am I so pissed about Zach?

"Wooh." Ben shuts his eyes. "So good."

"The best," Jones says.

Ben inquires about a restroom, which Jones indicates is past the red desk. As soon as Ben gets to his feet, he nearly loses his balance. "Woh."

"You okay?" I ask.

"I'm fine," he says, his face grayish yellow. "I'll be right back."

"Naomi wore a remake of this dress on the runway last year, you know," Jones says, taking Ben's place next to me. He gives my shoulder a soft squeeze. "One of my favorite collections."

Then, he's on top of me, shoving his tongue down my throat, making me gag. "Where," he starts to say, "is your"—he sucks at my bottom lip—"father's—his hand slides to the top of my thigh—"bed?"

I push him away. Then I see it clearly in his face. He's not interested in me. It's the bed. "Why?"

"No reason." He comes at my face with his, again. This time, I turn my head away.

The bathroom door bangs open. Jones switches back to the big chair. Ben makes it to the bed, but rushes back to the toilet. He wretches, the vomit splashing loudly into the bowl.

"There's got to be a reason," I say, getting up to check on Ben. "Just tell me."

"He'll be fine," Jones says, catching me by the wrist. "There's nothing you can do for him."

I shake Jones off.

"It was commissioned by the Queen," he finally says. "As in the Queen of England." He explains that Her Majesty's bed was accidentally damaged at Buckingham Palace. It was returned to Hong Kong for repair. Around that time, Jones saw it in the store. He ordered the replica. "But there was a mix-up," he says. "Long story short, I received the wrong order. The little Chinese man telephoned me requesting it back, explaining that in fact, the one I received was the original."

"What's the difference? I mean, it's the same bed."

"Ah, but that's where you're wrong. One of the beds already had her Majesty's seal on it."

"So you sent it back?"

"No, because mine didn't have a seal," he says. "Even if it had had one, I would have kept it. But it didn't."

"I don't get it."

"I didn't either, but years later, I heard that the son had secretly made a third bed and had kept the original for himself."

The room tips. I can hardly think and it hurts to try. Is the bed Ma chopped up and barbecued really the one he's talking about? I go into the bathroom where Ben is praying to the porcelain god. I try to wake him, but he's passed out. Impossible to lift. I leave him and find Jones sitting on the red desk.

"That bed should be mine," Jones says. "Those Chinese can be so goddamn cunning. You have to watch them."

"I'm sorry. Did I lose my face or something? Because the last I checked I was Chinese." I lean against the bathroom doorway. Either he's inebriated or he's just plain stupid.

"Oh, you're not one of them," he says. "You're obviously one of us. I'm talking about the ones over there."

"You're not getting the bed," I say, crossing my arms.

"Not immediately," he says, shrugging me off. "Eventually."

So now he's tossing around his one liners.

Behind me, Ben rustles and vomits into the toilet again. I could kick him I'm so annoyed. He's the one who told me not to mix, and now look at him.

"You don't deserve it," I say.

"And why exactly not?"

I start to laugh. "You're a fucking racist."

"Me, racist? That's absurd. Everyone *knows* how much I appreciate East Asian culture."

"Appreciate or appropriate?" I think of Zach downstairs with his girlfriend. Was I a girl he was fucking or an experiment, a stereotype, a geisha?

Jones watches me a moment. "You're beautiful when you're angry."

"No, I'm beautiful, period," I say.

"You are," he says, softly. Downstairs, there's a lull in the buzz of voices. Someone famous has arrived. Jones glances at his watch. "I really didn't intend—"

"What *did* you intend?"

He stares me straight in the face and crosses his arms over his chest. "To fuck you, of course."

"Oh, really?"

He nods almost imperceptibly. There's a smugness; a crooked smile. The way he leans back, crossing his arms casually and propping himself on the desk. The casual manner in which he tosses his head, his hair sifting to the side. There's a bubble of confidence, a knowingness, around him. Life is his oyster. How many women does he want—and get —like they are his personal toy things? Here he is, a cat batting me around with his paw like I'm a fuzzy toy mouse on a lead. And here I am, practically bending over for him to screw me up the ass.

"Sorry, darling," I say. "Not going to happen."

"Mm hm." *Not immediately. Eventually.*

"It's not."

"Well, then, shall we?" he says, waving a hand in the direction of the spiral staircase.

I push away from the doorway, fix my feet apart just right so that my stance is firm, and I'm grounded like I've got roots growing deep into the floor. Nothing can knock me down. "Take off your clothes," I say.

He looks at me, his face full of boredom.

"Do it," I say, my voice perfectly steady.

He fixes his gaze on me, and I can tell he's doing some quick mental calculations. Without another word, he unbuttons his shirt and removes his cufflinks. His bronzed torso is covered with silvery hair that stretches like a rug into the front of his pants. He removes the shirt, revealing his sinewy limbs and tired flabby midriff. He unbuttons his pants, draws the zipper down to reveal tight black briefs, and as he steps out of them, I see his left leg is slightly thinner than the right. The knee has a pale, cross-shaped surgical scar. His eyes narrow slightly, and with his chin up, he removes his briefs. Naked, he stands before me, the withered worm of a penis dangling between his legs.

"Shit, you're *old*," I say.

Instead of deflating, his dick expands and rises, the ruddy pink top spreading like a ripe mushroom.

"I guess you don't work out either," I say.

The more disdain I show, the more erect and larger he becomes, the tip of his penis pointing straight at me like a finger.

"What?" he says.

"You disgust me."

"You're just upset because I'm already fucking you and you're already coming, and there's nothing you can do about it."

"You wish," I say. "Get on the desk."

He lies back, his hands touching the base of his penis. "You're right here," he groans. "Oh, so small and tight."

I remain rooted in place.

"You know you want it," he says, nodding for me to come to him. "You feel me there inside you."

"Touch yourself," I say.

"Filling you up."

"Do it."

He spits on his palm, then slides his hand up the shaft of his penis, then down again. "You feel so good," he says.

"Harder," I say. "Faster."

He pumps and pumps. Each time it seems he can't get bigger or harder, he does, and then I can see him about to explode.

"You want me to make you come?" I say.

"No," he says.

"Yes."

He stops. It's like he flipped the off switch. He still has the erection, but he sits up, and calmly, without a hint of urgency, says, "You're the one who's coming."

"Ha."

"Mh." He stares at me, and for a moment, I feel penetrable, like he can see straight into the bleeding part of my heart. He touches himself, again, and starts to lose himself in it.

"Come," I command.

He laughs. "You think you can get me to come from over there? Get over here and fuck like a grownup little girl."

What did he just say?

"You're a bad little girl," he says. "A very naughty little girl."

My voice catches.

"What's the matter?" he says. "Did your boyfriend find out and break things off? Did he realize you've got loose Oriental pussy?" I go to strike him, but he catches my arm. "It's hopeless. You know it is. You need this. You know you do."

"You ignorant—"

"Asian pussy is always so *ripe*," he says. "So small and fuckable."

Tears rage down my cheeks.

"Oh," he utters. "No need for sadness."

"I'm—" I quake with rage "—Not—" Brush his hand away "—Sad!"

He gathers himself together, and starts to dress.

I've lost; I'm lost.

"What you think about me," I say, drying my face. "You know what *you* are?"

"Pray tell." He feigns a smile.

"You are the great Jeff Jones," I say. "You have everything and everyone. But underneath it all, you've got nothing and no one, and you're alone. No one wants you. Not even your parents. You're the loneliest person in the world."

He pauses, then tugs the jacket center front into place.

"The only way you can get anyone's attention," I continue, "is by being an old, controlling, white guy asshole because that's all you've got left."

Fully dressed now, Jones crosses his arms and leans back on the desk. The smugness is gone, and in its place, a glassy, bewildered look filled with darkness and devastation. We stare at one another, not speaking, and yet, sharing something words can't communicate.

He pats his jacket until he feels the bag on the inside pocket, then takes it out, unraveling tin foil and sniffing powder from the spoon. He offers it to me, and this time, I try it. There's an intense burn that cools and transforms into a lightness I've never felt before. It's like I can feel my soul; indestructible, joyous, loved.

A lull downstairs catches Jones's attention. "It's Naomi," he says, getting to his feet. "Ladies, first," he says.

At the top of the spiral staircase, I pause at what feels like the top of the world. My mind and every cell in my body wakes up. The world brightens. The invisible pack shackled to my back falls away. The party pulses; I'm part of it. The warm elixir spreads through me. It extends out of me to Zach and everyone here, then outward to Rick and everyone everywhere.

I descend. Glance up.

"Feel it?" his eyes ask.

Oh, yes. I smile. The spiral steps circle down, down. The world is watching, and yet, for the moment that is tonight, I don't stop to consider tomorrow; I ascend the steps between us and touch my lips to Jones's.

All that matters is a kiss.

Prenups and
Other Engagements

Boxes within boxes. Boxes stacked upon boxes. Open boxes. Closed and labeled boxes. Boxes and more boxes. I seal up the last of them, brush sweat from my brow with the back of my wrist, then text Ben: Done. He's on his way with a U-haul. We're going to move him to his boyfriend's place and me to storage because I'll be couch surfing with Georgie and Ma until I nail a job. It's the last day, the last hour. The Dean sent around a notice: Graduate students need to vacate by 5 PM. Maintenance has to turn around every second-year studio in time for the incoming group this fall.

Seventeen boxes. Not bad. Ben helped me organize by numbering and labelling everything: Boxes 1,2,3 Completed Designs; 4,5,6 Incomplete Designs; 7,8,9 Fabrics, Muslin & Leathers; 10,11 Sequins, Beads, Appliqués; 12 Threads, Yarns, String; 13,14 Hand Tools, Sewing Machine; 15 Mannequin #1 (Full body); 16 Mannequin #2 (Torso); 17 Shoe Projects; 18 Miscellaneous.

Two years ago, I started the program with one box. Now there are 18. It's amazing how much a person can accumulate so quickly. Equally amazing is how much dust it all collects; I'm covered in it.

There's a tap at the door. "It's open!" I yell, squeezing between two boxes and then stacking one on top of the other. The door opens. He's tall, silver haired, and wearing almost exactly what I'm wearing—a black T-shirt and jeans—only the British and tailored version. Not GAP nor streaked with sweat and dust. I *know* him, but from where?

His eyes light up.

My stomach clenches. Oh, shit. It's Jones. I haven't seen him since the party last fall. He seems different out of context. "I—" I stammer. Everything that transpired that night rushes into the space between us. "I, uh—"

Of all the times he could possibly see me, and he sees me *now*? Like *this*? Perspiration trickles from my jaw, dangling, ready to drop. With my shoulder, I rub it from my chin. It's too sickening.

"I'm glad I caught you," he says, glancing at all the boxes.

"*I'm* not," I say, and when I notice the stunned look cross his face, I quickly add, "I look like shit." My voice trails off. I feel so helpless, and so helplessly ugly on top of it. Why the hell is he here, anyway?

He gives me the once over. "You look—"

I cross my arms, tilt my head, and steel myself for the pretense about to come.

"You look like a coal miner," he says.

"Ha!" I laugh. "I actually feel like a coal miner."

There's an awkward pause, and then he says, "I was just speaking with the Dean. She said you were one of the last men standing."

"Yeah." I dig my phone from my back pocket. "Technically, I still have forty-three more minutes."

"One can do a great deal in forty-three minutes."

My gaze wanders over the shuttered boxes. If only it were forty-three more days. Or, months. The uncertainty of "real" life beyond the safety of these walls fills me with dread.

"It's a ghost town around here," I say. "Most people were packed up and out of here by lunch. But, I don't know. I mean, packing can be so overwhelming."

"Less so, perhaps"—he smiles— "if one wins the Jeff Jones New Star Award."

I stare at him for a moment and try to make sense of what he just said. He said "if." If one wins. What, exactly, does that mean? He can't possibly mean me. Can he? Do I dare even think it? Because most of the graduating class wanted this. Ben did, too, and while several students won contests and internships, Ben's the one who got a prestigious internship in Milan for the summer. I figured if anyone won the JJ New Star, it would be Ben.

Yet, Jones is here, talking to me. In my head, I hear Ma: "You think you're so special?"

"You don't mean me?" I say.

Jeff winks.

"Really?" My voice rises an octave. "Me?"

"Why are you so surprised?" He leans against my boxes. "I was informed the committee was unanimous."

Unanimous. Did he actually say that?

"I thought you'd want to know," Jeff says. "The official announcement will be made tomorrow at graduation."

Oh, my god. It's real. I won. Me, Amy Wong. I actually won! "Thank you, oh my god, thank you—" I leap at him, and the next thing I know, I'm hanging on his neck and jumping up and down and squealing like a child.

"It's—" Jeff utters. "Hm."

I catch myself, then, and pull back. "Sorry," I say, feeling myself blush.

"It's quite all right."

Heat rushes to my eyes. Maybe it's hope? Most contest results were announced by now, and I realize that since I didn't win anything, I had somehow given up.

"God, you're beautiful," Jones says, cupping his hand at the back of my neck and drawing me closer. "How can you roll around in the muck and still come out so beautiful?"

I feel like I'm high. Floating. In love.

"Kiss me," he says.

Is this love? Can it really be? It's something; maybe it's everything.

"And that night," he says. "That wasn't really me."

I start to laugh. "You mean racist?"

"I was coked-up, high." He rolls his eyes.

"So you're not really racist," I say. "Only the coked-up you is racist?"

"Something like that, yes," he smirks.

"Or maybe the real you is racist and the coked-up you is just honest about it?"

"Possibly." He sighs, sits back on box 15: Mannequin, Full body. "But, no."

"You seem pretty sure about that." I catch his gaze.

"It's interesting," he says, crossing his arms. "As different as we are…background, age, etcetera, etcetera…when you look at me, I feel like you get past my bullshit to the real me. No one else makes me feel that way."

"No one?"

"No," he replies, the glossy bewildered look I saw the night of the party coming over him again.

I kiss him. I kiss him and I don't hold back.

Once a week. Twice, tops. It's the most we can manage to see each other. He's busy building his empire, and I'm trying to find a job. We're both seeing other people, too. Jeff's divorce went through; he just wants to play. That's okay with me. I'm determined now to fuck who I want, when I want.

I decide.

So, it's a shocker when Jeff shows up at Georgie's apartment, unannounced, and luckily when no one else is there, to say he's rented a place at The Cape for the rest of August. "You absolutely have to come," he says. "I've been working around the clock to make this happen."

"That sounds fun," I say, picturing a house on the beach. "I guess I can come for the weekend."

"Don't be silly. Stay the week."

"That's sweet," I say. The thought of being alone that long with any man I'm fucking—just him and me facing one another the whole time—makes me queasy. And then to be totally reliant on him and at his mercy? It's not like I have a car. If things go bad, I'll be stuck. I shake my head. "Really sweet, but—"

"I won't take no for an answer," he says.

"Look, I need to find a job." It's been a month since graduation. "Or find an internship."

He waves me off. "You have the rest of your life to get a job."

"That's easy for you to say. You have one. You have a whole fucking business."

"That I do," he acknowledges.

"Besides, I have the rest of my life to not get a job, too, and I'm pretty sure I wouldn't like that very much."

"Not to worry, I'll put out some feelers for you."

"Really? That's so sweet."

"You've associated me with the word 'sweet'," he says, drawing me to him and holding me close. "Allow me to correct that immediately." He kisses me, his hands reaching into the band of my skirt, cupping a buttock in each hand. We bang onto the kitchen table.

So, then, it's settled. I'll go up with him in a rental car. I'll spend a week and then return to New York via bus to Boston. From there, I'll take a train to Penn Station.

The drive to The Cape is long due to traffic, and it doesn't help that Jeff turns out to be a tailgater. It's not that he's aggressive or mean about it. He's impatient. And it's obvious by the way he clasps the wheel—his knuckles are practically white, he's gripping so hard—that he's beyond anxious.

"I detest driving," he says. "I rarely do it."

"Don't worry, it's not like I can tell," I say, trying not to sound too sarcastic.

Jeff pulls so close to the car in front of us that he has to break abruptly when traffic stops.

"Maybe you could give a little more space between them and us?" I suggest.

"If only these cars would get out of the way."

"If only." I can't help but laugh.

"I'm glad you find this humorous."

"I can drive," I say. "I'll drive if you want."

"No, I'm fine," he says, shrugging me off.

We travel I-95 through Rhode Island. Eventually, we cross the Bourne Bridge onto The Cape, where the highway turns into a single lane. We go around a rotary and take Route 6 all the way to Wellfleet. When we finally locate and pull up to the house, the look of frustration on his face gives way to disappointment. It's a small, grey-shingled, single-floor building. He cuts the engine. The keychain swings back and forth in the ignition.

"This looks great," I say. "Let's go inside."

Jeff remains mute and unflinching behind the wheel of the car.

"Come on," I say, getting out and waving for him to join me.

Jeff reluctantly steps out of the car and walks sluggishly up to the house. The owner lives in the house next door, so the entrance is left unlocked. Jeff lets us in. The facing wall is made entirely of glass, and looks out over an oyster cove. A sandbar separates it from the ocean beyond with its curved, protective arm.

The living room itself has a cathedral ceiling with exposed wood beams and a stone fireplace. Everything else is white, including the sofa, coffee table, and walls. Even the bowl containing shells, starfish and sand dollars. White on white on white. Overlooking the silvery blue water outside.

"Wow," I say.

"This," he says, drawing me closer, "I can get used to."

The first couple of days, we drive to the bayside public beach. We lay out on the sand, heavily armed with sunblock, and sleep until the heat forces us out of our stupor and into the chilly New England water. Around 1:00 PM, we eat the sandwiches we picked up with our morning coffee. In the late afternoon, we head back to the house, wash up, and enjoy a glass of wine before going to meet his friends and acquaintances for dinner.

The next couple of mornings we decide to spend at the house. A small beach appears at low tide. It's private—only the owner and the oyster farmer have access—so we forego the bikini and the bottoms, which helps to get rid of the lines and produces a smooth, even tan. I've never baked in the buff before. I'm self conscious at first, but Jeff finds an umbrella to block us from being seen by neighbors, and after a glass of wine, we're having sex, only it's different somehow. It's the hot sun and the cool ocean breeze; my knees digging deeper, deeper into the soft warm sand, and my sweaty, lotion-covered body slipping over him. There's the taste of salt, the taste of him, in my mouth. He bookends my legs between his, pinches my nipples harder than I expect, and says, "Feel all of me, baby."

"I feel you," I say, because every nerve ending comes alive. "God, I feel you."

It's more sensual than I've ever felt, and as soon as I rock forward and back, the friction between us sparks something. Then I'm coming faster and more furious than ever. A stranger inside me tucked away so deep and so filled with sorrow rushes out—*out, let me out*—and then my body goes slack. I shut my eyes and try to pull back, all the way back. But Jeff watches, energized. He continues to slide me by the hips over him. "Again," he says.

"I'm done," I whisper.

"Fuck me."

"No."

"All of me." He clenches his teeth, restraining himself. "Say it."

"All of you."

Then it happens again, the gushing from within, only deeper and darker. Ecstasy. Anguish.

Stop; don't stop.

For a moment, I'm lost. And when he comes, the sound of him brings me back. I see straight to the suffering caged animal inside him, and then the release and bliss, the escape, that comes after.

Suddenly, I feel something unsteady happening inside me. I'm not sure what. I wrap myself in a towel, excuse myself to use the rest room, and climb the stairs up to the house. It's hot and bright outside and cool and dark inside. The shift feels like the floor swoops upwards. I'm going to either throw up or pass out. I curl up right where I am, at the edge of the jute rug, and close my eyes.

"Jesus, what's happening?" Jeff asks, appearing over me.

"I'm fine," I say, forcing myself to sit up.

"You're crying."

"I'm just being stupid."

He watches me, concern etched in his brow.

"It's just…" I grab his shirt in my fist. "It's so damn frustrating, you know? I mean, I thought it was just biology. Attraction. Fucking. But it's like I hardly know you, so why do I feel like I *know* you?"

"Because you know me." His face glows with sunburn. "And I don't mean just literally."

He lies at the edge of the carpet. Balances there. He looks at me, and I feel like I'm actually here, I'm real, and he can see me. *Me.*

"You're open, so it allows me to be open," he says.

"I mean, what are the chances a person like me would be with a person like you?"

Jeff nods. "After the party, I wasn't certain I'd see you again."

"Me, neither."

"I asked Zach about you, but he said he hadn't seen you before. He didn't think you were in the program."

"Really?" The fucker.

"When I saw that you had won the New Star, I put two and two together."

"And voila!"

"Fate."

"Here I am," I shift toward Jeff, and thinking about Zach, feel victorious. "Naked except for a towel."

Jeff tugs it off. "Plain naked, now."

At the beach house, there's a languidness to everything we do. We drink, fuck, talk, love. Memories shuffle like those in a deck of cards. The days flow into and over each other like the ebb and flow of the tide. Time expands. Days roll out ahead of us. Then suddenly they contract and are gone. One night we go to the beach with large rainbow swirl lollipops we bought in town. Jeff sucks at the edge of the candy and opens up about his mother, who left him to be raised with nannies while she busied herself with women's club activities. He says his father was concerned he was a "faggot" for having creative interests in clothes instead of the typical love affair boys have with football or soccer.

"My father was pretty fucked, too." I tell him about an ice cream incident I had with Dad. I must have been five or six. Dad, Georgie and I were eating ice cream after dinner. Dad finished his, then asked for a lick of mine.

"So, I held it out to him," I say, using my lollipop to pantomime what I say. "Dad licked it, but as soon as I reached for it back, he stuffed the entire thing into his mouth. He even made a sucking sound, like he was relishing its sweet taste."

"Heartless," Jeff says.

"Isn't it? I sobbed and accused him of eating my whole ice cream, and you know what he said?"

"I'll bet he called you selfish."

"Exactly," I say. "He said, 'Yours? Your *nothing*. Everything here, everything that's yours, is mine.'"

"My mother was like that," Jeff says. "After I started my company, my mother told me the only reason it did well was because of her. She said without her, my business would fail."

Jeff and I continue to swap stories. I recount what happened with the phone call. What Dad's girlfriend, now wife, said to Ma.

"Can you believe she'd have the balls to do that?" I ask.

"Who knew Chinese women could be so vicious," Jeff says.

"You have no idea."

"Hm," he says, raising a brow at me.

"That bed I told you about? We don't actually have it, anymore."

Jeff sets down his glass. "You haven't sold it, have you? Please tell me you haven't sold it."

"No, I mean it doesn't exist anymore. My mother chopped it up with the cleaver and barbecued it in the back yard."

Jeff emits the kind of sound a person might make if he were hopping on a bed of hot coals.

"Yeah," I say, "When my father finally came back to get his things? He found the charred, black pieces, and guess what? He actually—"

"Cried," Jeff blurts.

The words catch in my throat. He's correct, only I don't remember telling him this story. In fact, I know I haven't, because there's a tiny part of me that still frets he's interested in the bed more than me.

"Well, *I* would," he says, offering an explanation. "It's not just a bed, Amy. It's *art*. It's *history*."

"Right," I say, more sarcastic than ever. "It belonged to 'Her Majesty'." I wink my pointer and middle fingers to indicate quotation marks. "You think the value would go up if she'd fucked in that bed too?"

"Absolutely," he says.

"Honestly, Jeff," I say, punching him. "He didn't cry about us. Oh, no, not *us*—we were only his girls. But the bed? Bawling. Totally heartbroken."

"Well, isn't that perfectly…" He struggles to find the correct wording to complete the sentence.

"Shitty? I mean, what a fucking narcissist."

He watches, silent. Then he tops off our glasses with more wine. "A toast," he says, holding up his glass. "To narcissism! May it thrive universally for generations more to come!"

A couple days before I leave, Jeff asks me again to stay a few more days. He has the house rented through Labor Day. But my head's already back home: Where else can I send my resume? Does career services at school have any new job or internship listings? I need something. Living with Georgie and Ma is no picnic. Ma cooks constantly, but when Georgie binge eats, Ma nags about her weight; they never stop. Ma gets back from Hong Kong tomorrow, so I need to find a job and get out of there, pronto.

One afternoon after we come back from the beach, Jeff jumps into the shower to clean up first. There's a computer in the loft upstairs, so I log onto my school's webpage. I check career services for new postings. When I don't find any, I check my email. Ben writes, telling me how gorgeous it is in Milan. Would I like to visit in August? Possibly backpack through Italy? Rick, whom I haven't heard from in a year, emails to see if we can talk. Would I please get a drink with him? There are also emails from two of the other guys I'm seeing.

Jeff appears, unshaven but smelling of Dove soap, and in freshly laundered clothes. His hair is downy soft and combed back. "Checking in with your other boyfriends?" he asks, and even though he seems to be teasing, we're now treading dangerous waters. An unspoken rule is that the mention of others is off limits.

"Maybe," I say.

"You can tell them I'm fucking your brains out." He turns abruptly and descends the steps to the living room. I follow him downstairs to the couch. He offers me a glass of Chardonnay, then pours one for himself. He leans back into the sofa, sips the wine, and stares blankly out at the water. He's silent.

"You're seeing other people too, aren't you?" I finally ask.

"Of course," he says. "Why? Are you jealous?"

"What?"

"Oh, you *are*."

"No," I say, "I was just asking because—"

"It's okay, darling."

"Wait," I say, flustered. My pulse beats in my ears. How the hell did he flip things around like that?

"Truly," he says, touching a finger to my chin. "I get it."

He looks at me, his eyes shimmering with—with what?—Oh, my god, it can't be. Can it? He takes my glass and sets it next to his on the coffee table.

He kisses me, and whispers, "I have a surprise for you later. You're going to love it."

"What? Tell me."

"Later. Tonight." Then he takes my glass and sets it on the coffee table next to his. He climbs over me and unzips his shorts. I'm still in my bikini and cover up. He doesn't bother to pull down my bottoms. He tugs the material aside and slides inside me. His eyes roll back. Then he rocks, my head between his elbows. "Oh, darling, I... I..."

"You love me?" I whisper.

"Oh, yes."

I stare straight into his eyes and ask the big question I've mulled over in therapy ever since the day he appeared at my school studio. "What? What do you love?"

"This. God, I love this. I need this."

"No, me, Jeff. About me?"

"You're always so wet."

"Jeff!" I push him away.

He sighs, aghast, and rolls off. He combs his hair back with a hand. "Must we really discuss this right now?"

"I just—"

"You just—what?" He shakes his head, fixes his shorts and pours himself more wine.

"I don't know." My face prickles with heat.

"Maybe I was wrong about you. I really thought you were different from the others, Amy. I really thought we could skip such sophomoric, soporific bullshit. Can't we just share this moment? Can't it just be about us?"

I cross my arms. Hug myself to keep warm. He has no right to act like I'm making this about me.

"It *is* about us," I finally say. Yet, something inside me wavers. Is it? In my head, I can hear Dad calling me "selfish" and Ma criticizing me for not appreciating all that she has sacrificed.

"No, it's about you and your insecurities," Jeff says. "You can't tell how I feel about you?"

"Can't we just stop fucking for a minute."

"Why the hell would we do that?"

"To maybe talk?"

"About what, huh?" he exclaims. "What the hell is there to talk about?"

"It's simple. What do you love about me?"

"Nothing right now, damn it. You're just like my nagging ex for fuck sake. God help me. This is too fucking tedious."

Lumping me in the same category as his despised ex. My hands involuntarily cover my chest. It's like he stabbed me.

"I shouldn't have said that," he quickly says, shifting closer. "I was frustrated. I didn't intend to say that."

"I'm *not* your ex. I'm nothing like her."

"I know. I know that."

"Look," I say. "It's been fun, okay? Time to move on, that's all."

"Just like that—it's over? So what are you going to do now? Go home and fuck one of those idiots?"

"You were one of them," I say.

"I absolutely was not."

"Right. You're Jeff Jones. Woooh. And, I'm one of a dozen good fucks, so—"

"You have no right to be jealous."

"There you go with the jealousy thing again. How about you go ahead and call one of those other girls and fuck her instead of me from now on? Hm? How's that for jealousy?" I get to my feet.

"Stop," he says.

I head toward the bedroom. He remains in the living room as I locate my things. After a couple of minutes, Jeff appears in the doorway.

"So, you're leaving."

I pack the bikini I wore yesterday at the bottom of the suitcase.

"You're beautiful when you're angry," he says.

Something in me snaps. I grab a Manolo and throw it at his face. He darts out of the way and it hits the door frame.

"Jesus," he says. "I meant all of you."

"Me, too, Jeff. Fuck all of you." I grab the clothes in my designated drawer—three neat stacks—and set them into the suitcase.

"What I meant is that you're beautiful both inside and out. Every aspect of you."

I retrieve the shoe I threw and tuck it, along with its mate, into matching airline socks; I do the same with six other pairs lined up in the closet. It's a packing trick I learned from Ma.

"You're brilliant," he says. "I've never seen anyone use airline socks in such an ingenious manner."

My dresses are hanging in the closet. I tug one from the bottom, allowing it to slip from the hanger.

"And obviously hugely creative," he says. "*Especially* with design."

I shake out the wrinkles in the dress, fold it in four swift motions into a perfect rectangle.

"And you can fold clothes like they're origami."

I set the dress on top of the shirts.

"And you're not like other girls," he says, and when I continue packing, he adds, "Especially my ex."

I pluck another dress from the closet and fold it.

"Okay, fine—you want to know what I love about you? I'm not going to make any apologies. You're sexy as hell," he says, "but you're fierce, too. You fuck ugly. I'd say like a guy, but really, I mean like *me*. Not pretty. Most beautiful women fuck pretty. And until I met you, I've never met anyone who relishes and needs it as much as I do."

"Why don't we just call it for what it is, okay?" I stop what I'm doing. "It's okay to say it, Jeff. You're going through midlife crisis, and, well, I make you feel young again."

"You do," he says. "I'm not ashamed to say it. You're fearless. You challenge me. You make me go places I've never gone before. Places I don't necessarily even, eh, want to go."

His gaze briefly and involuntarily flitters toward the bathroom. The harness I bought for the trip is hanging from the towel rack. I'd brought it with me, kept it in sight as a teaser leading up to tonight, and so I realize he's alluding to that.

"Then you bring me there, and I find, well, I see that I definitely want it."

Something hard and cold rises up inside me. I'd like to bring him to his knees.

"Even outside the bedroom," he says. "You're making me 'talk.' Most women don't expect that of me."

"Except your wife."

"Ex." He flushes. His face, ears, neck. "Please leave her out of this."

Fine with me, I think, going back to folding the last of the dresses.

He watches as I lay the shoes on top of the clothes within the suitcase. From the drawer, I remove the lingerie and panties, squeezing them between the shoes so things don't slip around during the bus ride.

"Will you look at me? Please?" he asks.

I march to the bathroom and pack up my toiletries. When I return to the room, Jeff says, "Okay, then, you want to hear me say it? I don't want anyone but you."

I toss the toiletries bag into the suitcase.

"And, I don't want you to want anyone but me," he adds. "So there, I've said it. We've talked. Happy now?"

"What time is the bus?"

Jeff sighs, glances at his watch. "Wups. You missed it."

"Fuck."

"It's that bad," he says. "You can't survive one more night?"

I set the suitcase upright and sit at the edge of the bed. "What time does the bus leave tomorrow?"

"Eleven," he says, settling next to me, his shoulders slouching forward. "I'll drive you over after breakfast."

"Well, okay," I say. "Friends, then?"

"With benefits?"

"Don't push it."

He hugs me, and the smell of him feels so good, so familiar, it nearly breaks my heart.

I shower and get ready for dinner, and then we drive out to a place in Orleans called Land Ho, which is one of his favorite fried clams and oysters restaurants. It's a little after 6:00 PM and it's already packed.

There's a twenty minute wait. We consider leaving, but by now it's likely the situation will be the same anywhere we go. Jeff and I wait at the bar. He orders a scotch on the rocks and I go with a Cosmo, which is high in calories, but delicious, especially after a long day of sun, love, and a sudden and intense breakup. The music is loud, and adds to the din of voices, making it difficult to hear.

"To our last night," he says, once we have our drinks in hand.

"It's been fun," I say, trying not to get emotional.

"You're absolutely right, you know. You're young, you're beautiful. You don't need to be saddled with me."

"Saddled? With the Great Jeff Jones? I'm not sure I'd put it like that."

"Well, I regret being such a cretin."

"Stop."

"Because I meant what I said." He jiggles the ice in the glass. "The other girls don't mean a thing to me."

"Why? They don't fuck as well?"

"Or get fucked as well."

The host arrives to take us to our seats. For the appetizer, Jeff orders raw Wellfleet oysters. I order a stuffed clam. For dinner, I choose fried clams. Jeff goes with the oysters. When the appetizers arrive, he adds sauce and forks an oyster into his mouth. On a bed of ice, each of the six wet, fleshy mollusks lies within the mother of pearl interior of its otherwise rough, layered shell. "You know what I love?" he whispers, leaning close. "I love the way you taste."

"Will you stop, already?" I say.

"What's with the prudery all of a sudden? Yes, it's just 'sex'. But sex is a microcosm of life. It's a metaphor for everything." He brings a shell close to his mouth and slurps the oyster into his mouth.

"Everything?" I smirk.

"Yes, and if you separate the good designers from the best, you'll find it comes down to understanding that difference."

Was that true? I wondered.

"You'll see," he says. "Oh, and by the way, my friend Josie Chu emailed to say for you to go in and speak with her. She said she may not have anything right now, but…"

"Oh, Jeff," I say. "See? You can be really sweet."

"Yes, well, let's keep that our secret."

Jeff orders another round of drinks, and by the time dinner is over, I feel like we really can be friends. He tells me about women he's been involved with, some one-nighters, others he's dated for longer periods. What's amazing is that he can not only recall funny anecdotes or meaningful details about each of these women, but he never says a negative thing about any of them. He doesn't bring up his ex, and this time, I let it go.

We return to the house early. We stink of fried oil from the restaurant, so while Jeff makes some calls for work, I clean up in the bathroom and step out of the hot shower wrapped in a towel. Steam is rising off my skin. Jeff watches me from the doorway. "You don't believe me, do you?" he says. "We belong together."

"We'll see," I say.

"Can we at least be together," he asks, "one last night?"

"I don't think that's a great idea."

His eyes shine like flashlights.

"I want to," I admit. "It's just—"

"You're afraid."

Afraid? My head whirs. I groan, hold my head in my hands. Too many emotions. Too many thoughts. I can't hold onto it all.

"You want me," he says. "You don't want to, but you do."

"Fuck you, Jeff."

"Fuck me? Really? Darling, I know how you're feeling because I feel it too. It can't be denied."

"It can't be denied," I mock.

"Fine," he says, moving toward the door. "I'll sleep on the couch. But you love me, Amy Wong. That's why you're so scared."

"Jeff." He turns.

I throw him a pillow and shut the light.

The next morning, Jeff and I drive to the General Store to pick up some breakfast. It looks rustic from the outside, but like a Balducci-type New York specialty store on the inside. Chef-prepared foods, deli meats, fresh produce, baskets of fresh fruit, bins of coffee beans with a commercial grinder, and a breakfast area where one can order bagels, pastries, and coffee to go. Jeff grabs the *New York Times*. We pick out our breakfast—protein shake with strawberries for Jeff and yogurt and a peach for me. For the ride home later, I also grab an iced tea and order curried yogurt chicken. Jeff approves because it's labeled "Oprah's Recipe," and is both low fat and low calorie.

We bag the breakfast separately from the meal I'm taking on the bus. On the way out of the store, we pass an old-fashioned gum ball machine. The kind that every grocery used to have at the front of the store. It's filled with plastic bubbles, each with a different prize inside. Tattoos, stickers, rings, rubber balls. "Wait, wait," Jeff says, tucking the newspaper under his arm and handing me the groceries. He reaches into his pocket for change. He pushes two quarters into the slots and turns the knob. There's the sound of a bubble clambering down the metal shoot. He plucks off the lid.

"What'd you get?" I ask.

It's a plastic ring. Pink and with a smiley face.

"Here," he says, kneeling and offering it to me. "You're wedded to me for another week."

I laugh all the way to the car, and biting into the juicy peach, try to chew and swallow it down with the sweet-and-sour desire to stay longer.

Jeff stops at the bayside beach. We get out of the car and sit at the top of the steps leading down to the ocean. The sun is up, but it's still cool. A woman on the beach steadily walks toward Orleans. We watch the ocean and eat our breakfast. "Thanks for inviting me out here," I say, finishing my peach and dropping the pit into the bag.

"It's going be lonely without you."

I smile. It's too late to change my mind now. He'll think my life is totally malleable. That he can always get his way. As soon as I think it, I worry if it's already true. He can already get his way with me.

"You can call, you know," I say, opening the yogurt and spooning it into my mouth.

He stares out at the water. "My father used to bring me to this exact spot at this exact time," he says, sucking the shake through the thin straw. "We'd have breakfast and he'd tell me shark stories that made me afraid to go near the water without him."

The wind blows. I have to hold my hair back to keep from eating it.

"I always thought I'd be bringing my girls here," he says, shaking his head. "But…"

I tuck my hair into my shirt and continue with my breakfast. The night of the party, I'd seen baby toys in the storage ottoman. But since then, Jeff refuses to talk about them. I made the mistake of asking once, and Jeff responded angrily, the way he does at the mention of his wife. But today he's brought it up on his own, so I ask, "Why can't you bring them?"

"They're in London." He explains that his ex wife moved shortly after the divorce went through. She, too, had met someone new. "I wanted to fight it, but her father happens to be J.C. Moorehouse, one of the top divorce attorneys in the U.S."

"Whether he is or not, you still have the right to see your kids," I say, finishing the yogurt and tossing the spoon and plastic yogurt cup into the bag.

He shakes his head again. "In order not to get fleeced financially, I was forced to sign away visitation rights."

"That's crazy."

"What's crazier is that on my last business trip to London, I arranged to see the girls, but they clung to their mother's legs and refused to come to me."

"They didn't recognize you?"

"I've become a stranger to my own children."

"That must be depressing," I say.

"Not as depressing as when one of your girls is too afraid of you to let you hold her and the other one tells you you're bad, she doesn't like you."

"Wow."

"She's filling their heads with rubbish and lies."

I understand now why he can't talk about it. He must hate her. I know I would.

"There's a heavy pain right here," he says, tapping his breast bone. "It's so dense, almost as if my heart is hardening, and sometimes I think at some point it's going to stop."

Wave after wave. I take his hand in mine. The waves crash down on the sand and rush up onto the beach. The edges foam. The rest gets towed back into the ocean.

"I need you," he says. "You certain you can't stay just a few more days?"

I smile sadly. "Some of us actually have to find a job, and to find one, I actually have to, you know, look?"

"Okay, then," he says, finishing the last of his shake. I open the bag and he tosses the cup in with the rest of the trash. "I give in, darling. Forget professionalism. You're hired." He gets up and starts toward the car.

"Jeff," I call, hurrying after him. "Wait."

We get into the car. "Whatever you want," he says, starting the engine. "You name it."

Whatever I want? I say to myself. What the hell does he mean by that? He takes my hand and sets it on his erection.

"Personal secretary?" he offers.

"You *have* a personal secretary."

"So?" He leans across to kiss me. He slides a hand beneath my skirt.

"Oh, I know," I say, clamping down on his fingers. "How about 'designer who fucked her way to the top'?"

He frowns. His erection instantly dies. "Why do you have to be like that?"

"Like what?"

"Forget it." He makes a disgusted, throaty sound as we pull out of the lot. Silence. There's less than two feet between us, and yet, a vacant space sprawls out so wide, I don't think I can possibly reach him. He turns off the main highway. The car wends its way up the sinuous road. When we arrive at the house, Jeff gets out, grabs my curry and iced tea from the back seat, and enters the house. He doesn't shut the door on me, and yet, I hesitate to follow him inside.

I stand there a moment, trash in hand, wondering what to do. Finally, I go inside. The bag with the curry and drink are on the sofa, the sliding doors drawn open. I watch as Jeff disappears down the steps to the beach. What exactly is going on here? The glare off the water stings my eyes. A tepid feeling sifts through my heart.

I get my suitcase from the room and roll it out to the car. It's too heavy to lift into the trunk myself; I manage to shove it in the back seat. It takes half and hour to forty-five minutes to get to the bus station. There's still an hour before I need to leave, but maybe I should go next door and call a cab?

When I return to the house and Jeff's still not back, I head down to the beach where he's sitting in the shade of the umbrella. I hug my knees beside him. It's low tide. The oysters are there for the picking. In the distance, beyond the sheltered cover, the ocean looks like long shards of floating glass.

"Give me the ring," he says.

I slip it from my finger and hand it to him. He gets to his feet, winds up, and throws it into the bay.

"What was that for?" I demand to know. When he doesn't respond, I get to my feet. "You know what? Fuck you." I march up the stairs, through the house and out the front door to the car. See? I tell myself. You were right. You put yourself at his mercy coming here. Now, you're stuck.

I'm about to knock on the neighbor's door when Jeff finally appears. He gets in, starts the car, and we drive in silence all the way to Hyannis. When we get to the bus depot, he asks me to wait, he needs to talk, but I shove the door open and get out. I tug my suitcase from the back seat. "Amy," he calls, rushing around to my side of the car. "Please. I'm sorry, okay?"

"Yeah, whatever," I say, marching toward the station, dragging the suitcase behind me.

"I love you."

Three small words. Is he kidding me? In a movie, this would be the part when two quarreling lovers run into each other's arms. I turn to face Jeff straight on.

"I do," he says, crossing his arms over his chest. "I don't want to. I don't want to be that guy who needs the girl who doesn't need him."

Heat rushes to my face. I feel sunburnt, even on the inside.

"You know me, remember?" he says.

"Well, you don't know me."

"I do," he insists. "I do."

"Really? Well, then go back and get my fucking ring back." I tug the suitcase into the bus depot where I buy my ticket. He waits as I board, trying to hug me, but I push past him. He waves me off, but I shut my eyes until we're moving at a steady, even clip. I spend both legs of the trip home—bus and train—replaying everything in my mind. It's pure, unadulterated torture. I don't want to ever see him again, and yet, maybe I'm going to die if I don't. My eyes are swollen practically shut from crying. I don't arrive at Georgie's until 10 PM. Ma's back from her cruise, so I put on my sunglasses and hope she's already asleep. All I want is a shower, a shot of NyQuil, and a bed.

As soon as I walk into Georgie's apartment, I know something's wrong. Ma and Georgie are sitting together at the kitchen table, each with a mug of Chinese tea. Ma's wearing a silk nighty with butterflies that someone younger might pass off as an evening dress. She's got a dour look on her face like maybe her boyfriend broke up with her. Or maybe something's up with Dad?

"What's going on?" I ask.

Ma and Georgie exchange glances.

"What?" I insist.

Ma holds out a ring box, hand delivered from Tiffany's, with a small card attached.

"Maybe you should tell *us*," Georgie says.

I open the card. It says: I can do better than that—J.

Damn right, you will, I think. No one's ever going to treat me like that again.

"You look terrible," Georgie says, a line usually reserved for Ma.

"Ni ku shen me?" Ma asks. What's the crying about?

"It's just an apology of sorts," I say, taking the box. "Just a guy I'm dating, that's all."

"The boy just now at this Cape Cod?" Ma asks.

"Friend," I correct, worried that if Ma ever meets Jeff, she'll automatically judge him for being so much older than me.

"He wasn't nice?" Ma asks.

"A total jerk," I say, unwrapping the baby blue paper, and prying the box open. The cushion is white silk. Set inside it, a diamond ring. Rectangular-shaped. Framed by small diamond chips.

Ma gasps.

"Correct me if I'm wrong, but that looks like an engagement ring," Georgie states.

"Like, duh."

Georgie frowns.

Ma stares at it, then back at me. "What have you *done?*" she accuses.

"Are you asking if I prostituted myself for a diamond ring so that I can scare off nice Chinese boys?" I ask, angrily, snapping the box shut. "Because that could be true."

Ma strikes me across the face, catching me totally off guard. The last time she slapped me was in high school. I press my stinging cheek. "I know it's hard to believe that someone might actually want to marry me," I say, grabbing the phone from the stand and locking myself in the bathroom.

Jeff picks up on the first ring.

"This is *not* funny," I say, sitting on the toilet.

"I didn't intend it to be," he replies.

"You made me feel like shit. Like trash."

"I screwed up, okay? You're dealing with a hopelessly screwed up person. You have me in knots, I'm scared."

I sigh. "I miss you. Why do I miss you?"

He chuckles. "Have you tried it on?"

I remove it from the box and slip it onto my finger. "It's beautiful."

"Then marry me," he says.

"I never imagined I'd be proposed to over the phone while I'm sitting on the john."

"Well, you are. If it's not romantic enough for you, we can see what we get out of the bubble gum machine."

"Do I have to come up for another week if I say yes?"

"Absolutely. In fact, the dues have gone up to three weeks."

"Then, yes," I sigh. "Yes."

How beautiful and radiant I feel in front of the three-way mirrors. Jeff's favorite seamstress, Mona, makes the final alterations. It's the strapless wedding gown he designed just for me. It took a year to create this dress. Since Jeff Jones is getting to be a household name, he wants more than ever to push the envelope. He's certain the right dress would appear in the top fashion magazines. To his dismay, I asked for something more traditional—at least for the wedding itself. As requested, he created a modified A-line dress cut straight across the neck line, which drapes to the floor. The cut of the dress made it frightfully pedestrian, so he focused instead on the material itself. Using a lotus motif from a Chinese textile dating back to the Qing Dynasty, he designed a lace pattern and had it crafted by hand. The result was stunning. Jeff was so delighted that the lace became the dress.

Sheer, so sheer that a lace bra with silk edging needed to be sewn into it, and a pair of matching bikini briefs made to go with it. Most skirt lines start just above the hip, but part of Jeff's genius is to drop it mid thigh, using long layers of the thinnest Bengali muslin he could find, which drape over the lace to the floor, extending into a short train. Just below the bra line, and just above the skirt line, there are strings of ribbon made of miniature flowers. They could be lotuses, but they have the innocent quality of the daisy.

Critics declared that while Jeff dares to suggest the erotic, "Amy" is both sophisticated and elegantly balanced with both youthful purity and ancient spirituality.

Today, for the first time since the Cape Cod trip, all of Jeff's attention is on me. On this wedding gown—the one made just for me. I feel hopeful, as if I'm about to finally step into my real life. To celebrate after the fitting, I'm wearing an open gusset thong so we can fuck with the dress on if he wants. No one can tell by looking, so it's discrete, and will be a wonderful turn on for Jeff.

Which reminds me: I forgot to take the pill today. Yesterday, too. I better remember to double up tomorrow. Wouldn't want a bun in the oven while I'm traipsing down the aisle. Then again, we are getting married, and it wouldn't be so bad having a little Jeff inside me, would it?

Jeff circles around me, his hand brushing over the lace, indicating to Mona in a matter-of-fact manner to take it in a bit here or a pinch there. From my reflection, I see the dark areolas around my nipples, which show through the lace. "You don't think my mom will think it's too risqué, do you?" I ask. "Chinese, especially the older generation, can be ultra conservative."

"Of course not," he says. "She knows fashion."

"Yeah, but all her friends from Hong Kong and Taiwan will be coming."

I could already imagine the gossip: Scandalous! *Naked.* Can you believe?

"Thank you, Mona," he says, now, excusing her.

She takes the pins from her mouth, sets them back in the box, and leaves.

"You have the perfect body for this," he tells me, cupping my cheeks in his palms. "I made it explicitly for you. You know that, right? The perfect dress for the perfect body."

I lean in for a kiss.

"I love you, you know that, right?" he asks, shifting away.

"I love you, too."

"Do you?" His eyes tear up.

"Of course."

He sighs. Looks away.

"What?"

"It's—" he stammers, "well, I—"

He sighs again, moving behind to unzip me from the dress. The back opens, the lace slipping from my body. Maybe it's the central air conditioning. I shudder, automatically clutching the dress to my body. We had an argument last night. We made up—or so I thought. Can he be having reservations about the wedding?

But then why go through with the fitting?

It's too confusing. Why is everything with Jeff always so confusing? One minute hot. The next cold. So cold. There's less than a week left. What do I tell Ma? Many of the guests have already flown in from Hong Kong, Taiwan, and the Philippines. I can already hear Ma crying, "What will people think?" Oh, the gossip. Heat rushes to my face.

"It's nothing serious," Jeff says.

I brace myself.

"I spoke with the lawyer today, and he strongly advised, due to complications around the company and of course my ex—" Jeff brushes a loose thread from the cuff of his shirt. "He suggests we do a prenup."

It takes a moment for it to sink in. We are not breaking up. Everything is still okay. I swallow, and the rock in my throat gets lodged inside my heart. There's a sudden, sharp pain, then nothing. "A prenup?" I ask.

"The lawyer was saying it's not personal," he explains. "And I told him you're not like that. You wouldn't take it that way, right?"

"No," I hear myself say, "of course not."

"And we love each other," he says, "which really is all that matters, right? You love me, don't you?"

"Of course."

"I knew you loved me," Jeff says, hugging me tightly. "I knew you were different. I knew it wasn't about the money."

"Of course it isn't."

Jeff kisses me. I keep my eyes open. Maybe it seems he will, too, but he doesn't. His eyes remain shut until he shifts back. He helps me out of the dress. I stand in front of the mirrors, naked except for the panties and three-inch strap sandals. Jeff handles the dress reverently, clipping it between his fingers as if it's as delicate as tissue paper. He leaves to find Mona. Her workroom is at the end of the hall. I dress into my T-shirt and skirt. Jeff returns with a large manila envelope from which he produces the document. There's enough paperwork to make a book of it. The lawyer has tagged all the places needing my signature with red Post-it arrows. I don't understand any of the legalese.

Jeff hands me the pen. "Here," he says, indicating where to sign. "And here."

I sign.

Afterwards, Jeff tells me he has a few more things to finish up at work. If I want, I can wait. Otherwise, he'll meet me back at his apartment, and we can go to Red Farm, my favorite restaurant, for dinner. I say I'll meet him at home. I still have a laundry list of wedding errands.

But as soon as I step outside into the street, I feel as if I stepped into a fog. The subway is only two blocks away. Everything feels too raw, and yet, muted at the same time. The sidewalk is crowded with people rushing home from work. Traffic's thick. A cab honks. The subway is two blocks away. I pass boutiques and restaurants, a yoga center, bodega, and a gym. People talk with one another. They work out. Shop. Laugh.

I get on a train heading to my own apartment, but midway, I feel claustrophobic and jump off, walking aimlessly until I find myself at the restaurant where Rick works. I haven't seen him since we broke up. In fact, I haven't seen any of the men I was dating. I place an order with the new hostess up front, and, not seeing Rick anywhere, ask if he is working tonight. She calls his extension and sends me to his office at the back. The room's cramped by an oversized wood desk and chair and a bookshelf containing seasonal odds and ends: Mardi Gras masks and party supplies, Valentine Cupids and red hot candies, Christmas lights and star-shaped candle fixtures, Halloween decorations. There's also an ancient printer and copier, as well as a shelf dedicated to organizing the couple hundred menus, all separated by color into the dozen different renditions. Open on his desk is an oversized account ledger and a stack of receipts.

Rick pushes the chair into the corner to make room for me. He sits back. The seat creaks beneath his weight. "How was the wedding?" Rick asks, getting up and squeezing past me to shut the door. "I saw something about it in the paper."

"It's the end of this week."

"Congratulations."

"I was just at the fitting."

He smirks. "I'm sure the dress is beautiful."

"It is. He designed it for me."

"I'm sure he did."

I describe the dress to him. "Yow," he utters, his hands at my waist. We shift positions. It's swift, even comfortable, like an old, familiar dance. "I'm sorry I don't get to see you in it," he says.

"You've seen me in other things." Heat rushes to my face. Rick has a fetish for tall boots, buckles, lace and ribbons. He is one of the few guys I've ever been with who enjoys getting me off more than actually coming himself. "Um, how's Shadow?" I ask.

"I had to take her back to the pound," he replies, shaking his head. "It just didn't work out, you know? The landlord nearly evicted me."

"I bet." With all that howling whenever a woman sleeps over, it's no wonder. "Getting a dog. It's gotta be a good fit."

"Isn't that the truth," he says.

He probably couldn't find anyone else stupid enough to walk her for him, I think.

"Nobody tells you getting a dog's like getting married," he says. "You wake up, it's there. You come home, it's there. You go to sleep, it's there—"

"You fuck—"

Rick makes a whistling sound through his teeth. His blue eyes bug out, a characteristic Chinese consider unlucky. "That was some crazy shit, wasn't it?" he laughs. I laugh along, but as soon as I do, a trap door swings open inside me. Hot tears swell to my eyes, catching me off guard, and then there's a hurt so big, so sudden, I'm crying. I've never cried in front of Rick before, and in the back of my mind, I know I'll regret it, but at the moment, it's happening and it's too late to stop.

"No," he says, drawing me to him and kissing the tears from my eyes. "This won't do."

But I can't stop.

The more he sees my heartbreak, the more he needs to make things better. He needs to love things right. Rick kisses my neck, moves his hands up my legs. It has been more than a year since we've had sex, and now, his fingers grope the lace hungrily, stumbling upon the hidden slit. He unzips his jeans. His penis isn't long. It's stubby, thick and full. His testicles contract into hard candies.

"I can't," I say.

In one motion, he lifts me, perches his weight at the edge of the desk, and brings me down onto him. We both sigh. The fabric shifts between us. It's distracting and yet stimulating at the same time. I hang there on him, my legs not reaching the floor, afraid to move, afraid to not move. Jeff, the wedding, Ma. There's nothing I can do. I feel so helpless, so sad. Rick rocks, the fullness of him touching the many aches and desires, lost wants, abandoned hope. My body cups around the base of his penis like a mouth. Our bodies cling together, awakened by the lace between us, and then he leans back, tipping me toward him. Something snags. Maybe the sound's coming from inside me.

My entire body tenses, and then all at once, it breaks open. It's the cool ionic spray of a waterfall over my skin, the tingling sensation stretching to the tips of my fingers and toes. And yet it's charcoal hot and so sudden and violent that, while Rick clamps a hand over my mouth to mute the sound, he, comes, too, a range of emotions surging through him and appearing over his face. Desire. Desperation. Rage. Release.

Then, it's over. I've never felt uglier nor emptier. Nor more starved.

Later, Jeff arrives at my apartment bearing flowers and takeout Chinese. The smell of food nauseates me. While we watch TV, he whispers all the things he wants to do to me tonight and all the things he wants me to do to him, but I pretend to fall asleep so I won't have to say no.

A Wedding

"Oh." It's all I can manage. Jeff is best man at his friend's wedding. All well and good, except tomorrow night is the rehearsal dinner, and I'm not invited.

"The restaurant she chose is really intimate," he explains as he spoons the last of the spaghetti into a container. "They have to limit it to close friends and family."

It's 7:30 PM, Thursday. We've eaten, so I scrape the plates, rinse the dishes, and stack them in the dishwasher. Jeff hands me a pot. I make room for it in the dishwasher. Basically, I've survived another week with Alexander, our two year old, but am being denied the get out of jail free card.

"I could have sworn I told you," he says.

"No," I say, locking the dishwasher. "You didn't."

Do I look like the fucking babysitter? I want to yell. I'm sick of being the fucking sitter. The part that hurts most is that I actually know the groom. He is one of Jeff's designers at work, one of the guys who has been with him the longest. He came to my wedding with his former girlfriend. Back when I used to go to industry events with Jeff, I used to see him often.

The house is quiet all of a sudden. Too quiet.

"Alexander?" I rush into the living room. He's got the dog by the tail and is dragging her across the floor. She's a Shih Tzu, a wee little thing, and yet she doesn't yelp or even whine. Instead, she stares with googly eyes.

"Hey!" I yell, freeing her from his grasp. She scampers away, her tail tucked between her legs. I brush off the long locks of hair caught between Alexander's fingers. "Don't do that again, you hear me?"

Alexander rips free, races into the den, and yanks a rack of DVDs from the shelf. The stack clatters to the floor. Instead of being propelled forward to catch them, however, my body goes slack. I look on helplessly. I could run after him. I could clean it all up. But, what's the point? Nothing's going to stop him. The shit's not about to end.

Alexander picks up *The Lion King.* "Watch," he says.

I shake my head no. "Time for bed."

"Now!" He stamps his foot. "Watch *now.*"

"Brush teeth," I say.

Alexander's face reddens and puffs. He pitches the DVD, which hits my right shin, and runs away. I sigh and throw up my hands.

"Don't take it personally," Jeff says, picking up the DVD and moving to the den to gather up the rest.

"I don't," I say. "Actually, I'm taking him to get evaluated next Monday."

Jeff looks at me, confusion twisted in his brows, and I realize he was referring to the wedding.

"I mean Alex," I explain, and then I'm wondering about the rehearsal dinner again: Is it me? Am I just being insecure? Because this is personal, as personal as it gets.

"Didn't you already speak with the pediatrician? Didn't he say everything's okay? Alexander's hit all his, what's the word, markers?"

"Milestones," I say. "That's true, but, really? I mean, what does he know? He doesn't live with the kid."

Jeff watches me, something between patience and pity coming over his face. I can feel him straining to keep his composure. "He's a good kid."

"I'm not saying he's bad." My voice trembles. I notice a Thomas the Tank Engine sticker stuck on the neck of the floor lamp. With my fingernails, I attempt to pick and peel it away. "I've never said that."

"He's a boy, Amy. Boys are rambunctious by nature. They need to run and jump and shoot things. I wasn't so different."

"Really? Did you already have a concussion by the time you turned two?"

"Accidents happen."

"Whatever," I sigh, shrugging it off. "Forget it." My attention flitters back to the stupid wedding. Maybe I am overreacting. After all, it's just a wedding. Ceremony. Reception. Maybe, just maybe, I won't bother going. Ever since we moved out here to the suburbs, I rarely get to see Ben or my other friends. Finally, here's my chance. Why should I waste it on people who obviously don't care, or possibly don't even like me?

"Look, why don't you call the new sitter tomorrow night? Maybe get a massage?" he offers.

"A massage," I repeat. Like, really? Six months ago, I got a call from our previous sitter exactly 15 minutes into the film I was watching. She was frantic.

"Forget I mentioned it," Jeff says, waving me off.

"Considering the fact that Alex nearly bit the girl's hand off—"

"Will you please stop exaggerating."

"Her hand was bleeding through the towel, Jeff."

"Yes, and god only knows what she did to Alex. Bennett said his nanny set his kid on the hot radiator. The kid had burn marks on his legs."

"That's awful, but—"

"Damn right, it's awful. It's criminal. And remember how withdrawn Alex became?" This is true. I found Alex upstairs in my studio, cowering behind a dusty, headless mannequin. Since the pregnancy, I've been blocked creatively, and rather than draping it with muslin, I drew intricate, paisley-like arrangements with tailor's chalk, embellishing it with silver-tipped, ball head pins.

"We need nanny cameras," he says. "That would put us at ease."

I stare at the transparent figure reflecting back at me in the window—hair asunder, sweats, slouched over with discouragement. "Yeah, maybe," I say.

Jeff stacks the pile of DVDs on a higher shelf, then settles onto the couch.

My mind swarms with a mishmash of random, nagging thoughts. Call Georgie about Ma's birthday gift. Add "sugar" to the shopping list. Ask that new mom in the playgroup for the name of her pediatric allergist. Call the tree company to test the towering oak hovering directly above Alex's bedroom.

There's something inside me, something important I need to say right now, if only I could figure out what it is. Only three years ago, I was an aspiring designer fresh out of grad school. I combed through fashion collections, reading up on various designers and working straight through the night, testing fabrics, cutting, pinning, and sewing. Often, I'd still be there to watch the sanitation trucks do their early morning pickup. I pored over drawings with friends, savoring delicious cups of coffee while we took turns commenting on each other's work. We gossiped about lovers and partners, talked about books and movies, and discussed life—what it was, and what it possibly could be—as if we were at the beginning and it would last forever.

But then, Jeff and I moved to a house in the suburbs.

"A boy needs space enough to throw a football," Jeff said.

"You don't even like football." I wasn't happy. I was just beginning to get some "new designer" attention in the industry. But, I didn't say anything. What could I say? My belly grew larger and more bloated each day. Suddenly, I was fat and ugly. Something to be hidden away, and in truth, I was okay with hiding. I had a secret. The pregnancy occurred around the time I messed up taking the pill. It was only one exchange with Rick compared to the many I had with Jeff, so chances were Jeff was the father, but I didn't know for certain. Maybe Jeff sensed it, somehow, or maybe he fell into his old patterns. He started to look elsewhere. He came home reeking of sex and Coco Mademoiselle.

Fashion is a small industry. Everyone knew, which made me feel all the more helpless and ashamed. *Everything here, everything that's yours is mine,* Dad used to say.

So, this is what I understood: Everything that was mine was Jeff's; everything that was Jeff's was not mine. I had signed the prenup. Still, one of the tabloids doctored a photo of me dressed in one of Jeff's "Empress" gowns. The heading read: "Down with the Dowager." The article described me as controlling and "money grubbing." It said I married Jeff for social stature and to get a leg up in the fashion industry.

I kissed Jeff at Helena's party four years ago. Now, despite everything, I could never live it down.

On TV, Jeff tunes into one of the food channels. Chef Donatella Arpaia prepares her famous meatballs, using ground beef and pre-moistened bread. I should watch this and learn to make something Alexander will actually eat. The show has barely started and Jeff's already snoring his way to la-la land. Alexander's still running around like he's got a propeller on top of his head, and Jeff's gonzo.

Something like rage balloons inside me. *He's* tired? While he's at work and then enjoying his extra curricular activities, I'm stuck dealing with Alex. All day and now all goddamn night when Alexander's misery is often at its very finest—and *he's* tired?

Arpaia takes the time to remove her wedding ring. With bare hands, she works her fingers through the beef and bread. She cracks an egg into it, adding fresh, flat-leaf parsley, parmesan, and "lots" of fresh chopped garlic. In my mind, I run the list of injustices I have endured, starting with the fact that we don't have a nanny. The Great Jeff Jones needs privacy. How could he be expected to tolerate strangers in his house?

I hear Alex in the play room next door, hammering at his Bob the Builder work table. On TV, Arpaia continues with the meatballs saying Italians don't measure ingredients. They go by feel. Maybe it's not just the Italians because Ma cooks that way. Since Georgie was the smart daughter and I was the stupid one who was going to get married and have kids instead of a career, Ma forced me to sous chef every night. "A pinch of salt," she would say, intentionally vague, it seemed, or, "add water up to your knuckle." Then she'd wonder why the result was over-ly-salted Chinese broccoli or rice so dry it crunched between one's teeth.

"Now, if you get into a fight with your husband, not that we get into a fight with our husbands," Arapia says, digging into the mix and strangling it with her hands. "You really have to get in there."

Yes, I think. Now, we're cooking. Frustration. Anger. Knead, baby. Strangle it into oblivion.

Suddenly, the house is too quiet, again. Where's Alexander?

As soon as the thought comes into my head, Alexander appears, flying into the room with a toy plane. "Vroom!" he cries.

"No stickers on the furniture, Alexander," I remind, catching him by the arms and pointing out the sticky patch on the lamp post. "You know that." Though I've removed the face of the sticker, the glue remains stubbornly fixed to the lamp.

"Where do stickers go?" I ask. "Where is it okay to stick them?"

Alexander stares blankly back at me.

"On paper," I say.

"Paper," he replies.

"Right, on paper. Not on lamps, or walls, or anywhere except pa-per. Understand?"

"Vroom…"

I grab him by the arm before he takes off again. "Next time it's going to be a time-out for you, Mister. Understand?"

"Ow!" he yells, struggling to get away.

"Understand?" I insist.

"'Stand,'" he finally says.

I let go and Alexander zooms out of the room.

Jeff snores all the more loudly. I stifle the urge to yank the cushion out from beneath his head. Wake up, I want to say. I'm getting royally dissed by your A-hole friends. If I'm going to live in purgatory and take this shit, then the very least you can do is help me figure out what went wrong. Did I inadvertently say something to upset the bride-to-be? There had been an awkward exchange at the end of their engagement party. Could it have been that? The Maid of Honor had thrown a poolside "Hawaiian Luau" at her house in Queens. It was a casual barbecue with bamboo-skewered meats and frozen strawberry daiquiris, each decorated with pineapple and a mini paper umbrella. The day was memorably hot—in the high nineties, and humid. Perfect for swimming. And yet, Alexander refused to get in the pool. He insisted I carry him, screaming any time Jeff or anyone else so much as offered to hold him. I didn't mind. Despite the fact that there were no new toys or other children to play with, Alexander was cheerful and well-behaved. I was proud of him. The bride-to-be said he was so cute, she wanted to pinch him.

Then, as we were about to leave and Jeff had gone to get the car, she finished the last piece of chicken from a skewer and asked if she could poke Alexander with it. He was asleep in my arms.

"That's funny," I laughed, but she stared back, more serious than ever. I switched Alex to my other hip.

"Just a tiny pinch." She pressed forefinger to thumb.

I glanced at the Maid of Honor. Is she really serious? I wanted to ask.

"Oh, stop," the Maid of Honor said. "You're scaring her."

"It won't hurt, I promise."

"How many daiquiris have you had?" the maid of honor asked.

"Come on," the bride-to-be said. "He's so pinchable, I just have to."

The Maid of Honor and I exchanged another glance.

"What?" the bride snipped, defensively.

"You're scaring me," the Maid of Honor said.

"You guys are so funny," I laughed, playing it off as if it was a joke. Later, in the car, however, I recounted the story to Jeff and noted how ironic it was that Alexander hadn't gotten in one of his moods and stabbed someone with a skewer himself. "She wouldn't have thought he was cute enough to poke then," I huffed. The following morning, however, after waking with a hangover that felt like I'd jammed a cup of buttons into my brain, I realized the maid of honor had been right: the incident had a lot more to do with the daiquiris than anything else.

An indistinguishable, thudding sound comes from the kitchen. Jeff wakes. When he sees me, though, he mutters, "Okay," and sinks back into sleep.

Okay? Please, God, not another concussion. I race into the kitchen and find Alexander standing on the marble counter. He's used the bottom cabinet drawers as steps to climb up and reach the cupboards, and is helping himself to a bar of chocolate. The loud sound was a Costco-size bottle of agave, which, now cracked along the lid, is draining across the tiled floor.

"Fuck," I say.

"Fuck," Alexander parrots.

I remove him from the counter and pry the chocolate from his hands. "No chocolate before bedtime," I say.

The kid screams. He flails his arms and tries to kick me. Clutching him to my body football style under one arm, I pick up the bottle of agave and set it on the counter, then throw a paper towel down onto the mess so Jeff won't step in it before I have a chance to clean it up. Alexander squirms and struggles, continuing to writhe as I lug him upstairs, brush his teeth, and dump him, kicking and screaming, into bed. I take the plane from him.

"Give me!" he yells.

"It's right here," I say, setting it on the end table.

He grabs the plane and attempts to climb down from the bed.

"If you do that, no book," I say.

"Book," he insists.

"Then back in bed."

"No."

"Which book?" I ask, showing him the books. "*Where the Wild Things are? Native American Children's Poems? Trucks?* Or *I am a Bunny?*"

"Time to play."

"Play tomorrow."

"No," he says. "Now."

I take the plane from him again and shut the light. He screams, "it's mine!" and flails around so violently that he headbutts me in the mouth. There's an electric shock of pain, then throbbing numbness. My eyes tear. Am I bleeding? I check in the mirror over the bureau. No blood, no swelling.

"Ice," Alexander says. I pick him up and return downstairs. In the kitchen freezer, I dig out two toddler ice packs, each the shape of a different animal. Alex wants the mouse. I take an elephant. We head back upstairs to his bedroom.

Who was it who said that there is nothing to fear but fear itself? Oh, yes. That's right—FDR. The bombing of Pearl Harbor. One of America's "darkest" hours. Well, here, it's bedtime for Alex, and after two years, there is still no bigger and darker hour for me than now.

Alexander holds the mouse ice pack up to his head while I keep mine to my mouth. He chooses *I Am a Bunny*. My voice is muffled: "I am a—"

"Bunny!" he finishes.

I fix the pillow behind me. "I live in a—"

"Hollow tree!" he yells.

We read to the end of the book, and then, taking the ice packs and setting them on the end table on top of the books, I say, "Okay, time for night-night."

"No!" He tries to jump out of bed.

"Yes." I block him with my body and hold him back. "We can read more tomorrow."

His arms flail. His legs kick. I remain beside him, keeping at a safe distance, using my hands to block, if necessary. I shut the light. "It's okay, Alex," I say. "I'm right here."

"No," he says, hitting me.

I catch hold of him firmly by the wrists. "No hitting," I say, looking him in the eye. "That's not okay, you hear? Not okay."

He struggles for another fifteen minutes. When he finally gives in, I can feel the tension drain from his body. It's dark now, but the moonlight comes in from the window, and his face seems soft and peaceful. I release him.

"Nai nai," he demands. Milk, more milk.

"No nai nai," I say, gently.

"Yes," Alex insists, tugging at my shirt. "Yes."

"No," I say more firmly, taking hold of his hands. But he claws at my clothing, at me, at anything, until my arms and hands are raw.

"Stop," I say. "It's okay, Alexander. Stop."

After half an hour, he finally relents and starts to drift off. The Sleep Lady promised this would get easier each night if we followed the routine she laid out for us. But it's been three—almost four— weeks now. Maybe we should try Ferberizing again?

"Mommy sleep here," he begs, patting the space beside him. He clenches my hand.

"I'm right here," I say, sitting in the rocking chair beside him.

"No here," he cries. "Mommy here."

I try to pry his hands free. The Sleep Lady's instructions were for me to sit beside and talk to him, if necessary, but no hand holding. And then, over the course of days or weeks, I would gradually move away from the bedside toward the door. Simple, right?

He tantrums again. And, again. I check the time. It's 8:30pm. Then 9. Then 10. I try to remain patient. I close my eyes, and while I'm not religious, I find myself praying, "God, please help me. Please, please help me." I need to see some kind of progress, some kind of change, just to keep from giving up entirely.

Some time after 11 PM, when Alex starts screaming again, Jeff roars from our master bedroom: "I have to work tomorrow, God damn it!"

My body feels like lead. I lie down next to Alex, and as he falls asleep, let myself drift away.

A sound wakes me. I'm alone in bed. Where's Alexander? Then I see him in the corner of the room. What's he doing? He's got markers in his hands. Where'd he get markers? Then, I see him scribbling on the wall.

"Fuck!" I yell, and I jump to my feet, grab and slap him on the behind. "Alexander, no, fuck, no!"

He turns and I get the back of the marker straight to the rib. A rage wells up inside me so deep that I spank him on the backside until I'm panting for breath. My parents used to hit. They said they had to "beat out the stubbornness."

"I'm doing this for your own good," Ma said.

"Do you think I would bother if you were the kid next door?" Dad asked. "It's because I care that I do this."

And then he left us for good.

I always swore I would never hit my own kids. Ma hit, and now, as much as I love her, there's a sliver of me that despises her, too. I don't want that with Alex. I want something different. Better.

Hopelessness, I realize, is a swamp I've lived in so long that maybe it's who I now am.

In the morning, as soon as I drop Alex at pre-school, I call Ben to see if he can meet me for dinner tonight. No luck, he's dining out with his new boyfriend. I feel foggy and exhausted, yet at the same time, I am buzzing with nervous energy. I try another close friend, but she's going with her son to a party in Red Hook. I check with my masseuse, but he's fully booked. The aesthetician already has a 5 o'clock appointment and can't work past 6.

There's a scene in one of my favorite movies, *The Hours*, when actress Julianne Moore, who plays a woman feeling trapped by motherhood and life, checks into a hotel in the middle of the day. She needs time to read and re-claim herself. I could do that. Just go somewhere for some peace and quiet, a hot bubble bath, and some sleep. Or, I could go to the coffee shop, load up on caffeine, and read. As I walk the dog, I realize that neither option will work: I'm too exhausted to read and too anxious to sleep. A dull headache extends from the top of my head down the back of my neck.

Later, I stop at the pharmacy to pick up some Motrin. While I stand in line at the register, I double check that Jeff hasn't called. Any minute, now, he'll ring to tell me he spoke with the groom and that it was all a silly misunderstanding. Or, he'll just surprise me and show up, unexpected, in the late afternoon to say: "I told him to have a great rehearsal dinner without me, and I'd see him tomorrow morning at the wedding." It's stupid and naive, but there's still hope; a part of me's holding out for love.

On the magazine rack, I notice the latest issue of *People*, and realize I'm no longer familiar with the personalities on the front cover. I used to feed off the latest designer fashions to inform my own closet, but somehow even these seem foreign to me now. I glance down at the sweats I'm wearing. My hair is back up in a messy ponytail. I feel myself slump lower. I don't need a mirror to know what I must look like.

There used to be a beautiful, sexy woman inside this body. Where the hell did she go? Did she truly exist? If this dis-invite had occurred pre-marriage, I wouldn't have minded in the least. So why am I upset now?

Then I realize. This would never have happened pre-marriage. Jeff would have known I'd be out with someone else the second he walked out that door. Jeff would never have allowed that to happen. But, now, I'm married. There's a kid. I'm not going anywhere.

"You okay?" the clerk asks, as she charges the Motrin.

"Headache," I say, trying to hold back tears. How is it possible for a person to devolve from believing that anything is possible, to someone who believes nothing is possible? The morning of our wedding, final pages of the prenup were still being faxed to me. I signed. Faxed them back. During the ceremony, as the pianist played the wedding march, I walked down the church aisle, fatherless and alone, and felt a confusing sense of mourning.

It was us, I realize. The romance—*we*—were dead.

I drive to the health food store and traipse up and down the aisles of the market, filling my cart with items on the list. I made a mental note to add something to the list last night—I remember that clearly—but what it was, I can't recall. Come on, think, Amy. *Think.* Finally, when the time nears pickup, I give up.

I check the phone. Jeff hasn't called. Instead of brooding about how clueless I've become, I search the internet for possible movies to see. Usually, I can find a film at the Jacob Burns Film Center, which is close enough in Pleasantville. Tonight, however, nothing seems right.

It's 11:45 AM by the time I get out of the store. It's already time to pick up Alexander.

"Playground," Alex insists, as we leave the red, brick building of the pre-school.

"Later," I promise. "We can go after lunch."

"No," he says, pulling away from me and running to the playground. His favorite is the twisty slide.

"Alexander," I call, running after him. "Stop."

He runs to the slide and climbs up its ladder. My phone rings. It's Jeff! My heart balloons.

"Hey," I answer.

"Everything set for tonight? You getting a massage?"

"Maybe," I say. Alexander dives head-first down the slide. Jeff starts to speak, but I tell him I have to go and hang up.

I arrange for the sitter to arrive by 3 pm, telling her when she arrives that I'll be home by 9 or 10 pm. There's a new Star Wars Lego set in the closet. I give it to the sitter, then prepare dinner and run an early bath. When Alex is in his PJs and building the fighter plane, I shower and get ready even though I'm still not certain for what.

The first thing I try on is a white Theory dress. It makes me look fat. The second is a Helmet Lang jersey dress, but that makes me look frumpy. Finally, I step into what I originally planned to wear to the wedding, a form-fitting, black Herve Leger dress with white piping. But this, too, looks wrong. How could I have possibly considered this dress for the wedding? I wonder now. I walk the dog, give the sitter my cell phone number, along with my permission for Alex to watch TV if things get hairy. Then, I drive straight to The Westchester mall and valet the car at Neiman Marcus.

Everything seems quieter the moment I step inside. The marble floors. The clear glass counters displaying jewelry and makeup. I ride the escalator up a floor to the apparel section, being careful to avoid the Jeff Jones Collection. Today, there's a sale. Even Helmet Lang has a rack. My hand is drawn to a tight-fitting black dress: compressed twill, sleeveless, and with the sexiest, yet most elegant back ever. In the fitting room, I try it on. The salesperson zips me up. It's like skin. I feel my old self coming back. I smooth my hands down the front, turn to check the rear view from over my shoulder, then turn again to check the other side. The body is still there after all.

"Wow," she says.

"How much?"

"$268.80. Down from $448."

"I love it." I hand her the credit card and my old dress.

"You'll wear it out?"

"Hell, yeah," I say.

When she's gone to the register, I take off my wedding ring and drop it into my change purse. Tonight, I'm not a wife or mother. I'm me. I call the Japanese salon in town to ask if my hairdresser can squeeze me in. He says yes—he's had a cancellation!—but only if I arrive within the hour. "I'm there," I say.

The sales clerk returns with my receipt and a scissor to cut away the tags. I stop next at the shoe department and immediately gravitate toward a Jimmy Choo sandal. It's made of snake-embossed leather with black contrast piping and a 4" metallic heel. The design and detail, the sheer craftmanship, makes these more—much, much more—than just a pair of shoes. As Armani once said, "To create something exceptional, your mindset must be relentlessly focused on the smallest detail." Here is proof of it. Something like awe fills my chest. *This* is the power of beauty.

It's my size. I slip the one shoe onto my foot, and, oh, yes. I'm in love. In the full-length mirror, I see a transformation of myself back into the person I once was.

"How much?"

"$925."

Ouch.

"This is the last pair," the salesman says.

How to justify? Well, I did save more than two hundred on the dress. Besides, I don't have a pair of sandals like these. And I'm Jeff Jones's wife. I need to be presentable. I can't be looking like a mismatched FOB. "I'll take them," I say, handing over the card.

I go 70 mph on the Bronx River Parkway, and arrive at the hair salon with minutes to spare. My hairdresser is a man named Morita. His clients refer to him as "the Magnificent." He wears a long, neat ponytail down his back and sunglasses perched on top of his head.

He assesses my hair critically—the way a designer might examine the seams of a coat—and asks what I'd like. It's been almost a year and a half since my last trim. "Long layers?" I say, which is vague, considering the many kinds of layering techniques. Then, glancing over at the dye-job next to me with plastic wrap around her head, I add, "Highlights."

He sets to work, lightening the hair, then cutting while we talk about our kids. I tell him honestly about Alex: not only about how tough it has been, but how clueless my husband is about the situation. "I don't know who I am anymore," I say, as he paints and foils the side of my head. "It's like the real me got lost." I try not to cry because it's not Japanese to lose control, but my mind snags against the prenup and the many other injustices. The assistant needs to give me a Kleen-ex. I feel mortified that I may have embarrassed Morita, and yet, I confide that nothing I do, nothing I endure, will ever be enough to prove my love to Jeff. "I'm done trying," I explain, and once I say it—once it's out there—it becomes obvious. I'm not in love with Jeff, anymore.

An hour and a half after he starts, Morita's angling a hand-held mirror behind me so that I can see the back of my head as well as the front. My normally long, flat hair falls in what seems like waves. The highlights are subtle, but they brighten my entire face. I'm free.

I smile, and the person in the mirror radiates pure love back at me.

"Okaerinasai," he says, nodding with reverence. "Welcome back."

What to do? Nothing comes to mind, even now, but it would be a waste to go home so soon. It's only 6:45 pm; too early. The June weather is warm and beautiful—picture perfect for a rehearsal dinner, and so filled with new life and hope that I'm overcome with melancholy.

I get in the car and drive. For a moment, I consider calling Ma to meet for dinner, but one look and she'll know what's going on. The last thing I need right now is Ma railing about Jeff and how she told me so.

Within twenty minutes, I find myself at a restaurant on the Hudson.

The hostess asks if I have a reservation, and when I say no, she indicates there is an hour wait for a table. However, if I like, I may enjoy a seat at the bar, or, since the weather has been so accommodating, perhaps I'd prefer the rooftop bar?

"Perfect," I say.

On the roof, I lean against the wall with a glass of Sancerre and watch the sun set over the mercury water. Right about now, Jeff would be enjoying drinks and appetizers. Possibly toasting the wedding couple. "Here's to your future together," he'd say.

I finish my drink. The river seems huge under this blanket of dark sky, the water silvery in the beam of moonlight. I think about the rainbow lollipops that night at The Cape. I can almost taste the cherry sweetness. That was the moment, I think now. That was the moment when I chose Jeff over the others. When I fell in love.

How young, I think. Naive.

The Hudson drifts, strong and steady, and I think: in a thousand years, when my bones are nothing more than dust, the river will remain, unchanged, indomitable. A breeze whips my hair. Is it possible to fall out of love with someone over a single incident? One which, to be fair, is not really that person's fault?

My mind shifts gears, landing on the practical issues of divorce. What would I do and where would I go? How could I possibly handle Alexander on my own? Should I wait a couple years until he is older?

I think about Ma. She's bitter and alone. Full of blame. What, exactly, do I tell her?

"Would you like another glass of wine?" the waiter asks.

I turn to say yes, and find it's not the waiter after all. The stranger's a lean 6'2" or so, late 30s or early 40s, light brown hair, brown eyes. He's wearing a grey suit that fits a little too loosely about the sleeves and torso, but with his height he can pass it off.

"William," he says, offering me one of his two glasses. When I hesitate, he adds, "It's Sancerre. I asked."

My phone rings. It's Jeff. I realize it's already close to 10 pm. The dinner is probably over and either Jeff's on his way home or he's at a bar with the wedding party. I drop the phone back into my purse and take the glass offered to me. "Thank you, William," I say. "What brings you here tonight?"

"Fate?"

We laugh. Our glasses touch. His gaze is so intense, I can feel him reaching, trying to take root inside me.

I don't look away.

Blood

"Get him a full day private," I tell Jeff as I check the blind spot and change lanes. We're on our way to Stratton. It's 6 PM and getting dark out. The snow's coming down like sticky balls of cotton. In the three years since our last visit, Jeff has opened retail stores in London and Hong Kong, and Alex, now ten, plays travel hockey. The tournament in Massachusetts got cancelled this weekend due to rink issues, so Alex wanted to ski. The resort's projecting heavy snow: eight inches overnight, another three to four in the early morning, and late-morning sunshine. What luck. Jeff and Alex are thrilled.

"Yes, seven," Jeff says. He's on the phone with the lodge, making dinner reservations.

"I don't want a private," Alex says from the back seat, too busy gaming to look up.

"Tell them to transfer you to the ski school," I tell Jeff.

"No, don't," Alex says.

"For three, correct," Jeff says, louder, gesturing with a wave of a hand for us to be quiet.

"We can get an instructor who can ski at your level," I say, glancing at Alex in the rear view mirror. "That guy Tommy, remember? The college kid. Maybe he's still there? You really liked him."

"I don't need a babysitter," Alex says.

"How about 6:30, then?" Jeff asks, plugging his ear with a finger.

"It's your first time out in years, Alex," I say.

"I'll be fine."

"What was that?" Jeff asks, into the phone. "Six? Nothing later? You sure?"

"Don't worry," Alex says. "For once, just trust me."

"I do trust you," I say, which isn't a total lie. What I don't trust is the ADHD. In my mind, it's like a giant, frenetic glob. When Alex gets excited, upset, or shaken up, he gets swallowed up by its static. By the time he was seven, he'd suffered three concussions. The first when he was 1 1/2, from climbing onto a kitchen chair and falling; the second when he was three, from swinging on the furniture. And the third when he was five, from playing Evel Knievel on his bike.

"Now look what you made me do," Alex gasps.

"What?" I ask.

"Nothing," he groans.

"Jones," Jeff says. "Yes, Jeff Jones."

"Alex," I say, lowering my voice and watching him in the rear view mirror. He glances up and catches my gaze, his brows furrowed and mouth pinched tight. "I want someone with you the first few runs. Just until you get your ski legs back, okay?"

"No," Alex states.

"Oh, you do?" Jeff says into the phone. "I think that might work."

"I'm fine." Alex turns his attention back to the game.

"But—" I say.

"I said, I'm fine!" he yells.

"See you this evening," Jeff says, slipping his phone back into his jacket pocket.

"You hung up? Didn't you hear what I said?"

"About what?" Jeff asks.

Behind us, Alex starts another round of Minecraft. I can't see it, but I can hear the rapid motion of his thumbs over the keyboard.

"A private," I say. "For Alex."

"Oh, he doesn't need a private," Jeff states, checking his email.

The corner of Alex's mouth twitches upward, just slightly. The dynamic duo. Nothing penetrates the two. I get a flash of him snow-boarding down a black double diamond—pure recklessness and inten-sity—and feeling suddenly dissatisfied, veering off trail into a woody thicket.

"Jeff," I insist.

"It's fine, Amy," he says. "I'll go with him."

"Yeah," Alex says. "He'll go with me."

I stare at Jeff. He turns 64 next month. With the aid of Viagra and his latest "secret" affair, he has the notion that he's as virile as he was in his twenties.

"You can really keep up?" I say.

Jeff stiffens. "Of course I can."

"Of course he can," Alex parrots.

"Okay," I shrug. In the past, this kind of exchange with Jeff would frustrate me. Make me resentful. Today, however, I feel a strange mix of detachment and resignation. Neither of them knows, but this is our last weekend together as a family unit. I'm leaving. No more hemming and hawing. This time, it's for real. My suitcase is already at my sister Georgie's. So, in the end, do I really need to win this battle?

"Welcome to Vermont," the sign reads. "The Green Mountain State."

Jeff's phone rings. Whenever his office calls, there's a strum of the guitar. At the moment, however, it's a regular ring tone. "Hello?" he answers with his fake voice. "Mm hm... mm hm... a very *big* order... Yes, that's right...Okay, then, see you Monday."

Whatever. I actually feel sorry for him. He still thinks I'm going to be jealous or hurt about his escapades. But, really, it's like that quote the Jewish Community Center put on the facade of their building by writer Elie Wiesel: "The opposite of love is not hate, it's indifference."

The only thing I'm uncertain about is why *he* hasn't asked for a divorce. He's the one with the prenup, and yet, despite his infidelities and mine, he's careful never to put the "D" word on the table. Whenever

I do, he always finds a way to assuage the situation. Two years ago, he immediately dropped the affair, swore he wouldn't cheat again, and brought me up to the same house in Cape Cod where we spent our first summer together. It's like an elevator. Every time I get inside, he jams his foot in the doors, jarring them back open.

When we get onto route 279, I follow the trail of other SUVs with skis or Thules bolted to the rooftops. The car directly in front of us has an "Of course I'm awesome, I'm a Stratton" bumper sticker. We pass a stream I don't recall ever seeing before. Could we have all missed the exit to route 9? The snow's coming down harder, forcing traffic to slow to 30 miles per hour. My chest aches with tenderness. I've decided Alex will stay with Jeff. He's older; in all likelihood he'd want to be with Jeff anyway. There's really no choice. I start as a floor salesman at Bloomingdale's next week, and it will be a while before I have enough saved to get my own place.

"Oh," Alex startles, looking up from the game now.

"What's wrong?" I ask. Guilt is like the snow. Sticky, cold, and silent as it falls.

Jeff turns to Alex.

"My swim trunks," Alex says. "You pack them?"

"Oh, no," I say. "It slipped my mind."

"Mom!" Alex barks. "How could you forget? You know everyone hangs at the pool at night—"

Jeff shushes him. "It's fine."

"No, it's not," Alex says. "You always say everything's fine when it's not."

Alex does have a point.

"Your mother will pick one up in the morning," Jeff says.

"I will? I mean, I was planning to rent skis."

Jeff's brow twitches. Typically, I spend these weekends catching up on sleep, getting a massage, and running errands. It's the reason I don't own skis.

"Fine," Jeff says. "I'll get them."

Alex makes a tsking sound through his teeth and shoots me a hostile, penetrating look. Jeff purchases clothes based on design taste. He remains unaware, almost belligerently so, of Alex's sensory issues. If the suit isn't loose enough or the fabric is anything other than sweat-wicking or breathable, Alex's eczema flares up. To a certain extent, it will anyway; Alex is sensitive to chlorine. He needs the "right" suit in order to reduce potential misery.

"Which stores carry swim apparel?" Jeff asks.

Alex catches my gaze in the rear view mirror. *Please*, he says, silently.

Fine. I roll my eyes. "I'll take care of it."

"Thanks, mom." Alex smiles and pats me from behind. I would have done it anyway, but today, there's the added reason of making this weekend as perfect as possible. If he's going to remember something, I don't want it to be that I wouldn't run a simple errand for him.

The next day, the boys are out the door by 8 AM. They want to hit the slopes as soon as the lifts start running. I remain in bed, aching and exhausted. Not just the physical body, but the soul. I dread hurting Alex; possibly even losing him.

Jeff texts at 9 AM. He's made a reservation for noon at the Japanese restaurant. If I'm going to rent skis and hit the bunny slope, I need to get going. A long, hot shower fogs the bathroom mirror. I wipe a hand over the glass. My reflection appears, then slowly, slowly vanishes.

By the time I get skis and poles from rentals, it's close to 11AM. Only an hour before lunch. God forbid I'm late, and we lose our reservation. The Great Jeff Jones would get stuck eating cafeteria fast food like everyone else. Since I'm going on the bunny slope, the easiest and shortest trail of them all, there's definitely time for a run. The guy paired up with me on the lift line has hair down to his shoulder blades, the front pulled back into a ponytail holder. No mustache or beard, but the type Ma would derogatorily refer to as "Jesus" because she hates men with long hair. There's something about his eyes. One's green, one's blue. We get to talking. I tell him about Alex, whom Jeff's probably killing himself trying to keep up with right now.

I ask Jesus what he does, and he tells me he teaches a personal development course. All the while, I pay attention to the timing of the lift. For every pair of skiers who get off, another gets scooped up and carried away. When we get to the front of the line, I'm nervous about pushing off and timing it so that I make it onto the lift correctly. "Put the poles in your other hand," he advises.

I switch hands. The chair circles toward us. The attendant grabs hold of it and scoops it beneath us. I'm seated, but the tip of my right ski dips forward and I lose my balance. Even as I feel myself lifting into the air, my ski dangles like it's going to tow me off.

Jesus draws me back with one arm and tugs the safety guard down with the other. My heart pounds so hard that it's all I can hear. For a moment, I'm lost, full of trepidation. Maybe it's how I'll feel when everything comes crashing down. When I'm alone.

"You all right?" Jesus asks.

"No." Tears gush down my face, "Yes, oh my god, I'm so sorry, it's just—" I choke it all back.

"It's okay," he says. "We all have our moments."

Then I'm crying in front of a total stranger and I don't care. All the hurt and sadness I've hoarded throughout my marriage comes flooding out.

The lift jerks to a standstill. The chairs rock in unison. Forward and back. Forward, back.

I brush the tears away with my fingers. "What's happening? Why'd we stop?"

Jesus shrugs. "At least we can enjoy a moment of sunshine."

Sunshine? I hadn't noticed the sun was out. The world felt grey and ominous. Now with the warmth on my face, I notice that, suspended in the air, over the blanket of white snow below, everything seems more quiet. Almost serene. Broom-swept clouds fill the azure sky. Sequins of sunlight reflect off helmets of those rushing down the mountain. For a moment, nobody knows anything and it's okay.

Forward and back.

"Feel better?" he asks.

"Yes, thanks." Skiers and boarders rush by below us, carving S shapes down the mountain. Fast and slow. Old and young. Edges and V's. I think about Jeff and how it's been over and yet not over since the night we met, and wonder if that's what life is, just people rushing past and meaning nothing, except for those select people, who, for some reason are on the same lift as you, and for what? Because in the end, even they have come only to go, and what's the meaning in it all? The trail of skiers tapers off. The mountain grows quiet.

I introduce myself to my lift partner and he tells me his name is Cameron. He just moved to New York City. When I ask about his personal development coaching, he tells me it's called The Masters Class, which conjures images of bald men with orange robes and nonsensical koans.

"What exactly gets mastered?" I ask, barely able to keep a straight face.

"Life."

I have to give it to him. It's not a bad response.

"It's about learning to live one's life consciously and deliberately," he says. "And examining one's beliefs."

"My friend Ben would be into that," I nod. "He attends those Tony Robbins things."

"It's quite different," Cameron says, and by the way he says it, I'm guessing he doesn't think much of Tony Robbins. "But he might find it helpful all the same." He hands me a couple business cards from his wallet. "You may benefit from our methods as well."

"Thanks." I glance at my watch. It's 11:45 AM. Even if the lift starts immediately, I won't get to the restaurant in time. For all I know, Jeff and Alex may be stuck on the lift themselves. My phone indicates there's no cell service on this slope, but Jeff has texted: "CALL ME."

My anxiety spikes. He must be at the restaurant already.

In the distance, there's the beating sound of a helicopter. White with a red cross, it passes overhead, disappearing to the other side of the mountain. "Someone must have gotten hurt," I say. "The last time we were here, someone skied into a tree."

"It must be serious," Cameron nods.

It's past noon. Alex will be famished by now. The texts aren't going through, but I write one anyway: "Eat without me. I'll see you back at the lodge." Again, the message is not delivered.

After another fifteen minutes, the helicopter reappears and returns from the direction it first came. The lift heaves to a start. I get off at the first exit area. Cameron continues up the mountain. People say skiing is like riding a bike. Once you have it down, it's down for good. That must be true for young people. Or those who are athletic. For me, the baby hill seems like Mt. Everest. I start off snowplowing. Kids and other beginners zig zag around me. I stiffen, determined to maintain control, nervous they'll crash into me.

Easy, Amy, go easy.

Plow right, then left. Right, left. Half way down, my body eases up. More confident, I parallel, taking the curves smoothly. It's all in the hips and knees. Almost effortless. Then, I'm at the base of the mountain. I've done it. It's over.

After lunch, I'll try again. Maybe I'll try the green trails next.

I step out of the skis, stand them against the rack, and walk as swiftly as possible to the restaurant. It's nearly 1 PM. They may be finishing up. When I arrive, however, I see they've gone. They must be back on the slopes. I walk to the village area. As luck would have it, I find a long pair of surf boarding pants that feel extra silky soft. The length will make it safe to cut out the netting, the part that causes Alex the most discomfort.

After picking up a salad for myself, I walk back to the lodge, snow crunching beneath my boots. I call Jeff, just in case he has phone reception.

"You still in the village?" he asks.

"Got em," I say, about the swim trunks. "I'm headed back to the room."

"Wait, you need to come back." He pauses. "Alex is in the emergency clinic."

Everything stops. Breathing. Heartbeat. A chill razors through me. The helicopter. My Alex.

In the ER clinic, the doctor goes through the concussion protocol, checking pupil dilation, vision, eye tracking, knee reflexes, and memory. "How many fingers am I holding up?" the doctor asks, holding up index and middle fingers.

"Two," Alex states, his face yellowish-grey.

"Now?" the doctor asks, holding all digits except the thumb.

"Four." Alex lurches forward, vomiting onto the doctor's black clogs. The doctor cringes and stiffly steps back.

"I'm so sorry, doc," I say.

"It's fine," he sighs. "I buy these in bulk."

The doctor instructs the nurse to start an IV to keep Alex hydrated. "We can give him an anti-nausea medication," he says.

"Fine," Jeff says.

"Ten milligrams, Metoclopramide," the doctor tells the nurse.

"Shouldn't we be getting an X-ray or something?" Jeff asks.

"I'm putting in an order for a CT scan," the doctor says, monitoring the pulse.

I know from the last concussive experience that scans are to rule out internal bleeding. If they show injury, the diagnosis changes from concussion to "mild traumatic brain injury." The doctor finishes his assessment. He types his notes into the computer.

"Okay, Alex," the doctor says. "I'm going to say a few words. I'd like you to repeat them back to me in the correct order."

"I want to go home," Alex whines, squinting from the fluorescent light.

"We're at Stratton, Alex," Jeff says.

"Like, duh!" he snaps.

Jeff startles. Derision is usually reserved for me.

"It's a figure of speech, Jeff," I say. "He means the lodge."

"I realize that," Jeff retorts. "I wanted to be certain he wasn't having a memory lapse."

Typically, I back off from confrontation. Today, however, I lock my gaze with Jeff's until he looks away.

"Okay, Alex. Repeat these back to me: Finger, penny, blanket, lemon, insect," the doctor says.

"Finger—"

"Penny," Jeff silently mouths.

"Lemon, insect…" Alex pauses. "I don't know."

Skin sags around Jeff's eyes. Worry lines bracket his mouth.

"Okay." The doctor types into the computer. "Candle, paper, sugar, sandwich, wagon."

"My head hurts," Alex complains.

"We'll discuss that, I promise," the doctor says. "Let's get through this assessment, first."

"Okay," Alex says.

"Candle, paper, sugar, sandwich, wagon," the doctor repeats.

"Candle…" Alex says.

Paper, I think. Jeff mouths the word.

"Keep going," the doctor says.

"Candle…" Alex says, starting to cry. He holds his head in his hands. "My head's going to blow up."

"Okay, enough," the doctor says, typing more notes.

"You can lie down, sweetheart," I tell Alex, helping him get settled.

The nurse has brought a warm blanket. He curls up with it over his face as I gently rub his back. When he seems to be asleep, I turn to Jeff. "What happened?"

"I told you," he says. "He went off trail into a thicket."

"And?"

"And, what? He's okay."

"What the fuck happened, Jeff?"

"Well, you can see what happened." He waves a hand at Alex.

"Um, the last I checked," I say, through gritted teeth, "skiing into a thicket doesn't cause a head injury. That is *unless—something—happens*."

"He jumped a ledge, all right?" Jeff booms. "There was a 60-foot drop."

"A what?!"

"He would have landed it, except the edge of his ski caught a rock," Jeff says, deflating. "He flipped and hit the back of his head."

If only I could hit the back of *your* fucking head, you stupid, arrogant prick.

Alex buries his head under the blanket. I switch the bucket to the other side of the bed.

"Did he lose consciousness?" I ask. More than 20 minutes is considered a more serious injury.

"Barely," he says.

"Exactly how long?"

"I don't know. Maybe a few minutes."

"How long?" I yell. "Jeff!"

"15 minutes."

"Fifteen minutes!"

"He's going to be fine," Jeff says.

"We are in the ER," I say. "He is not fine."

"Why do you always have to..." His voice trails off.

"Have to what?" I challenge. "Don't act like I'm making mountains out of molehills, Jeff. Didn't I *say* we should get—"

"We didn't know this would happen," Jeff argues.

"I knew this could happen. I told you, but you didn't listen. You never listen."

"Listen to what? Are you psychic?" He throws up his hands. "This could have happened to anyone."

"You were trailing behind Alex," I say.

"So? An instructor would have been too."

"An instructor would have caught up to him as soon as he went off trail," I argue. "He would have known about the cliff and cut him off before the pass."

"So now you're the expert," he says. "You don't even ski, but you know better."

"Excuse me," the doctor reluctantly interrupts. "Do you know Alex's blood type?"

"His what?" I ask.

"Don't worry about it," he says. "I put in the order for the scan, but in the meantime, I'm sending you to the lab for bloodwork."

"Us?" I ask.

"In case we need a match," the doctor says.

Beneath all the lies and deceit are justifications and heartbreak. The chance that Rick's Alex's biological father is one in a million, but, however minuscule, the possibility exists. Secrets, I realize, live in every moment, lurking within the buffer of months and years. They grow like parasites. Wait to be exposed.

That day. Every thought and emotion, every sensation comes back to me. The lofty feeling of being in front of the mirrors; Jeff's hands brushing the lace, tucking me here and pinning me there. The prenup, which needed to be signed here, and here, and here....

"You really think he needs a transfusion?" Jeff asks.

The word "transfusion" draws me back to the room. "What?"

"It's possible," the doctor says.

"What exactly are you looking for on the scan?" Jeff asks.

"Indicators of internal bleeding," the doctor says. "Swelling. Trauma to the brain."

I swallow.

"If so, we may need to put in a stent," he says.

"A stent?" Feeling suddenly lightheaded, I close my eyes.

"He's fine," Jeff says. "He's not going to need a stent."

"Yes, first things first. Let's start with the scans," the doctor says. "If there's little swelling, this may be a moot point."

"Please, god," I pray.

Jeff's phone sounds. He lets it ring until it goes to voicemail. Alex throws off the blanket and vomits. It sprays the blanket and floor, missing the bin altogether.

"It's okay, sweetheart," I say, using a paper towel to wipe the spittle from his mouth.

"I don't feel good," Alex whimpers, hiding under the blanket again.

"I know, baby." I remove the soiled blanket. The nurse spreads a clean one over Alex and me. Transport arrives to take Alex to radiology. Alex wakes when I get up from the bed. "Don't go," he says, so exhausted he can barely open his eyes.

"I won't," I say.

"Daddy," Alex moans, blindly reaching with a hand.

"I'm here," Jeff assures, from the other side of the bed. "Mommy and Daddy are right here with you."

Transport wheels Alex down the corridor to radiology.

"Don't leave me," Alex cries.

"We won't."

"Promise," he cries.

"Promise," Jeff says, and he doesn't let go.

Black Ice

It's 6:30 PM and snowing again. As I leave work, the sales manager waves goodbye through the glass window. I acknowledge her with a nod, wrap my scarf tightly around my neck, and check to see if Alex texted back yet. Options for dinner tonight include Chinese, Japanese, or Greek. If I call and order now, the food will be ready by the time I get off the subway. The wind has picked up. There's an ugly edge to it. This morning, before the hustle of rush hour, the beauty of the city snowscape nearly brought tears to my eyes. The soft downy whiteness coating the streets. The crunch of snow beneath my boots. The hush, as if I were sharing some kind of secret. I felt so grateful about life: mostly about the job, but Alex, too. For a moment, I glimpsed a future. While my current position was only Assistant buyer, and while Monarch was not established like JJ or other boutiques like Intermix, there would be more opportunity if I did well. There was hope.

But now, the wind smacks me so hard in the face that I'm not feeling quite as positive nor hopeful. Head down, I barrel toward the subway. The cold seeps through my down coat as if it were nothing but tissue paper. I hold my breath with each gust. Slush pools at the curbs, starting to harden. There are footprints where people navigate around them. It's still rush hour. Despite the heavy flow of pedestrian traffic, people wait their turn to follow in these tracks. I'm wearing fur-lined, knee high Aquatalia boots, which are famous for their resilience to the winter elements. They're warm and keep my feet dry, but there's a heel, which makes me more cautious. At the subway where there's salt over the sidewalk, I hurry down the steps and check my phone. Alex has texted back: "Korean."

There's no cell service in the station, so I return up the steps to call the restaurant. The wind rages with such ferocity, the person at the other end of the line can hardly make out what I'm saying.

"Two bibimbaps!" I yell.

"What's that?" he asks.

Ugh. I hang up, my eyes tearing from the cold. The restaurant is exactly four blocks from my stop and then there are another four blocks—two long ones—to Jeff's. I race down the steps, pause to reconsider, then return back upstairs.

I text Alex: "Freezing. Lemon chicken soup, Greek salad, gyro, ok?"

People rush past, brushing against me and disappearing down the steps to shelter. I resist the urge to race after them, and when I don't hear from Alex immediately, I text again: "?"

"Please?" he responds. "BIBIMBAP."

"K. B3 it is." Alex hasn't eaten much, if anything, today, so it's actually a good sign he wants to eat at all. Jeff started Alex on some kind of listening therapy this morning. It was at least 45 minutes by car, way out by the Woodbury outlet stores, during which Alex apparently got car sick. Ever since the accident two years ago, Alex suffers from frequent migraines and motion sickness. Jeff called me because he considered staying the night at an inn, even though it's actually my night with Alex. Technically, according to the "agreement," I get Alex Monday to Thursday. But Jeff rented a place two blocks east of the hospital, and on my nights, I visit Alex there. It's better this way. Alex refuses to visit Georgie's because her apartment is practically on top of the hospital ambulances. The sirens and whirling lights trigger symptoms for traumatic brain injury. Jeff works from home and takes Alex to all his appointments at the hospital. He also researches different alternatives. Jeff is so hands-on that I was able to take an internship last year. And now, as of three months ago, this assistant buyer position.

I retreat into the subway, shivering, my knuckles red and my hand so stiff from cold I can hardly make a fist.

At Jeff's, Alex is asleep on the sofa. Jeff is on the phone, speaking with his assistant from the office. He gestures to be quiet by touching a forefinger to his lips. I remove my coat, and while Jeff disappears into his office in the other room, I make myself a cup of hot tea. The prenup had made it easier to separate and divorce. That day in the hospital, before Jeff and I got results back from the lab, I confessed about Rick.

"When?" he asked.

"The day of the fitting. After I left."

"The fitting," he sighed.

"I was confused… Devastated, actually."

He was quiet. No doubt, he remembered the prenup. Finally, he said, "So, now you've decided to be honest."

"Yeah, you should try it sometime." "You might actually like it."

We started to argue, but the doctor arrived to say Alex would need surgery. We sat, mute, staring through people and walls.

"You don't think…?" he finally said.

"Rick? It's possible."

Jeff got up like a pained old man and walked out of the hospital. A couple hours later, the nurse appeared in the waiting area to send Jeff to the lab to draw blood, but by then, I figured he was gone for good. I wanted to kick myself for having said anything. I should have waited for the results.

Not even half an hour later, however, Jeff marched back into the waiting room. He had gone back to the hotel, showered and changed into a clean polo and loafers. "You can leave me if you want, but you can't take Alex. He's my son. Nothing can change that."

"They need you in the lab," I nodded.

"Because I'm his father," Jeff asserted.

True to his word, Jeff stepped into the role. The apartment itself reflects exactly how much Jeff has changed by having a child with TBI. The rooms themselves are minimalist in style—everything white, everything rectangular—but the countertops, which, in the past Jeff would have insisted be kept clear, are now crowded with medications, supplements, and kitchen appliances, including a juicer, blender, panini press, toaster oven, microwave, and, of course, a top-of-the-line, restaurant-grade cappuccino maker. I set my tea down at the kitchen table, take the containers of Korean food from the bag, and set three places at the table in case Alex wakes up. The smell of Korean beef makes me hungry.

There's the muffled sound of Jeff's voice in the other room. It's already 7:40 PM. I have work tomorrow. I crack a set of disposable chopsticks, but it breaks unevenly, causing one to be much shorter than the other. No matter—they still work. I help myself to one of the bibimbaps. *Oh...* A perfect mix of rice, crunchy bean sprouts, sweet sesame oil, and spicy kimchee. It was worth the trip. Almost.

Pressed up against the wall behind my chair is a folded massage table, on which Alex now receives cranial sacral massage three times a week. Initially, we pursued only conventional medical treatments like PT, OT, vision, speech, cognitive therapy. But after many months and thousands of treatments without any major improvements, Alex showed indications of "therapy fatigue." Desperate, Jeff decided to try alternative therapies. Three months ago, the first time Alex received cranial sacral massage, he fell asleep during the treatment and woke feeling pain-free. The cumulative effect seems to have helped Alex's chronic, daily migraine. We were lucky; the injury Alex sustained was mild to moderate. While he still gets irritable and is easily fatigued, interventions like HBOT—Hyperbaric Oxygen Treatment—have helped to improve his memory. He no longer suffers from vertigo, and recently he concentrates well enough to have a tutor. Alex no longer plays video games, which cause blinding headaches, but he enjoys lying in his darkened room, listening to all kinds of books on tape.

I take up a small cube of lotus kim chee, and pop it into my mouth.

Jeff finally reappears. "What a day," he mutters, combing his hair back with his fingers.

I glance at Alex in the other room. He could use the calories. Even lying beneath a blanket, he seems more gaunt, his edges more sharp. He lost weight after the accident. No surprise, but what's concerning is his overall growth rate. It never bounced back. "Should we wake him?" I ask.

Jeff shakes his head. "He started to get a migraine. Hopefully, he'll sleep it off."

"How did the therapy go?" I ask.

"It was interesting. Alex said it helped, but when I asked how, he couldn't articulate." Devoid of any facial expression that suggests any kind of hope or excitement, Jeff spoons his food onto his plate and starts to eat. I figure as hopeful as he may be, there's a part of him that's putting up a self-protective wall. Many therapies seem promising at first, but the results don't last. Jeff offers an explanation of Tomatis Listening Therapy. As usual, he's obviously done a lot of research. The therapy was originally developed to rehabilitate opera singers who suffered some kind of trauma and then lost their ability to sing.

"Trauma, as in, to the *head*?" I ask, pausing mid bite. Now *this* is worth listening to.

"Correct." Jeff nods and feeds a piece of steak into his mouth.

"It definitely sounds worth trying."

"I'm glad you think so—" He pauses. "I would feel sorry if we didn't at least try—"

I feel something disagreeable about to transpire, even before he mutters another word.

"The company needs me now," he continues. "We postponed going corporate because of the accident, but now I need to get back…"

His lips move, and while I can hear everything he says as he goes on and on, the words bounce off me.

"A critical juncture" … "Going public" … "It's time to take the IPO plunge"… "Strong management and accounting teams"…. "successful transition"… "Now or never"….

All last year, I think. Interning at that design company way out in Connecticut. Having to take out a loan for a car. And for what? Grunt work that any high school dropout could manage?

"A nurse can handle it," I say.

"Who will get him to and from all the appointments?" Jeff points out. "HBOT is down in the financial district. Listening isn't even in the city."

"Isn't that why you have a driver?" I ask. "So you don't have to drive?"

"He's finally getting on track, Amy. We can't drop the ball now."

Drop the ball. Finally, I have a job. It doesn't pay well, but it's a start. Only, now, this.

"I've done everything," he says. "I got him back on track, and he's faring so much better."

It's true. Jeff *has* done everything for Alex. The only time Jeff's not with him is Monday mornings when he needs to be at the office for staff meetings. Aside from the Met Gala, which he attended simply because he's now a board trustee, Jeff no longer attends industry events or charity fundraisers. According to Alex, Jeff's not even involved with other women. What's incredible about it all is that instead of disappearing into oblivion like most popular figures who shy away from society, Jeff's sudden and enigmatic disappearance produced the opposite effect: it transformed him into a transcendent, almost mythical figure.

"The company needs me now," he says. "I need to see this transition to fruition."

Jeff the savior. Then, I'm wondering: What is it that makes some people disappear while others become all the more sublime? Why can't he just sink like the rest of us?

Stop, I tell myself. He deserves it. It's true. He does. Unlike me, he changed his entire life to accommodate Alex's needs. The doctor, PT, OT, HBOT, listening, massage. Life revolves around the appointments. Jeff had said no one would ever take Alex from him; and, in fact, he proved his commitment—and devotion—as a father.

What have I proved? I tried to rebuild my life, "allowing" Jeff to take full responsibility for Alex. How selfish is that?

"It's your turn," he tells me now.

"But, my job." He must know I need the money.

"I've thought about it and I have an idea." He tells me his plan to give me a lump sum of money to pay off my debt for the car. Then he'll pay me a "salary" every month—he'll match what I'm making at Monarch.

"And Alex will be back in school soon," he says, using his chopsticks to place a thin slice of barbecued steak over my rice. "So you'll have the whole morning, the whole day, really, until three. Potentially, you could even work part-time."

I swallow. There's no way Maggie, my boss, will keep me part-time. I don't have the tenacity to even ask.

"I know this is difficult for you, but if the company doesn't survive this transition, well, then what are we going to do? How would we take care of Alex? Where would we get health insurance? How would we pay for all these therapies? I'm burning through money like there's a genie in a jar, but at some point I've got to push ahead or we need to cut back. Way back."

Jeff's thought out his argument. He knows I can't say anything because he's right. It's my turn. He handled Alex's care when it was the most critical—*and* the most difficult. All the guilt I've suppressed floods back to me. As his mother, I should have been there. I should have helped more. And now Jeff is generously making it possible. Who wouldn't want such an arrangement?

I stare into my plate and push the steak to the edge. The bibimbap comes with a fried egg over a bed of rice, minced vegetables, and shredded beef. I poke the yolk until it bleeds. There it is. My life diced into segments, smothered by the very splooge of life, resulting in a mishmash of total nothingness.

"What do you think?" Jeff asks.

I think behind that stony facade, you are a cold, calculating asshole.

"It's great," I say, forcing a smile. "Thanks."

"No problem. It'll be so good for Alex to spend more time with you."

"Who is he to suggest I don't see enough of my own son?" I rant, the next evening at Ma's and Georgie's. "That mother fucking asshole!" I pace between kitchen and living area. "He thought out every fucking angle. The whole fucking thing!"

"Enough," Ma snaps, banging chopsticks down on the porcelain spoon holder. She's in the kitchen, cooking tea eggs. "What a mouth you have," she gasps, crossing her arms. "Fucking, fucking."

"But it's true. I mean, what could I say, right? He's my *son*, right? Now, it's my *turn*, right?"

"It is!"

She may as well have smacked me across the face.

"He's your *son*," she says. "What's more important, uh?"

"Well, I'm your daughter. That didn't stop you from flying off to Hong Kong for half a year."

"I brought Daddy back, you forgot?" she says, her face red. "You have a funny memory. When Daddy went back again, did I leave? Ha. No, I stayed here with *you*. You forgot?"

So that's what this is about. She blames me. Ever since Dad left, Ma's been alone. She has a boyfriend here and there, mostly divorced men who wine and dine her, but nothing that actually sticks. Ma gave up her life because of her kid; now it is my turn to suffer.

I recall a moment in the hospital when Alex was still in surgery. I swore to myself, and God, that if Alex was okay, I would give up my silly antics and desires. I would dedicate my life to taking care of him.

"Your own son," Ma mutters. "You don't feel shame?"

It's like air gets sucked out of the room and I'm going to suffocate. I grab my phone from my purse and text my boyfriend, William. "Okay if I stay over tonight?" I type. I've been staying at his place a lot lately; it's an easy 35 minute drive up the west side highway to Hastings where he lives. William has a son two years younger than Alex. Not exactly romantic to have a nine-year-old around all the time, but he's very little for his age, and while I would never admit this to anyone, he's sweet and easy to be around in a way Alex never was. William and I had a short affair when Alex was two. We bumped into each other again a couple years ago, and even though he and I have been monogamous ever since my split with Jeff last year, William still wants to do everything "just the two of us." It's stifling at times. I try to sympathize, considering the roller coaster on-again, off-again relationship he had with Toby's drug-addict mother, which he's told me all about. She up and disappeared when Toby was six without so much as a goodbye. He came home from school one day and no one was home to let him in. I can't help but feel sorry for William. He's not the Daddy type, and yet, he has had to contend with a boy who suffers from night terrors and is prone to accidental falls; a couple weeks ago, he broke an arm while playing football with William in the backyard.

"Sure," William immediately texts back. "Come on over."

Then I remember the right tail light of my car is out. No way I can drive like that or I'll get a ticket. What luck. I text back, letting him know, and William answers that he can drive in to pick me up.

I texted back to say he was sweet, but not to bother. I was fine, and I'd see him this weekend. He texted back that it wasn't a bother and he could really use a hug. He'd had a tough day. Plus, he'd already gotten a sitter to watch Toby.

I indicate he should pick me up at Children's hospital across from Georgie's apartment and continue packing, so desperate to get away from Ma that I break a nail rushing to unzip the bag.

"Take the money," Ma says, hovering now. "He owes you."

"I don't want Jeff's money," I say, searching my purse for a nail file.

"You stupid girl," she says, "you never learn."

"Jeff doesn't get to be the hero. Not here. Not now."

"Who is saying 'hero, hero?' That's your money, stupid. It's, how should you say, uh? Your ali-mony. Maybe only little bit, but something."

"I didn't need it before, and I don't need it now. And *stop* calling me stupid."

"So *stupid*. I don't get to see my own grandson. Why? Because you can't afford a home for your own son. And you can say don't need, don't need?"

If I could slit my wrists in front of her—if I had a knife in my hand right now—I would do it just out of spite.

I chuck my phone into my purse, then head into the bathroom for my toiletry bag.

"Where you going?" Ma stands outside the bathroom. "You going to see that…that William?"

"It's 'William'," I say. "Not *that* William. Just William."

"I don't like him."

"You've never met him."

"I don't need to." She tries to block me from moving past her into the living area. "Every time you sleep in that man's bed you are less and less. You have no value."

"Just stop, okay? I know it's hard to believe but we actually graduated from the Middle Ages. Women actually vote in this country."

"For what, uh? To open their legs? To sign prenup? To get divorced with nothing like a beggar on the streets? Who you are, mh?"

I stuff a pair of pumps into airplane socks and pack them into the overnight bag along with a clean bra and panties. Just to get her goat, I dig out a silk blue teddy.

"Fine, ha che va dong," she says, accusing me of not appreciating her good intentions. "You don't want to listen. See how things turn out. How lonely."

Something inside me snaps. I stare her straight in the eye. "Lonely like you?"

Ma's hand whips back, then starts to swing at my face. As if in slow motion, I reach up and catch her by the wrist. I squeeze, the anger inside me causing her arm to tremble. "Don't you *ever* hit me again," I say.

She startles, registering the sudden shift in power. I release her with a slight shove, just enough to make her retreat a couple steps. She holds her wrist. Massages it.

I grab the overnight bag and my purse, then step into my shoes by the front door. Without another word, without even looking at Ma, I head out the door.

The rain comes down like ice picks. I'm standing in the covered area outside Children's Hospital, where, during the day, the valet meets visitors pulling into the semi-circular driveway. It's close to midnight now. The wind moves through me as if my bones are hollow. My teeth chatter. I refuse to step inside the empty lobby. Maybe it's the experience with Alex. Something about desolate hospitals, especially at night, spooks me. But another blast of cold, this one as vast and dispassionate as space, and I'm racing to get inside. My lungs burn so badly, I'm choking. Once I'm behind the seven-foot panels of glass wall, I hug myself and rub the shivers from my body. I may be safe from the elements outside, but my mind darts to dark, cold places. There's no protective guard to shield me from myself. All the things I should have done. All the ways I've failed. Jeff and Ma are right. I'm a terrible mother.

A car honks. It's William. He pulls into the driveway. He's wearing a blue wool cap and a down jacket. I wave and run outside. The wind whips hair across my face. By the time I'm settled in the passenger seat, my left eyeball feels as if there's hair frozen to it.

I give him a quick peck on the lips, then flip down the sun visor. The light goes on, and I finger strands of hair from my lashes.

"Okay," he mutters. The car jerks into drive.

"Something wrong?" I ask, as he turns down the street toward the West Side Highway.

"No." He fidgets with the heat, turning it higher, which immediately fogs the front windshield. He switches on the defrost. Cold air blows right at our faces.

"Sure?" I ask, shivering again.

"Positive." He flashes a big smile, returning his attention to the road.

I recount my exchange with Jeff yesterday and the argument I had with Ma tonight. "She actually agreed with him," I say.

"Don't let her get to you."

"How am I supposed to do that?"

He shrugs. We pass the entrance to the G.W. Bridge, on the West Side Highway. The Hudson is a wall of blackness.

I've got nothing. I am nothing.

We approach the toll. He slows as we move through the booth, then picks up speed on the other side. I set my hand on his thigh. He removes his right hand from the wheel and places it over mine. We follow the sinuous road that cuts through Riverdale. William slows with traffic, driving no faster than 35 miles an hour. With the drop in temperature, rain has turned to sleet. As clear as the road may look, it's probably covered with black ice. Pellets of ice ping off the windshield and car rooftop. The wipers drag across the dry glass, making a sluggish thumping sound. William shuts them off.

"I'm sorry I dragged you out in this," I say.

"Don't be," he says, taking my hand again.

I have to tell my boss I'm resigning. She's going to think I'm crazy. Then she's going to be pissed she wasted so much time and energy training me. What a perfect way to burn a bridge. "You'll never get another job in this industry again," she'll say.

"Why are you crying?" he asks.

"I fucked up. I fucked up my whole life."

"That's not true."

"It couldn't be more true." I tell him about Jeff's "salary," which is supposed to compensate for the possibility of an actual career. "I'm 38 years old. What have I got? I'm living with my mom and sister, sleeping on their *couch*, and I've got a grand total of $300 in the bank."

William exits the highway and turns left at the light.

"Can't your mother help?" William asks.

"She has. She co-signed for my car. She covered the whole year's expenses."

Finally, we arrive at his house. William pulls into his garage. Only a few hours ago, my life was filled with possibility. But now? Giving up this job, stepping out of the arena again, would mean a permanent dead end.

William leads me directly into the kitchen. The TV in the living room is on, and Toby is huddled with a duvet in the corner of the couch. He looks up at us with round terrified eyes. His hair's asunder and seems to be standing on end.

"Shouldn't you be in bed?" William asks, clearly exasperated.

"He had a nightmare." The sitter gets up from the recliner.

"Again?" William scowls. "You're nine. Get over it."

Toby burrows deeper beneath the comforter.

"I'm talking to you." William pays the sitter, and she leaves.

"I couldn't sleep."

"Which is it then," William accuses. "A nightmare or insomnia?"

Toby blinks. "It—" he stutters. "I…"

"Stop," William orders. "Enough, just be quiet."

William seems agitated. It occurs to me Toby may have an act to prolong bedtime every night. When Alex was little, he used to do everything he could to fight it, too.

William asks if I'd like a cup of tea. He keeps chamomile ever since I started staying over.

"Yeah, tea, perfect," I say, removing my coat.

William takes it and disappears to the kitchen. I settle on the couch at Toby's feet, fitting myself snuggly into the opposite corner. "So what are you watching?" I ask.

Toby shrugs. He has the comforter drawn up to his nose.

We watch an old Western. Toby snuggles up beside me. He seems to be shivering, so I put an arm around him and hold him close. Then, the cast appears from under the duvet, and the next thing I know, he's sharing it with me. When he sees that my far arm remains exposed, he leans across and with the thick cast over his hand and arm, he tucks the blanket behind my shoulder.

One little guy, I think, with so much caring. He's only a couple years younger than Alex, and yet, emotionally, he's lightyears ahead. Alex has never done anything nearly so thoughtful. Does it come from having had the responsibility of caring for his drug addicted mother? Or is it just an innate part of his character?

"Thank you, Toby," I say, putting an arm around him. "It's so sweet of you."

He smiles. He smells of strawberry shampoo. William returns with a mug of chamomile tea. "For Pete's sake, go to bed, Toby," his voice booms. I can feel Toby shake.

"William, it's okay. He's my buddy." I glance at Toby. "Right?"

Toby nestles closer.

William settles into the recliner, and within a couple minutes, Toby's asleep.

"He's *so* sweet," I say. "I wish Alex was this sweet."

"He'd be a hell of a lot sweeter if he were upstairs in bed and I was the one lying there in your lap. The things I'd do to you beneath that blanket…"

"Eh hum?" I raise my brows at the impropriety of saying such a thing in front of a child.

"He's asleep." He waits to wave me off, then shifts out of his chair toward Toby. "It's time he got upstairs."

"No, wait. Just a minute." I smooth my fingers over Toby's hair. It's been a year since I've been separated from Alex. How much I've missed him—the heartbreak and grief—nearly tackles me. The guilt has weighed on me this whole time, only now, it's crushing, unbearable. And for what? Everything I've worked toward. Gone.

But this little boy. The look on his face. He's not my child, and yet, there's an innocence about him, maybe about any sleeping child, which makes him mine, all of ours.

"Why don't you come stay with us?" William says. "Yeah, stay here. I can put a bunk bed in Toby's room for Alex," he says. "He'd be ecstatic to have company, especially at night."

I get an uncomfortable feeling. "That's nice of you, William, really generous, but—"

"Give it a try. If you or Alex don't like it, you can find something else then. Simple."

"I don't know." I get an uneasy feeling again, and yet, my mind races to do the math: I won't have to live with Ma and Georgie, anymore. Alex has been here and likes it. There are no loud sirens. He's got a buddy to play with. Plus, my car. What a relief it would be not to worry about alternate side of the street parking. I could leave it here in

William's driveway. I'll get a ride from him into the city every morning, then jump on the subway.

"What do you have to lose?" William asks.

It's spring, three months after I move in with William when Jeff finally puts his foot down and demands I tender my resignation, effective immediately. I meant to do it. I just couldn't. But Jeff Jones, Inc. goes public soon. He needs to focus on the transition and he needs me to take full charge of Alex's care. It's Sunday, 10:30 PM. Alex is asleep in the boys' bedroom, but Toby can't sleep, and is now on the living room couch with the TV on. It's been a recovery Sunday. William and I drank so much last night—he insisted on tequila shots after dinner—that I spent the day brain dead in bed. William surfed the internet, then finished some work. Since he's in the shower, I take over his desk with my laptop.

Letter of resignation. How to start? Name, address, date. Space break. Manager's name. Manager's Position. Company name. Company address. Maggie's the Buyer at Monarch who hires the Assistants. She and I hit it off during the interview, and even though I was older, she felt the responsibility factor and my fashion sense would more than compensate. She spent a lot more time training me than the others, familiarizing me with the label, company protocol, and understanding the target audience.

Maggie has the most amazing Asian eyes. Large and light brown, with a slight bluish rim around the corneas. I can only imagine the way they will look at me when she finds this letter on her desk.

Dear Maggie. No, too casual. Delete, delete, delete.

In the bathroom, the shower goes off. The shower curtain pulls aside. After a minute, William enters. Steam pours into the room. He rubs his hair with the towel, then tosses it onto the chair by the window. He knows I hate it when he does that. My work clothes are draped on the back of it. With something on top, especially something damp, my clothes will wrinkle. I get up from the desk to hang his towel back on the rack in the bathroom. He grabs me by the waist and tries to tug me onto the bed with him.

"Don't," I say, pushing away. "I have to write this."

"Suit yourself." He gets into bed directly behind me at the desk.

Dear Ms. Geller-Kitano, Please accept this as my letter of resignation effective

I check my calendar, find the date two weeks from Friday. When I finish the sentence, I draw a total blank as to what to write next. "Exactly how do you write one of these?" I ask.

"It's easy," he says, yawning. "Please accept this as my letter of resignation effective May 15th, yadda yadda yadda."

"Yeah, I got the beginning part. It's the yadda, yadda part I'm not sure about." I turn around. He's lying on top of the covers, naked, and with an erection.

Ugh. "The boys," I hiss. What if they walk in?

"Nothing like danger."

I turn back to the computer. I'm exhausted. The last thing I feel like having is sex.

"Just come to bed already. We can do that in the morning."

"No, I need this to be professional, but thoughtful, too."

I regret having to make this decision, but life circumstances

"Fine, keep Willy waiting," he says.

Delete, delete, delete.

This was a difficult decision to make.

I hear a slippery sound behind me. The pace of William's breath changes and grows louder, more exaggerated. He's masturbating.

My face heats up. In fact, my entire body does, too. My heart races. It's as if he pressed the "Go" button between my legs, and despite myself, I can't find the emergency lever to "Stop."

"I can do this in the kitchen if you'd like some privacy," I say, not turning around.

"You'll wake Toby." He groans loudly.

"Quiet," I whisper, spinning around. Some things the boys don't need to hear.

William rubs the shaft of his penis. There's a wavelike motion, and then a drop of semen appears, perching at the tip. He rubs it in his palm. "Ah," he sighs.

Then I'm in it. I get up from the desk, pull off my clothes, and get onto the bed. I try to move on top, but he blocks me with an arm. All at once, he explodes. Semen spurts onto the comforter. His body goes slack.

But I need this now. I reach for him, determined to make him hard again, but he holds me off. "You had your chance," he says.

The confusion must show on my face because he adds, "You heard me."

Shame or something like it floods to my face. The corner of his mouth twitches. He gets under the comforter, expecting me to clean up the mess, and turns away from me to sleep.

I get off the bed, go into the bathroom, and wet a towel. I come back and wipe off the mess the best I can, then throw it into the bathtub and rummage beneath the sink for my magic wand. I don't need him, if that's what he's thinking. I can take care of myself. He can watch for all I care.

I return to the room, unravel the cord, and plug it into the electric socket on my side of the bed. I get under the cover, lay back, and turn it on. I haven't used it in a while, and at first, the magnitude of it is nearly too much. But my body settles into it, and then I'm rocking as if a lover's on top of me. The world disappears. It's just me. Ah, yes. That's it. Coming is like music. There are pitches, and as I move toward the grand finale, it climbs, notes yearning to explode. I'm almost there, lost inside myself, when all of a sudden, the vibrator stops.

I open my eyes. William has just cut the cord. He's got my cut-through-anything Chinese scissors with the thick rubber handles. He drops it, and I hear the point peck the wood floor. He shakes out his hand. From the grimace, I realize he must have gotten shocked.

If this had happened a few months ago, I would have packed my things and walked right out of here. But I've got Alex. He's asleep. I can't just wake him in the middle of the night and drag him out of bed. Tears rush from my eyes. I don't want William to see. He's no longer privy to my anguish and fear. I slide under the comforter and turn away from him just as he did to me.

I'm a wall, I tell myself. Just cold, hard brick. No emotions. No tears.

William fusses with the comforter and nearly tugs it off me. I hold tight and refuse to give it up. As of tomorrow, I decide, Alex will stay at his father's until I find a place of my own. If Jeff is willing to give me a little more in rent, I may even be able to get a studio in his building.

"I'm sorry," William says.

That's not going to change the fact that I'm out of here, I think. Ice. I'm ice.

"Did you hear me? I said I'm sorry."

"I heard you," I say.

"Can we talk about it?"

I resist the urge to turn and slap him. "No, let's not."

Neither of us moves. The silence is so great, I can hear the TV on in the living room.

"Please," he finally utters, his voice breaking up. He reaches around and spoons me, kissing the side of my face. He sniffles, and when I feel the tears on my neck, I realize he's crying. I've never seen him cry.

I turn to him, and he kisses me with a desperation I've never seen from him before. He moves on top of me. Tears drip into my eyes. "I love you so much," he says, and then he enters me with a ferocity that makes me gasp.

I try to push him off, but he slams into me harder, making me wince.

"William!"

"I love you so much," he sobs, "I hate you."

He slams into me, again and again, punching harder, gritting his teeth.

"Stop," I rasp, my body clenched. If I scream, the boys will hear. They can't see this. I don't want them to see this. "William!"

He comes again. There's a sharp pain and sweat breaks out over my entire body. I'm shaking. He pulls out, and the sting from the friction makes me nearly pass out. I hold myself with both hands.

"Oh, baby," he says, now. "Oh, shit. What happened? What have I done?"

There's blood on my hands, on the bed.

"My princess," he says. "I'm so sorry. I didn't mean to hurt you."

He punches himself, smashes his forehead with his fists.

"Stop," I say, "Just get something to clean this up."

He hurries to the bathroom. I lie there. He returns with a towel.

"Oh, baby," he says. "I'm so sorry. Oh, God. You know I didn't mean it."

I bunch the towel between my legs. The pain dulls and starts to throb.

"Do you believe me?" he asks. "Baby?"

"Ice," I say.

"Do you forgive me?" he sobs. "Please. You have to forgive me."

I try to sit up, but the pain's so intense it feels electric.

"That won't ever happen again," he says. "I promise."

My body trembles. Sweat covers my face, drains down my scalp and neck.

"You believe me, don't you?" he asks. "I'll change."

I shake my head. Please stop.

"I am," he insists, "you'll see, I'll show you."

Ice, I try to say. Oh my God, ice.

"It's just that I love you so much." He buries his face in my chest. "I go crazy when I think you don't love me back. What are you doing with someone like me, anyway?" He punches his chest.

"Don't," I manage.

Wind whistles against the window pane. A spray of hail pecks at the glass.

"I'm a monster," he whispers. "Just like my father."

He's told me about his father. The guy put William in the hospital when he was nine.

"No," I say. "Please don't say that. It's okay."

"Do you—" He wipes his face with the comforter. "Do you love me?"

I shouldn't. I know I shouldn't. And yet, maybe I do.

"Yes," I whisper. Then: "Get ice."

Loved. Past Tense.

William refuses to see a psychiatrist because he's not "crazy," but I have to give him some credit because he actually signs up for an anger management course. He learns a breathing technique—in for four, out for eight—and the importance of mindfulness. Within months, he has downloaded and is using at least half a dozen mindfulness apps on his phone.

"Check this out," he says, showing me the latest. "You've got to get this. It's exactly the kind of thing you like."

"Guided mediation," I say, trying not to sound as skeptical as I feel. Meditation is a frame of mind. It's not listening to someone tell you to focus on your breath when you're honking at the driver in front of you and telling him to fuck off. "Have you used it yet?" I ask.

"No time," he says, "but I was thinking we could listen on the way to work in the morning—"

"I'll drive if you'd like," I say. "That way you can try the meditation."

"Maybe." William always needs to be the one driving.

"Oh, wait," I say. "I can't go with you tomorrow. I need to drive in also. Alex has an appointment in the morning and two in the afternoon. Upper East, West Village, then Upper West Side. He's going to be beat afterwards."

"Why don't you take public transport? It's so much easier."

"It's too much for him."

"How do you know? Have you tried?"

William doesn't understand traumatic brain injury; I can tell he thinks I'm spoiling Alex.

"You have a few minutes now, right? " I say. "Why don't you try the meditation? It's quiet enough in our room."

"Maybe," he nods, scrolling through other apps. "So, have *you*?"

"Tried? Yes." It's not a total lie. "It's too much stimulation. The therapies are hard enough on him already. He gets maxed out and shuts down. Have you signed up at the gym yet?"

"Yesterday." This gets my attention. I've never seen William do any kind of exercise whatsoever. He drives everywhere, even if it's to a neighbor's house down the street.

"Ron says exercise helps a lot to relieve stress." Ron's the therapist who runs the Anger Management course.

"And it's good for you, too."

"He also said I should start walking two or three times a week. He wants me to create a set schedule, maybe Monday, Wednesday, and Saturday."

"That sounds like good advice, but...aren't you overextending yourself a bit?"

"Walk three days, gym three days, and one day of rest and guided meditation."

"Well, okay…"

"Come on, it'll be fun," he says. "We can do it together."

"I wish I could, Will, but Alex's appointments are all over the place. You see me rushing to the city at 8 some mornings, and some nights I don't even get back until 10 or 11."

A pink blemish appears on his neck.

"But I could join you on the weekends," I offer, bracing myself for an explosion.

William breathes. I can tell he's counting up to ten. Finally, he draws in a deep breath, then sighs it out. "It's all right," he says. "I was hoping for your support, but, it's fine."

"You have it."

"Ron says we're only as successful as our partners make us."

It's like I'm biting into a lemon ripe with guilt. I'm living with William because I can't afford my own place and Jeff can't right now, either. He just liquidated most of his assets, funneling the capital back into the business; he has only a few months before the company goes public. I considered moving in with Ma and Georgie again, but Ma said no. "If you want to stay for a few days, that's fine," she said. But long term? "Too crowded."

"I'll see if my mom can stay with Alex a couple nights," I say. "Jeff gets home by 7 Tuesdays and Fridays. That wouldn't be too late for her."

"Yes!" he cheers. "And maybe another night you could let Alex take care of himself. He is 12, after all."

"I don't know. What if he has a seizure?"

"He hasn't had one in a while, has he?"

"Not since last year."

"See? He's fine. You should stop worrying so much."

"Well, he does seem better," I say. "I'll talk with Jeff. We'll figure something out."

"I knew you cared." He buries his face at my shoulder.

"Of course I do."

"I love you," he says, in an almost child-like voice. "I'd do anything for you, you know that?"

"Breathe," I remind him.

He shuts his eyes; he must be counting to ten.

I can understand his frustration. Toby's a smart boy; it's true he should be doing a lot better academically than he is.

"Ten," he sighs, blinking his eyes open. He calls Toby to our room. "Why aren't you doing all your homework?"

"I do them. Most, anyway."

"Most? You think homework is optional?"

"No."

"Then what's this?" He holds the report card out for Toby to see.

"A couple times I just forgot," he explains.

"And the others?"

"I printed them out, but forgot to bring them to school."

"Oh, *that's* why your stuff is always in the printer," I say. "I thought you were making copies for your own records."

"No," Toby replies, his hands digging deep into his jean pockets. "Just forgot."

"From now on, print everything the night before," William says, "and double check everything's packed before you go to bed."

"Uh, okay," Toby says.

"That went pretty well, don't you think?" William says, once Toby's left the room. He seems to have surprised himself.

"I'm really proud of you," I say.

"Yeah?"

"Yeah."

"I'm a changed man," he says.

"You *are* changing. Keep up the good work."

"I can if you're here with me. I'd do anything for you, you know that, right?"

"You've got to do it for yourself."

"Yeah, right," he says.

For the spring break, William decides not to go away. Instead, we will do all the touristy things we've never had the chance to do in New York. We take the boys to the Cloisters, then stop at Arthur Avenue for dinner. We spend a day at The Brooklyn Museum and the Botanical Gardens next door. We pack a picnic and go boating on the lake in Central Park. The last day, we go to the Empire State Building. William's made a reservation at Keens Steakhouse for dinner afterwards.

We ride the elevator to the rooftop of the Empire State, which offers a panoramic view of the city. The boys point out the different attractions: "The Chrysler Building!" Toby calls.

"Statue of Liberty!" Alex says. They elbow their way through the crowd to get a better view.

"Boys," I say, using my "be polite" voice. I feel strangely disappointed. When we were on the way up, the recording touted the unobstructed 360 degree view. While it's true, it's also not: the entire rooftop is fenced six-feet high, with barbed bars above it that extend another six feet and curve inward. As if that weren't enough, there's netting surrounding the entire building. These obstacles keep the crazies from jumping, the daredevils from rappelling off the sides of the building, and kids from chucking toys that would instantly kill the pedestrians on the ground. It makes sense and is necessary; but sad. In movies, this place is one of the most romantic spots in the world, but in real life, it's like being in a cage with too many people.

"Isn't this incredible?" William asks, from behind.

I take in the New York skyscape. The Financial District. One World Trade. The Brooklyn Bridge. "It's breathtaking,"

"I'm glad you think so," William says, tugging my arm.

I turn; he's on a knee, a ring box bearing a gold band open in his hands. "Marry me."

The wind swoops over us. My hair whips into my face. I pull strands from my mouth and struggle to sweep the tangle from my eyes.

"Marry me," he says, again.

Tourists clap. They have their phones out, videoing this moment they are witnessing on the Empire State Building.

"I—" I stammer. "I—"

"Don't leave him hanging," a guy shouts.

"Amy Wong, you're the best thing that ever happened to me," William says. "I want to spend the rest of my life with you."

The crowd roars with excitement. They are witnessing something here in New York City that they will be able to talk about when they get home. *This couple got engaged.* "Say, 'yes'," a woman calls.

"Oh my god, like, how romantic is this?" a teen exclaims.

But it's *not* romantic. Not even a little bit. Can't they see that?

"Don't you want to?" William asks, getting to his feet now. "You love me, don't you?"

"Of course," I say.

"I don't make you happy?"

"Of course you do," I say.

"Then what is it?" he asks.

I gaze at the faces around us. Mortified, I wish I could disappear. "Can we talk about this at home?" I ask.

"It's him, isn't it?" he snaps. "Jeff!?"

"Oh, William," I say, shaking my head.

"The ex-wife of the great Jeff Jones. You think I'm not good enough for you, is that it?"

The crowd around us disperses, and yet I can sense them riveted, waiting to see what happens. *You'll never believe what happened…* Then, from the corner of my eye, I see Alex and Toby appearing through the crowd.

"Please, William?" My cheeks burn. "Let's talk about this over dinner."

"Fuck dinner." He snaps the box shut in my face. "Fuck this! Fuck you for doing this."

He storms to the elevator, muscles people out of his way, and gets inside. I watch, the boys behind me, as the doors roll shut.

"So stupid," Ma says, when I tell her William proposed and I said no. I stopped by their apartment because Alex has an occupational therapy session at the hospital across the street. He's at a stage when he doesn't want Mommy to be hovering all the time. It's the third time in a year that William has brought up marriage. We have been fighting about it almost constantly. "You live with a man, you should at least have health insurance," Ma says.

"Marriage is not a job." I pause. "Okay, well, maybe it is, but I'm just fine."

"Forty-five you are," Ma says.

"Forty's the new thirty," I say. "I'm strong, healthy, and haven't had so much as a cold in years."

"Linda's daughter—"

"Who's Linda?"

"Oh, you don't know her."

Bet I'm gonna know her now, I think.

"Her daughter got the breast cancer," Ma says. "She's forty. Younger than you."

"I'm not getting cancer."

"You know this? You are God now, ah?"

"I'm not God." I'd like to bang my head against the fucking wall. "All I'm trying to say is I'm fine."

"So shame, such pretty girl. The chemo makes all her hair fall out." For emphasis, Ma plucks imaginary tufts of hair from her scalp.

I shudder.

"A whole year she's in the hospital," Ma says.

"I get it, okay? I hear your point."

"You hear what?" she utters. "She's die."

Defeated, I finally say, "I just don't think it's a good reason to marry someone, okay?"

"Not good reason or best reason?" Ma says. "You tell me what is so good—love?"

"I know that's hard for you, but, yes, love."

"You love Jeff, what is that getting you?"

"Loved, Ma. Past tense."

"What so difference? In the end, what do you have?" She sniffs. "Nothing."

Please, God, I think. Don't say it.

"You give to him the prenup," she says.

Banging my head open would make this stop, anyway. "I was young," I say.

"Young?" she says. "Or stupid."

"Will you leave her alone?" Georgie tells Ma, shuffling out of her room in robe and slippers. Must you two bicker so early in the morning?" It's 11 AM; during her days off, she typically sleeps until mid-afternoon.

"Who's bicker?" Ma says. "I'm just saying."

"That's the problem," I growl. "You're always 'saying.' For once in your life, can't you stop meddling in other people's lives? Don't you ever learn?" I'm referring to Georgie—the catastrophic destruction of the only romantic relationship she's ever had. Instantly, I'm sorry; Georgie squints, a reaction that betrays her impervious facade. Even Be-a-Robot Georgie has that dreaded thing called a heart. It's been twenty years since Marc. Since then, she's been too busy doctoring to date; it's her only form of defiance.

"You don't love William, why you live with him?" Ma asks.

"I don't know," I say, "maybe because you won't let me move back in with you?"

"I'm going back to bed," Georgie utters, retreating to her room.

"Why would a grown daughter want to live with her Ma?" Ma says.

"*Georgie* lives with you."

"Georgie takes care of mommy. You want to take care of mommy? You can't even take care of yourself, your own son."

"I knew you were going to say that. You always have to get that in, don't you?"

"What Americans like to say? If the shoe fits?"

A week later, I feel a sharp pain in my left breast. It happens sometimes the days before menstruation. Some women in their 40s go through menopause, but my menstrual cycles are still going strong. Except, three days pass—still, nothing. There's nothing to worry about, I know there's nothing to worry about, and yet, my conversation with Ma plays like a loop inside my head. What if I *am* sick? As annoying as Ma can be, she's right. What exactly would I do? Are the uninsured in this country expected to roll over and accept a death sentence? I've been healthy since the divorce. I never worried about healthcare. But I need to be more careful, take better care of myself.

The next couple of days drag out. The pain in my breast comes and goes. Whenever it happens, I grow more convinced that something's wrong, and yet, as soon as it stops, I laugh it off as nothing but paranoia. I consider making an appointment with the gynecologist, but when I call, I find out that without health insurance, the doctor's fee is around $200. God only knows how much a mammogram would cost. It's a lot of money to drop if it turns out to be a false alarm.

"What's wrong?" William asks, noticing me cringe during a moment of phantom pain.

"Nothing," I say, because the last thing I need is for health care to tip the balance.

"Why's marriage so important to you?" I ask.

"Just is."

"It's just a piece of paper."

"It's more than that and you know it," he says. "A marriage license validates a union between two people."

"I guess I don't really believe in it. I've been there and done that and it's not for me."

"Been there and done that," he mimics. "Can you hear yourself? We're not talking about backpacking through Europe, Amy."

"I don't know what you want me to say."

He looks me in the eye. We both know exactly what he wants, and yet, I can't bring myself to give it to him. Am I just being stubborn? Selfish?

"Look, William. I loved Jeff—"

"Love."

Why does everyone keep saying that?

"I was in my twenties. None of the men I was involved with were anything like him."

"You mean, plebes like me, right?"

Yes.

"No. He swept me off my feet, you know? It was all pretty over-whelming and confusing, but, yes, I did love him and I think he loved me, too, but—"

"He's such an arrogant prick."

"Maybe, but he was *my* arrogant prick."

"You can say that after the way he's treated you?"

"That's what I'm trying to tell you. Jeff and I were good, William. We were having fun. It was up and down and all over the place. A fucked up kind of happy."

"Happy?"

"*Until* we got married."

"Funny how he's a good guy now."

"Jeff is Jeff," I say. "But, yes, he's changed a lot and I'm proud of him."

"I've changed a lot. Or haven't you noticed?" He sets his beer down, the force of it causing it to splash onto the table. "But I get it. It's not like I'm rich and famous."

"William, don't."

"God knows, I'm no Jeff Jones."

"Please don't drag Jeff into this again."

"Why not? You're still in love with him, aren't you?"

"Oh, my God, stop it."

"You'll go back to him," he says. "I know it. I saw how you looked at him when he came to get Alex."

"Can we please stop? We're going in circles. If I wanted so badly to be there with him, I would be. He's told me I'm welcome to stay if I ever need…"

"Oh?" Red splotches creep up William's neck to his face. "When did you talk about it?"

"He's always said that," I lie.

"I'm not stupid," he says, spit spraying me in the face. "You think I didn't realize you moved Alex out of here after that night? To what— protect him from me? Like I'm some kind of monster?"

I'm not sure what to say. Is that why I moved Alex to Jeff's? It is, isn't it? "No," I say. "I told you. Rushing to the city every morning and then schlepping back after his therapies was too much for him."

"You expect me to believe that? He'd been staying here for months. Then all of a sudden, he can't take it any more?"

"We were trying to make it work, but he was getting nauseated and sick. He wasn't making the progress he needed to be making. It just wasn't fair to him."

"And what about me?" He starts the breathing. In—two, three, four; Out—two, three, four… "During the week I hardly see you any-more."

"It won't always be this way." I hope.

"All I want is a family with you. Is that so bad?"

No, I realize. Jeff never cared about family until he nearly lost it. William actually wants one, with *me*, and yet, I have no faith to go through with it. Why? I think about Jeff, how much we've gone through and grown, and the truth is we are finally getting to be friends. People can change. Relationships can change. So why do I keep Wil-liam at arm's distance? What matters is that he's trying. That counts for something, doesn't it?

"Fine," I say. "Let's just do it."

He looks at me, his eyes dull, and then it's like the experiment I used to do with the boys when they were little: a drop of dish soap in a bowl of oil-saturated water forces the oil out to the sides; suddenly there's clarity.

"Really?" he asks.

I smile.

"Yes!" His face brightens. He pumps a fist. "We're getting married!"

"Just no reception," I say. With Jeff, I had the perfect fairytale wedding. But it proved to be nothing more than an elaborate lie. "Something simple."

"Town hall?"

"Can we do it in the city? On Wednesday, Alex's PT appointment is in the Financial District. We could walk over afterward."

"City Hall it is," William says.

"Just you, me, and the boys."

"What about your mom or sister?"

"Hell, no."

"But we'll need a witness."

"I'll ask Ben."

"You won't regret this, baby," he says, racing to our bedroom and returning a minute later with the ring. "From this day on, we belong to each other. I'm all yours and you're all mine."

The band fits, but with the spike in humidity, it feels too snug.

The City Clerk's Office is essentially a massive, albeit well-designed, waiting room. It was commissioned by Mayor Bloomberg in 2008. The fact that it has stood the test of time speaks to the incredible talent of the interior decorator, Jamie Drake. Ben likes the pastel accents and drooping chandeliers. I love it all, even the display of bouquets. Often, arrangements are a mix of different flowers. Here, each species is celebrated apart from the others. There are the typical pink roses and blush, but also simple handfuls of daffodils, Picasso lilies, hydrangea, and even a lovely arrangement of bunched white carnations, a flower I usually despise.

There are forty-three couples ahead of us in the queue. The hall has the feel of the subway; always crowded, and with people constantly coming and going. Each ceremony takes only a few minutes, so we find ourselves in the east chapel within an hour. The sofa and walls are apricot and peach. There's an abstract painting at the front of the room. Indigo blue background. A petite yellow flower here, a cluster of pale blue and lilac scattered there.

William and I stand before the officiant. I'm in a strapless, cream-colored, knee-length sundress with silver-chain piping along the hemline, which I sewed on myself. No jewelry. A modest birdcage veil. For William, I chose a summer gray suit and tie. Ben, dressed in a black tux, is possibly more suited for the affair than either of us. He stands beside me. Alex and Toby remain seated on the sofa behind us.

"We are gathered here today to join William and Amy in marriage," the officiant says.

I stare at the petite fleurs behind him. How innocent and sweet.

"William, do you take Amy to be your wife?" the officiant continues. "To have and to hold from this day forward, for better for worse, for richer for poorer, in sickness and in health, to love and to cherish, till death do you part?"

"I do," William says.

"Amy," the officiant says, repeating the same words to me. I notice a loose thread on the lapel of his tan jacket. At some point, he must have stuck a pin through it, damaging the material.

I get a strong urge to step forward and brush it away. *Don't,* I tell myself.

"...till death do you part?" he asks.

"I do," I respond.

"Rings, please," he says. Ben sets the gold bands on our palms.

"William, 'with this ring, I thee wed,'" the officiant says.

William repeats what he said to me, then slides the ring onto my finger.

"Amy, 'with this ring, I thee wed.'"

"With this ring, I thee wed," I say to William, giving him his.

"I now pronounce you to be husband and wife. Congratulations, you may kiss the bride."

William leans in, but I peck him on the lips and quickly turn to the boys. Alex is bent over, holding his head in his hands, a sign that he's getting a migraine. Toby sits beside him, watching helplessly. Not a single aspect about this ceremony is like my first wedding, and yet it's as if my body remembers the sadness and confusion, as if it were happening now. That girl, Amy. I mourn for her.

I didn't cry then. But I do now.

A couple weeks after the wedding, Alex and I are at Jeff's when I get a call from Maggie, my former boss at Monarch. "Would you be able to meet me for dinner tonight?" she asks. "I know you want part-time and I need a hand with sales. We can talk."s

Alex has eaten and bathed. Jeff will be home within an hour.

"Sure," I say. I'm not certain I want the job. It doesn't pay much to be on the floor, but at some point, the boys will be more independent, and if I stay in the loop, I'll know if and when a buying position opens up. I call William to let him know I'm meeting Maggie and to have dinner without me.

"Where're you going to eat?" he asks.

"I'm not sure. She said she'd call around to see which restaurants are still taking reservations. She'll text when she knows."

"SoHo," William says. "That sounds fancy. You sure you're not going on a date?"

I laugh. "See you tonight, okay?"

"Don't do anything I wouldn't do."

"What?"

"Nothing, I'm just messing with you."

We meet at a restaurant called The Dutch. It's around the corner from the boutique. She arrives fifteen minutes late because she's finishing up with a customer. *Don't do anything I wouldn't do.* What did he mean by that? I fret. All through dinner, while Maggie tells me about the position and other opportunities she sees in the near future, William's comment curdles in my stomach and makes it impossible for me to enjoy my kimchi rice and chicken. Then, on top of it all, I feel a warm dampness in my panties. Shit, now? I excuse myself to the bathroom and confirm that, in fact, it's my period. Luckily, I have tampons in my purse.

Returning to the table, I ask the waiter to pack my meal to take home, but I'm so distracted that I forget it on the table.

Forty minutes later, I pull up to the house. The light in the living area is on. I figure Toby's watching TV, but when I come through the door, it's William on the couch. Empty, crushed beer cans litter the coffee table and floor.

"How was dinner?" he asks.

"Good, but I forgot to bring home my kimchi rice."

"What did you talk about?"

"The job. I think it might be nice to start working again. Part-time, anyway."

"Which restaurant?" he asks. "What time did you meet?"

"Reservation was at 6."

"You sure about that?" he asks. "Because I called the store at 6:10 and spoke with Maggie."

"Were you checking up on me?" Dread spreads like a rash over my body. "You know what? Don't answer that. I don't want to know."

"You were with Jeff, weren't you?"

"Oh my god, are we back to this again?"

"Just tell me."

I turn and walk away.

A week later, I'm in bed reading when William approaches to make up. I give him the cold shoulder. "Come on," he says.

"Just leave me alone."

"Come on, baby," he coos. He kisses my neck.

"No, I'm tired of this, William. I mean, what's wrong with you?!"

For a moment, he seems like he might morph into The Hulk. He squeezes my cheeks in his hand. "Don't ever say that again," he says. "I'll fucking kill you."

"Get off me." I shove him away.

He looks at me, his face red and nostrils flaring. Then, he pins me down by the hips. He tears off my panties and tries to eat me out. I'm frigid, as frigid as can be, and I visualize my body to be a hollow, empty cavern. I feel nothing. It means nothing. He seems all the more determined, desperate, even, and I find myself smiling viciously. He can lick and bite me until I bleed, but I'm already elsewhere. He has no access; he can't touch me. There is the old term "dead fish"; that's what I am.

"Oh, yeah?" he says. He forces his fist between my legs, thrusting furiously over the G-spot. My body tenses, then suddenly releases as if all the anger and rage inside me gushes from a prism between my legs. I scream, the sound as naked and raw as my heart. My *soul*. I feel it now. Sliced open, laid bare.

"That's right," he says, his nostrils flaring. He unzips his pants, entering me with a blow so violent, I hear myself yelp. He fucks using his dick like a fist. When he's done, he collapses. "Look what you made me do," he sobs, punching the pillow.

I lie there in so much pain I can hardly breathe, suffocating from grief and shame.

The Masters Class

Florida's so humid and hot the cab windows drip with condensation. We arrive at the hotel by 7 PM. Since we left New York, the boys have yet to stop arguing. As I check in, Alex grabs a bag of chips straight out of Toby's hand. Alex is thirteen. He should know better.

"Hey," Toby yells, "Those are mine." Alex has a longer reach. He holds the bag up, down, behind his back. Toby reaches this way and that, trying to snatch it back.

"Give it to him, Alex," I order. He ate his Doritos on the plane.

Alex shoves the last of the chips into his mouth.

I gasp. "That's it—no phone tonight." Ever since he discovered he can game again, it has turned into an addiction. He's trying to make up for lost time.

"What?!" Alex says. "It was just a couple chips. I'm hungry!"

Toby punches him.

"Enough!" I shift my body between them, grabbing them by the front of their T-shirts. "Phones," I order. "Now!"

The boys glance around self consciously at the people gawking at us in the lobby. Toby hands his phone over begrudgingly, but Alex stands with his arms crossed over his chest, refusing to budge. "Fine," I mutter, turning and walking away. "I'll call Verizon and shut off your data."

"No!" Alex moans.

We pass a glass wall that overlooks the pool. The boys stop. The pool is abuzz with people. I notice a hot tub at the far side. "Can we go swimming?" Alex asks.

"Please?" Toby adds.

"We'll see," I say, heading to the elevators. "We have to eat and unpack first."

As soon as we get into our room, I wash my hands and face, use the rest room, and leave the unpacking for later. We have dinner at the hotel restaurant. Keen on going to the pool later, the boys come together for a common cause. They order burgers and share the ketch-up. When Toby finishes his fries, Alex even offers some of his own. I'm enjoying a Caesar salad, but get paranoid that lettuce may get stuck between my top front teeth. The right is an implant and food tends to linger along the gum of the crown. It's happened so often that I'm now in the habit of brushing and flossing after meals.

After we eat, I tell the boys we can go to the pool as long as we get back to the room by 10. They agree. Tomorrow, they'll be at Disney all day with a hotel sitter. I'll remain at the hotel with Ben for The Masters Class, a self development workshop that supposedly focuses on how to create the life you want.

We return to the room to change into swimsuits and flip flops. Alex brings along his football. The pool has emptied out significantly. Alex and Toby jump into opposite ends and practice throwing spirals. Before long, other boys join in. A gaggle of girls appear. They're fully developed, dressed in the latest bikinis; they make the boys look like babies.

I soak in the hot tub. William and I wed one year ago, but it has been so suffocating, it feels more like eight. My lawyer's serving him the divorce papers tomorrow. I'm relieved the boys and I won't be there for it. William can put a hole in the wall if he wants; I'm fine as long as I don't have to be there to witness it.

Ben texts he's delayed at La Guardia.

"You'd better be here by tomorrow," I respond. "This was your idea."

Ben went through this program several years ago, and just like everything else he does well, worked his way up to being a Master. For the next week, he's *my* Master.

According to the signage we passed on the way to the pool, two conferences are being held at the hotel this week: The Master Class Workshop and The Florida Health Insurance Consortium. Clusters of men, some in their 30s and 40s, others mostly in their 60s, arrive around 9 PM. Some of them team up with the kids, and before long, they're chicken fighting in the pool. Some of the others join me in the hot tub. We exchange pleasantries. One of the younger guys, probably in his 30s, reminds me of Rick. Maybe it's because of this that I feel a strange charge between us. His name is Tim. He has brown eyes, and like Rick, he also has the stocky physique of a weight lifter. I would gladly converse with him, except that Ma calls, and I'm forced to get out of the water to speak with her.

"How can you be so stupid?" she asks.

"Oh, hi, Ma, and how are you?" I say, removing myself to the furthest beach chair from the pool. She's upset about the suitcases I dropped off at their apartment. She knows what that means.

"Have you thought about this? Really thought about it?"

"Ma, please."

"Do I have to remind you how old you are?" she asks. "Ai, you have no idea how lonely, Amy. Now, you will see. Ni chi ku." Taste bitterness.

"Look—there's a lot you don't know, Ma."

"What do I need to know? You tell me."

"This is the right decision. I should never have married him."

"But you did." She makes a sucking sound through her teeth. "Divorce, divorce. Tell me—who will want you now, mh?"

"Me," I say, finally.

Ma makes a throaty sound, something like laughter, but tinged with bitterness. She's angry I'm not more. She can't boast about my accomplishments; instead, she has to hide her shame.

"Look, I have to go," I say. It's nearly 10 PM. "I have to get the boys out of the pool." I explain that we're in Florida, at which point she asks, "Why is *that* boy with you?"

"Because he is," I say, as Toby lobs the ball over his opponent. "Now, I've got to go, okay?" As soon as I get off the phone, I give the boys a two-minute warning. Neither is happy about it, but they come when called without drama. The three of us are showered, unpacked, and in bed within half an hour. Both boys fall asleep almost immediately. My eyes feel dry and sandy. My body aches. And yet, I can't sleep. Why can't I sleep?

Suddenly the hotel phone rings. I grab the receiver before it wakes the boys. "Ben?" I ask.

"No, it's Tim," the voice says. "From the pool."

"Oh, hello, Tim from the pool." Does he realize it's nearly 11 pm?

"Would you like a glass of wine?" he asks. "I have a fine bottle of Merlot."

At one point in the hot tub, a younger woman wearing a neon tangerine one-piece joined us. The two were speaking when I left. "If you're looking for Orange, I think she's in room 1208," I say. Her room is directly across the hall. His is next to mine.

"No," he says. "It's you I'm looking for."

I'm awake at this point. Wide, wide awake.

I change into a cover up and go next door for the aperitif. Half a glass into the visit, he kisses me. Just leans over as if to get something on the table, and kisses me. He smells of shaving creme and chlorine.

With everything going on with William, I draw away.

"Look, I'm really flattered, but..." The reason I'm in Florida for The Masters Class is to develop myself and gain control over my life. Not the other way around.

"Relax, it's okay," Tim says, sitting back on the couch. He's hard. I pretend not to notice, but he looks at me and the energy is suddenly there. I can feel him; a deep tingling sensation. "You have an incredible body," he says.

"That's sweet of you to say." I shift to my feet. "I better go."

He gets up. As he moves past, his body brushes against mine. He leans to peck me on the cheek but then places a smacker full on the lips. He's a good kisser, gentle at first, almost teasing. His tongue reaches into my mouth, caresses and circles my tongue. He presses his body to mine, dances me to the bed and scoots me onto the mattress. His hands move up my legs.

"You're a runner, aren't you?" he asks.

"No, not really."

"A dancer."

"Actually—"

In one swift motion, he tugs the panties to my ankles. "Woah—" I say.

He dives between my legs, working magic with his mouth. Instantly, the tension lifts. I fall back and give into the pleasure.

"You're like honeysuckle," he says. "You ever taste honeysuckle?"

Holy shit.

He moves up, pushes his tongue into my mouth. The taste is familiar: Sweet, almost tangy, a hint musky, and with a pinch of salt. He slides inside me, filling me up exactly as I had imagined. Maybe it's the weight of him in all the right places, because he barely moves, and yet it's like my entire body expands into a million stars twinkling across the night sky.

Late morning the next day, Ben takes me through yet another Master Class exercise. We're standing in the hallway outside the conference room.

"That," Ben says, pointing at a wall sconce. It has an aged, silver finish with a mesh-screen shade. Flame-shaped bulbs flicker like candle light. "So, for this next exercise, what you're going to do is feel into it," he says.

"Feel into it," I repeat, because I have *no idea* what he's talking about. "Um, it's a light fixture."

"That's correct." Ben laughs. "It's a light fixture."

I glance around, half expecting someone to tell me this is all part of some elaborate, crazy scheme, just to video my reaction. "You're on Candid Camera," he'll say. Or, "You've been punked!" There are two hundred other participants milling about, either inside the hotel staring at wall sconces, oversized paintings, and hotel signage, or outdoors in the heat, seemingly mesmerized by benches, coconut trees, or the fountain separating the hotel from the beach and the vast ocean beyond. As crazy as all of this seems, no one else seems to think so. Is it me?

"I don't know if all of this—" I wave a hand at everything going on around us "—is really my *thing*."

Ben tips his head. "This is a chance to dig deep. Get to the root of things."

"It's just—" I stop. "I mean, shallow is working for me just fine."

He watches, and as usual, without judgement, which makes me feel smaller and more superficial than ever. In a matter of fact tone, he rattles off a mental list: "Two marriages, both to abusive men, then two divorces, two children—a son, who, until a few years ago, you thought might be out of wedlock even though you were actually *married* at the time, and the other, your step, who prefers you to his biological father because the guy is controlling, manipulative, and has major anger management issues." His gaze is so intense, heat rushes to my face. "I'm sorry, darling," he says, his voice softening, "but shallow, or however you want to label it, is not working for you 'just fine'."

"When you put it that way," I say.

"Sweetie, I know this is all foreign to you. A lot of it was to me, also, when I started. But give it a chance. I'll show you. It'll click, I promise."

Another Master hurries over to Ben with her student. "May I get your opinion?" she asks. Ben steps aside. They speak in hushed tones, but it's obvious what the situation is. Her student is a twenty-something-year-old male who is, without a doubt, totally baked. He's got blond hair. The whites of his eyes are bloodshot, the lids puffy and drooping. "Hey," he says, his eyes half closed as he speaks. I get Ben's attention, mouth the word "bathroom," and turn to go.

In the conference center bathroom, I brush and floss my teeth, pushing and pulling the waxed string between my real front tooth and the porcelain implant beside it. All of a sudden, something snaps.

It's the crown over the implant. Click, click. The porcelain nugget bounces over the marble, then drops into the basin. With the precision of a hawk going in for its kill, I slam my palm down, catching it on the concave rim of the basin. I drag it up, then grab it with my fingers.

In the mirror, I smile at myself to assess the damage. There's a gap where the cap once was. In that blank space, all that's left is a spade-like post sticking out of the gum. My stomach wrenches into a knot. When the original tooth had broken—it snapped almost a year ago to the day—I'd been eating an ice cream cone while driving to pick up Alex from school. I heard the *crack*, and my initial thought was: Oh, shit, I've chipped my tooth! But when I glanced in the rear view mirror, what stared back at me was a gaping hole. The person I'd always thought of as me was gone. In her place, there sat a much-older, hick version Ma would have referred to as a xiang wu nging. Peasant.

If I were alone with no one to witness such raw, uncompromising disgust and fear, I'd probably be screaming. But I'm not. A toilet flushes. A blond with a slender, willowy quality that screams yoga, appears next to me. I calmly push the tooth back into place and rush outdoors to call my dentist. My hands are shaking so badly it takes three tries to call up the correct number on my phone. The secretary answers. I explain the situation, and it takes every ounce of self-control not to get hysterical. She tells me he's with a patient; he'll have to call me back. I hang up, contemplate returning to the room, packing all of our belongings, and leaving for the airport as soon as the van returns. The boys will pitch a fit because I promised them one of the water parks for being good. Ben will be disappointed, too, but, friend or no friend, there is no possible way I can allow anyone to see me with a missing front tooth. I need home.

On the way to the elevator, I encounter Tim, the guy from last night.

He acknowledges me with a nod. How unlucky can I get? He's with one of his buddies, too. Doesn't that break some kind of guy code? The stranger you meet in a hotel and have sex with should remain just that—a stranger you had sex with. He's not supposed to be nice, nor good, nor considerate. And he should not—absolutely not—acknowledge you. In this kind of situation, you should both ignore one another and pretend nothing ever happened. Why doesn't he know this? Whatever happened to the good old fashioned asshole? You just can't count on American products anymore.

I stare down at my phone, as if to check email, but sense him coming closer. No it's worse. He's staring. I'm so sick with dread it's like I've been dunked head first into a pool full of ice. I look up and lock eyes with him, smiling just enough, afraid if I open my mouth the tooth might fall out.

Luckily, my phone rings. Saved! Haha, I'm saved! It's the doc, too, oh my god, it's the doc. I indicate by pointing at the screen that I need to take this, we'll catch up later. Tim nods, again, says something to his friend, and disappears into the restaurant. I hurry out of the lobby to the hotel van because the dentist suggests Polident cream, which can be obtained at any pharmacy. "Not the pink, but the white kind," he stresses.

"I can drop you off, but you'll need to walk back," the driver informs me. In fact, the pharmacy is less than a ten-minute walk, door to door, and is located directly across and five-minutes down the street.

"No problem," I say.

At the pharmacy, I pick out the correct dental glue, re-reading the box three times to be certain I have white and not pink. Since there's a mirror at the makeup counter, I purchase the cream and glue the tooth right on the spot. My hands are still shaking; it takes three tries, and one of the times, the tooth slips and nearly bounces off the counter onto the floor. I'm finally successful gluing the crown in, but I use a little too much. The tooth refuses to slide all the way up to the gumline, and sets crookedly. It's noticeable and I'm not exactly thrilled about it, but at least the tooth is in.

I walk back toward the hotel. I should feel relieved; happy, even. But I feel strangely dazed. Numb.

Random, disconnected memories and emotions flood back to me. Ma telling her friend that Georgie was the smart one who'd become a doctor one day while I was the social one who'd get married and have kids. I needed to look perfect, cash in on my beauty the way she had because I'd gotten it from her, after all, and I owed it to her now. And yet, once I was beautiful in my own right, on my own terms, Ma told me, "What's beauty, anyway? It fades with age."

There was Dad, who'd cheated on Ma, had a child out of wedlock—a boy!—and so left us for his other family in China.

I think about my first real pair of boots; what happened with Bootman all those years ago. The grit on the floor sticking to my back.

And, William. The mind games and manipulation. Luring me in and turning me on, only to withhold sex. Or having sex so rough it caused me to bleed.

Nothing makes any sense. Why does nothing make sense?

I'm choking on emotions. The shakes manifest even harder. I make it to a thicket of trees off the side of the road and cry. Maybe I'm there ten minutes. Maybe it's twenty. The sorrow. Regret. Dad stuck a knife into the very heart of Ma's confidence. She never got over the divorce. Is it my fault that Ma feels like a total failure? Because it's bad enough that Georgie remains unmarried, a spinster. Now, her other daughter is a serial divorcee.

When I finally calm down and notice where I am, I suddenly realize nothing seems familiar. There's construction across the street, a row of new houses going up, which I didn't pass on the way to the pharmacy. Or, did I, but was too freaked out to notice?

How long have I been walking? It's been more than ten minutes. Hasn't it? Did I pass the hotel? Take a wrong turn? Shit, I'm lost.

By the time I return to the conference room, I'm dripping sweat and hyperventilating. I'm intercepted on my way to Ben by a Master and accompanied to a line outside the course room until Ben is able to finally join me. The Big Master at the front of this particular line happens to be Chinese, and older, possibly in her sixties or seventies. She lived through the tail end of the Cultural Revolution. Unlike the stereotypical Asian woman, she's fat and aged; she's got a lot to be bitter about. I ask Ben if we can change lines to speak with a different Master.

"Effy's hilarious," Ben says. "I love her."

"You're not Chinese," I say.

"You're not really, either."

"That's exactly the problem. I look it but can't speak it." If there's anything a Chinese of that generation disdains more, it's the Hua Ciao, overseas Chinese, who can't speak the "home" language.

"That's an interesting belief you have," he says.

"It's not a belief. It's a fact." I go on to tell him about the time I went to the Taiwan consulate and was denied a visa because I couldn't write my Chinese name. Never mind that the guy in front of me didn't have to do it; he was white. When I pointed this out, in English, the clerk informed me that I would need my mother to return with my completed application. I was 21; I never had issues getting visas at any other consulate. Only Taiwan.

"Interesting creation," he says, nodding. "Very interesting."

My patience is wearing thin with this psychobabble. I'm almost relieved to find I'm at the front of the line. "She looks terrible," Effy says to Ben. Ben explains that I've been out of the course room for most of the afternoon. Effy demands to know why. I explain the chain of events that precipitated my getting so lost inside my head that I walked straight past the hotel for another fifteen minutes. I try to have a sense of humor about it.

"You don't speak Chinese?"

I glance at Ben. See?

"No, when I was growing up, the idea of melting pot was pretty big," I explain. "My parents were told by our teachers to speak English at home."

"You're lucky your parents raised you here."

"Uh, I guess."

"Guess?"

Uh, oh. I'm standing in a minefield.

"My parents have their issues," I say, cautiously, "but they really tried their best."

"There's the problem," she says.

"Problem?" I ask.

"You don't have gratitude," Effy says, and she stares at me in a harsh judgmental way. It's strange. You'd think it would be the number one cardinal sin at a personal development course. As one of the Big Masters, shouldn't Effy know better?

"I have plenty of gratitude," I say, trying to control my voice. "I said they tried their best."

"That's not gratitude."

"I'm sorry," I say. "I'm not sure what you want me to say."

"I want you to recognize how much your parents did for you."

"Look, it wasn't easy growing up here. We weren't exactly American, and we weren't exactly Chinese, either. It wasn't both worlds, it was neither."

Effy turns to a table of Chinese several yards from us. "You see all those people there? Do you realize how much they have had to go through?"

My body starts to shake. "Let me guess, their fathers beat the shit out of them."

"They got beat up at home," she states, "and then they got beat up at school, too."

I bite my lip and wait for her to have her diatribe. I recognize exactly what's going on. It doesn't matter what I say. It's lose/lose any way you look at it. I watch her a moment, steam whirring from my ears, and turn to Ben. Is he going to help me out here? Or is he going to stand there and let this bitch go at me like this?

"You have no idea," she says. "Your parents gave you an easy life. You can't appreciate?"

"My father is a narcissist of the highest order."

"Why can't you appreciate?" Effy repeats.

"For one, my father cheated on my mom."

"So?"

"He left because his lover gave him a boy."

"So?"

"He divorced my mom and started a new family. It was like we didn't exist anymore."

"So you blame him."

"Yes, I fucking blame him, okay? I blame him."

"You live in blame instead of appreciation. Can you see that?"

"I have no idea what you're talking about," I say.

"You're making a choice," she says. "You're creating blame."

"That's not fair."

"You have to choose appreciation to have appreciation," she says.

"I do have appreciation," I sob. "I appreciate a lot."

"You need to start with your parents. They gave you life."

"Life?" I retort. "My dad destroyed me!"

Silence. Maybe it's a sound coming from inside my own head.

"What do you mean destroyed you?" Effy asks.

"I don't know." I get this feeling like I want to die. "I'm just a girl."

"What was that?" Emmy asks, watching me with her shrewd eyes.

"I'm just a girl," I repeat, suddenly overwhelmed by emotion. Within those five words lie a prison of other beliefs: Who do you think you are? Accept your place. You're nothing; nobody. Your job is to nurture. Be a wife, a mother. Others' desires come first. Yours don't matter. You don't matter. Your career doesn't matter. What have you done? You're selfish. Not good enough. Be grateful for what you get.

Oh my god. It's everything I shouldn't believe and have told myself I don't believe, and yet, deep down I have believed.

Ben hands me a box of Kleenex. I dry my eyes, blow my nose, and compose myself. Effy asks Ben what drill I was working on before I left, then gives the okay for me to come back into the course room and start the next exercise.

As soon as I arrive at my floor, the elevator doors open and I hear the boys in the room, beating the shit out of each other and screaming "You're an asshole!", "No, you're the asshole!" The sitter tries to intervene. "Boys!" she says. "Stop this or I'll have to call your mother."

I rush down the hallway. But once I get to our room, I stop outside the door. Stop because I know as soon as I get inside, I'll have to pull them apart, assign "chill" spots, and then scream at whichever one won't remain in his designated zone. They'll do whatever they can to antagonize the other, I'll be forced to ref, and for some reason, this time, I can see how ridiculously serious I get about it all, and it seems funny now, like part of a larger, more elaborate joke.

"It's my turn!" Toby says.

"No, it's mine!" Alexander yells.

I tap a finger at Tim's door. A part of me hopes he's inside. Another prays he's not. Desire; resist. I need him; I don't need him. Past lovers. Former husbands.

"Who is it?" Tim calls from inside.

"Amy," I say.

The door opens. I step inside.

Toby

Me, Amy Wong, 45, divorced again, and at the precipice of my new life.

William signed. Five long, tortured years of waiting, and then, out of the blue, he finally signed. I kiss the documents and hug them to my chest. Thank you, God. A warm feeling of gratitude moves through me. It expands in my chest. I lay back on the chaise and shut my eyes. It's in the low 70s, warm for New York in February. I just returned from Florida this morning, so it seems cold, even with a down coat. Yet, it doesn't bother me. I'm free. This is what freedom feels like. Melting ice from the gutters drips. Otherwise, it's quiet, almost forgivingly so, as if time has stopped to be experienced fully.

Yes, I can feel it now. All the decisions I ever made, either consciously or by default, that led me to this one singular moment. The happiest day of my life. How many times, as a child, had I prayed for the happiest, the best, the most beautiful? Now, here it is. Earned. Appreciated.

I hear the neighbor leave her house. The back door shuts. Footsteps. I realize it must be the daughter. It's not necessary to open my eyes to look. I can feel her, the youth and lightness of being. When the car starts and the radio comes on, the sound of Coldplay confirms I'm correct. The car pulls out of our shared gravel driveway, the pebbles crunching beneath the rubber tires and pecking against the ground. The sun warms my face. Wisps of hair tickle my cheeks. I could lie here all day without a care in the world. In fact, Alex doesn't get home for another day. Right now, he's with Jeff in Vermont. And Toby—well, ever since the separation, he lives with William.

Despite that, Toby and I still see each other pretty much every week. I take him to lunch or the movies, sometimes with Alex, and other times without. Occasionally, his girlfriend, a debate champion and the mightiest of blushers, comes along. William sold his house and moved to a condo a town over and less than a mile away, which means Toby goes to a different school now. It's William's way of keeping Toby from Alex and me while also remaining close enough to maintain a menacing presence. His plan is backfiring, though. At 16, Toby is bigger, more mature, and unwilling to stand down during disagreements. This causes them to butt heads. Twice since September, Toby walked the mile and appeared at my door. When William arrived to claim him, I could tell the depth of his rage by how carefree and jovial he seemed to be, and it worried me that he might take it out on Toby all the more.

Three weeks ago, Ben called. He was going to Florida for another Master Class workshop, was I? I told him no, and when he asked why, I thought a moment, and said, "I'm worried about Toby. What if he shows up and I'm not here?"

A couple days later, though, I met Toby at the bookstore, bought him a sci-fi novel he wanted, and took him to lunch. He seemed to be in a good place, and he told me William was spending more and more time at his new girlfriend's apartment. "He bought her a ring," Toby said. This was the most hopeful news I'd had since I started the divorce process.

"Ah hah," I said, since he'd been dragging it out for years. William evaded the issue of divorce, and when push came to shove, outright refused. His actions weren't necessarily aligned with what would actually be best for him, but he was spiteful; he'd rather create a jail so that I would be sitting in it, even if it meant he would be, too. For this reason, I tried not to get too hopeful.

Toby didn't express many warm fuzzy feelings for Mandy, but when I asked how he felt about the possibility of his father getting married again, and if he was okay with it, he said, "Yeah, someone else can deal with his shit from now on."

"That's terrible," I said.

"It's true."

"Shit, it really is."

We both laughed. Since things were better, I told Toby I was going to be gone for a week, and booked myself a flight. One of the days I was on course, working with Ben on one of the exercises, I realized that as much as I wanted the divorce, there was a part of me that didn't want it as well.

The reason, I realized, was Toby. *I'm going to lose him.* The belief itself was irrational. Toby didn't live with me anymore. More important, though William and I were separated, it had not kept Toby and me from spending time together.

Yet, it was *there.* Once I became aware of the conflict within, once I could experience the fear and sadness fully, I worked with Ben to release it, using one of The Masters Class techniques, and then actively created what I wanted. It was similar to an exercise we learned from a book called *The Artist's Way,* which was a self-help book for blocked creatives. I hadn't worked on any design projects since I got married and started a family; Ben felt burnt out by his professional career as a magazine writer and editor. We worked together through this ten week course, and found an exercise called "blurts" especially helpful. Basically, it worked like this: if I gave myself a compliment like "Amy has incredible talent as a designer!" Something blurted back: "Oh, pa-lease." Or, "You suck." So the idea was to repeat the compliment, dig out all the blurts you have hidden away inside until you came away "clean." In the book, it was a written exercise, but Ben and I found we could run blurts back and forth out loud, in a fun way that made us laugh. We found the technique worked for things we wanted to create in our lives, too, because blurts dug out all the insecurities, limiting beliefs and negative voices that held us back. In fact, since the Master Course broke for lunch before we had a chance to work on a new exercise, I asked Ben to run blurts during lunch.

"What do you want to create?" he asked.

"My relationship with Toby grows deeper and more resilient each day," I stated.

"Blurt—"

"Yeah, right. Like William will allow that?"

Ben repeated the drill again, and I responded: "Toby's a teenager. He's got his girlfriend for support, he doesn't need his 'mommy'."

Ben and I worked through what turned out to be a half-hour list of concerns. I'd often felt closer to Toby than I ever had with Alex, and now, I felt a love for Toby as pure and resonant as if I'd carried him in my own womb.

"The only love I really believe in is a mother's love for her children," Ben said, using his fingers to bracket the quote.

"Please tell me you didn't get that from 'The Great Jeff Jones'."

"No, silly." Ben laughed. "Lagerfeld!"

"Oh yeah." I sat with it a moment. Realized Ben had just handed me a beautifully packaged gift. It was true. I could feel it.

For the rest of the week, Ben ran an even more powerful Master Course exercise with me. I created, created, and created the things that I wanted: "William and I are divorced"; "Everything works out better than I expect"; "I find a new job"; "I build a new career in fashion." I was so confident and at peace by the end of the week that I believed all of it already existed.

And here it is now. I squeeze the envelope containing the divorce papers to my chest. Life is waiting for me to come through a new door. I feel so strong. So powerful. So *me*. When I die, this is a moment I want to remember. I think about Ma and how lonely she feels not having a partner to share her life with. It's strange. For me, it has been the opposite. Both marriages were the loneliest periods of my life.

The day William and I got married, I felt like I had failed not only my first marriage, but my life. I rub the cold wetness from my face. There's a sniffling sound, and it takes a moment to realize it's not actually coming from me, but from outside of myself.

I squint my eyes open, shielding them from the sun, and all I can make out is an outline of a body.

"Toby?"

"Hey." He's cross-legged on the ground, facing me, his back to the sun.

"I was just thinking about you." I sit up in the chaise. "How long have you been here?"

"Only a few minutes."

"You didn't walk, did you?"

"Actually, yeah, I did."

I blink the glare from my eyes, and when they adjust, I see a shadow over his left eye. Only it's not a shadow. "What the fuck—"

"I'm okay," he says.

"You are not okay," I say, hysteria rising inside me. I touch his face, sadness rising from my core like dense lava. "That fucking monster…"

"Don't." He grasps my hand firmly. There's a jerking sensation, as if I'd leapt out of myself, and I feel myself almost bouncing back into the lounge chair. He winces, the motion wracking his body. "It's just something I created," he says. "You're the one who always says that."

I gaze into his eyes. My chest expands. Sadness, beauty, love. It's not the teenager that I see, but the soul beneath it all who comes packaged inside that body. Neither of the boys experience The Master Class because neither of their fathers agree to it. William in particular feels it's a cult, and I realize now that I assumed Toby did, too. But he doesn't. The reality is that I'd stuck that label on him. While he had believed in me and what I've been doing all this time, I had kept him locked inside a box that limited him to "helpless." I'd taken from him tools that I could otherwise have shared, which may have helped him handle his father.

But Toby isn't helpless. He's choosing not to be. I see that now.

"This may be your creation," I say, "but that doesn't mean I can't mother you." He squeezes my hand, smiles earnestly and with such openness and courage blanketing so much fear, frustration, and loss that I ache for him. Moments like this, I'm sure he thinks about his biological mother. She may have been a drug addict, and she may have died before he had a chance to know her, but she's still his mother.

"You'll always be my baby, you know that, right?" I say now.

"I've never been your baby," he says, tears shimmering in his eyes. "By the time I met you I was, like, already nine or something."

"Maybe in this life," I say.

He moves to hug me, wincing again, and this time, the color drains from his face. He hugs an arm at his side. The past two times he came to me, I sent him back to William because I believed that as a biological parent, William had more "right" to Toby than I. It's logical; the law.

But is that true?

"Let's get inside," I say. "Your father will be here any minute."

"Don't make me go back—" Toby attempts to uncross his legs to stand, but pain singes through him like a bolt of lightening, and he crumples back to the ground. He groans, clutching his side as if to keep it from collapsing.

"Oh, my god, don't move," I say, my hands skimming the jacket, afraid of setting undue weight on him. "Let me see."

"I'm okay." Toby's face reddens. His breath is quick and shallow.

Has William bruised a rib? It's hard to believe. William can be violent, I'm not discounting that. I've seen him push and shove Toby. I've heard him say cruel things. But outright physical abuse toward Toby just isn't his style. Or so it seemed. All this time, I figured his violent side revealed itself mostly in bed with me where others were not privy to his true nature. Now, I wonder.

"Just let me see." I attempt to peek under the jacket. But Toby puffs his cheeks, forces himself to his feet, and before I know it, he's racing toward the house. I hurry to hold open the back door. He grits his teeth, breathing laboriously, and once inside, goes straight to the kitchen table. The agony is so great that when he sits in the chair, hugging himself, he has to lean his forehead onto the table. Beads of sweat appear at his temples. Quickly, I double lock the door. William doesn't have the key, but I pull the chain across anyway. My purse is on the sink counter. I remove what I can from it—computer, notebook, novel, Master pack— and then dig through the rest of the mess to search for my cellphone. Makeup bag, receipts, protein bar, wallet, notebook, lipgloss, hotel bill, keys, flyers, lavender essential oil, pack of airline cookies.

"Shit," I curse. "Where is it?"

Without raising his head or looking up, Toby reaches over to grasp my coat. "Amy."

"It's here somewhere." I toss aside the cookies and a bunch of paperwork. "For god's sake, where is it?"

"Mom," Toby whispers.

I stop. The sound, the declaration in that single, precious word. Alex uses it in its many different intonations, yet strangely, it's Toby who makes the word "mom" resonate. It's always Toby who appreciates the things I do. It could be the Star Wars T-shirt I buy him or the corn dogs I make for snack. Even that time I sign him up for hockey camp with Alex despite the fact that he doesn't actually like hockey. Even then, Toby is the one to say, "Thanks, mom." I crouch down, dragging the purse to the floor, and kneel beside him.

"I'm not going back," he says, forcing the words through his teeth, and I can see that bruised ribs make it difficult to breathe.

"I'll speak with your father." I crack open the kitchen window to listen for anything outside the house. The sound of the Audi pulling into the driveway or the slam of the car door. The last time, I persuaded William to let Toby stay for the weekend before returning him home. William might allow that again. I rummage through the purse one last time, dumping my things onto the floor, my hands shaking, and determine that the phone is not in the purse.

"I mean it." Toby tugs me by the pocket of the coat. "I'm staying here with you."

Body, mind, emotion, energy. Who was it who said love is "life longing for itself" and "boundless"? Was it Yogananda? Kahlil Gibran? I spent my entire life with a hunger trapped inside my body, searching for something that could fill that black hole. Yet, here it is. Love. It has always been here. Unadulterated. Pure. From a being who has less and yet gives infinitely more.

"Please," he rasps.

"Let me see," I say, and this time, he lets me unzip his jacket and lift his shirt. My stomach turns. For a moment, I actually feel myself shift away from Toby. There's swelling along the left side of the ribcage. One rib in particular, just below the breast area, is pinkish purple and raised. Bruising underlines the length of the bone, extending beneath the armpit. "What did he *do*?" I rasp.

Toby opens his mouth, but words fail him, and he just shakes his head and gives up. His breath is short and shallow. My horror turns to sadness.

Right there, right then, I decide.

"You're not going back. I'm not going to allow it. Not this time."

The phone, I suddenly realize, is in the coat I'm wearing. It has been in my pocket the whole time. I comb my fingers through Toby's hair with one hand, and, locating the phone with the other, dial 911.

I barely hang up before William arrives, the car's tires plucking at the gravel driveway. "It's him," Toby says. I've given him an ice pack for his eye, and another that he has wedged beneath his jacket.

"It's going to be okay," I say, wondering how much longer it will take before the ambulance arrives. Why didn't I drive Toby straight to the hospital ER? My car is there in the garage so William knows I'm home. He knows Toby is here, too. I dial 911, again. William's car door shuts. I can feel him moving toward the front door.

"Hello?" I say when the dispatcher comes onto the line. "I just called for an ambulance. I think I need the police."

The doorbell rings. "Don't leave me," Toby says, tugging at my coat pocket.

I cover the receiver. "One minute!" I yell at the front door. The operator asks for information. I relay what I can before the second sound of the bell. This time, twice, more insistent, and then after a pause, once more.

"Amy!" William yells from outside. He knocks. "Come on!"

I whisper for the operator to hurry, please, my ex-husband is at the door. She asks me to hold for a moment.

"I'll be right there!" I yell, again.

William starts banging at the door, now. "I know he's in there," he says in a threatening voice. I realize that I'd always counted on William being quiet about things; I'd been willing to suffer in silence. Having the neighbors possibly witness a scene, especially Jenna, the gossip queen across the street, makes me panic. It fills me with shame.

The operator comes back on the line, indicating the unit is on its way. I hang up and move toward the front door.

"Don't go," Toby says, gripping my coat. "You don't get it."

"What don't I get, sweetheart?" I kneel on the floor beside him.

"She dumped him." He moves the ice pack from his eye. It looks mottled, purplish, and swollen.

"I thought—" I glance around nervously until I see the documents resting safely on the kitchen table. "Didn't he propose?"

"Toby!" William yells.

"Yeah, but they fight," he says. "He hates her going out with clients all the time."

"Oh." It makes sense, now. He had pressured me slowly, insistently, and I found myself isolated from friends, work, and especially Jeff. Mandy was obviously a lot smarter than I'd given her credit for. A lot smarter than me, anyway. She figured out how to extricate herself before getting lawfully bound. She had outmaneuvered William, and that's what was driving his rage right now.

"Toby, get over here," William yells. He kicks the door.

I jump. My heart races, my entire body tensing. But The Master Workshop is still fresh in my mind. Instead of giving in to the panic, I use the techniques to let go of the fear and overwhelm. Once I do that, a calmness eases me. I can move outside of what is happening, almost as if I were spectating. I think about the humiliation I felt a moment ago about my neighbors "finding out." It's the same strategy he used in the bedroom. He could force his way inside and I would be resigned to it. I wouldn't cry for help because I did not want anyone, least of all the boys, to witness my shame.

"Don't be *stupid*, Amy," William says, jerking the door by the knob. Toby flinches, then moans from the sudden motion. "Let's talk about this," William adds.

Stupid. There was an incident over Toby's 11-year birthday party. William had arranged 9 holes for Toby and six friends at the Country Club, but Toby had asked for a movie and sleepover instead, because they were planning to play poker all night; one of his friends was going to teach them how. "What will people think?" William exclaimed. "Your peers will be having bar mitzvahs with the Knicks or renting out MSG in a couple of years, and you're telling me you want a sleepover? What are you, five?"

Toby was visibly crushed.

"He's just a kid, William," I offered. "What does he care of social improprieties? It's his birthday."

"What are you, stupid?" he blurted back. "Did I ask you?"

"No, I—"

"That's right," he said. "If I wanted a stupid opinion, I would have asked you outright." The boys watched.

Humiliation danced like static across my face. "William—"

"You don't get it do you?" he said, raising his voice. "You're a pretty face and a good fuck, but between those two little ears of yours? Nothing much going on."

"Stop it," I said, my voice dying.

"What's the matter? Am I hurting your little feelings?" he mocked. "Oh, she's crying. Little Miss Pretty is crying."

"Don't call me that."

"What should I call you, hm? Stupid? Lazy?"

"I'm a designer."

"Correction," he stated. "You married a designer. That doesn't actually make you one."

I felt myself shrinking. Wishing I could disappear.

How is it that some people make all the right choices while others continually make all the wrong ones? I wondered. Why? What was wrong with me?

In this marriage, just as in the last, I'd lost parts of myself and grown weaker every day. I would never really get away. I was trapped, again.

Only, I'm *not* trapped, I suddenly realize.

William is counting on me opting for invisibility. He knows I'm uncomfortable making a scene in front of the neighbors; he's intentionally making a ruckus in order to manipulate me into opening the door. Shame. What a powerful weapon.

"Don't worry," I tell Toby. "I'm not going to let him in."

"Promise?"

"Promise."

Toby releases me. I move to the front door. "Go home and calm down," I say.

"Open the door, Amy. Don't be stupid."

"We can talk later, William."

"He's my son," William says. "You don't get to screw with my son."

"Just calm down."

"Let me in." William rams the door. "Now!"

My heart lurches into my throat, then pounds in my ears. Where is the ambulance? The police? I back away, retreat to the kitchen.

"They'll be here any minute," I tell Toby, who's sitting cross-legged on the floor and holding his side. I phone Jenna, and when she answers, I explain by saying my ex is at my door, and would she be so kind as to call the other neighbors and everyone step outside together to acknowledge what is happening? Within a couple of minutes, William retreats from banging at the door. I hear him saying, "No, no problem. I think she's got the music turned up. Yeah, I—"

"She's fully aware you are outside," Jenna says.

William quiets.

"She'd like for you to leave," another neighbor adds.

"Now," another neighbor says.

"This is a private family matter," William says.

"It's not sounding so private," Jenna says.

"Bitch," William mutters, under his breath. He starts ringing my door bell, again. This time, he lays on the buzzer.

"I hate him," Toby says.

"That's okay. I'm grateful to him enough for the two of us," I say. *My relationship with Toby grows deeper and more resilient each day.* "It's because of your father that I have you in my life."

"But the whole world knows now." Toby starts sobbing.

"Yes, everyone cares," I say. "Can you feel it?"

Toby thinks a moment, then nods. His forehead bobs on the tabletop, a tear hanging from the tip of his nose.

"It's all going to be okay," I say, kissing his hand. "I've got you, baby. We've all got you."

I hear a siren, then. Everything quiets. Out the window, I see the police pulling to the curb. The officers step out of the car and come toward the front of the house. William backs off, switching back into the man who behaves in a cordial, appropriate manner. The officers ask him questions.

"You will need to tell the police," I say.

Toby lays his head sideways on the table so that he's facing me now.

"When it comes right down to it, I know you may feel conflicted—" I say.

Outside, William points a thumb over his shoulder at us. Next door and across the street, the neighbors remain on their stoops, watching.

"He's your father, after all," I continue. "But, you absolutely have to tell them everything, okay?"

Toby blinks, the purple eye already closing and immobile.

An ambulance pulls up behind the police car.

"It's here," I say. "Ready?"

I step out the back door and wave down the paramedics.

"Here," I yell, waving my arms. "Over here."

Dust

In the room he shares with Alex, Toby sleeps on the bottom of the two bunks like he's dead to the world. Every couple hours, I check on him. 9AM. 10. 11. He usually wakes around 7AM as soon as he hears me in the bathroom. Maybe he's sick? I touch his forehead with the back of my hand. Cool, no temp. Oblivious, Toby continues to slumber. Alex is at Jeff's, so the top bunk is empty except for a balled-up comforter. I climb the two steps, and kneeling, make the bed. When I come down, again, Toby rouses, only to turn toward the wall.

That's enough. I draw open the shades. "Toby, wake up," I say, nudging his shoulder. "Sweetheart, you okay?"

"Stop," he groans, rolling and pulling the pillow over his head. "I'm tired."

I step back. Typically, Alex is the moody one. Toby's my helper, especially on weekends when Alex is at Jeff's, and he has me to himself. While I make pancakes or eggs, he pours us each a mug of coffee. We talk about school or friends or maybe Amanda, his girlfriend. Sometimes, Alex. Last spring, the morning after William beat Toby so badly he broke a rib, Toby sat quietly on a stool beside me, and as I fried bacon in one pan and scrambled eggs in another, he asked in an almost child-like voice if I would please adopt him. The judge ruled that Toby remain in my care while William underwent private therapy sessions as well as another round of anger management training. We go back to court in September, and since Toby is 17 now, the judge may agree to his wish to be adopted by me instead of getting turned back over to William.

"You feeling okay?" I ask Toby.

"Yes." His voice muffles in the pillow.

"Sure?"

"Fine."

The phone rings. It's in my room. I run to answer it. "Just picked up some tiles in Elmsford, so I'm in your neck of the Big Woods," Ben says. He's remodeling the bathrooms in his apartment. "I feel like matzo ball soup."

"Ready in fifteen," I say, hanging up and jumping in to the shower. Warm water rains over me, and I imagine it washing all the worry down the drain. Is such concern motherly instinct or is it the overbearing helicopter mom? I shut off the shower. Moodiness. Sleeping late. Lazing about. Toby's being a typical adolescent. Maybe it means he feels safe enough—a positive sign. I feel myself relax.

Exactly fifteen minutes after Ben's call, I'm practically dancing down the stairs to the front door. It's been ages since Ben and I had a chance to catch up. I've told him I got into FIT, again, and now is the perfect opportunity to get his feedback on some new sketches.

"Ma," Toby calls, as I'm checking that the folder with my drawings is in my purse. He's at the top of the stairs. His chocolate curls lie flat against the left side of his scalp. "Where're you going?"

"Uncle Ben's stopping by. We may go for a drive. Get a bite somewhere."

"Can I come?" Dark crescents shadow his eyes.

I stifle the urge to say no. "Okay, get changed," I unlock the door and step outside. "We'll wait."

Ben's already there, lounging on a patio chair, his fingers intertwined behind his head. He's in a worn T-shirt, loose jeans, and Prada leather sandals. "I always forget how bucolic it is out here," he says, staring at the row of colonials—replicated like Monopoly houses—across the street.

"Quiet, you." I settle into the love seat facing him. It's the dead heat of August, two weeks before Alex leaves for college, and the cool-ness of morning has already given way to heat and humidity. Cicadas sound like a symphony of shaking maracas.

"No, really," he says. "I'm not being facetious."

"Sorry, but the Hamptons is that way." I point south in the direc-tion of the Bronx River Parkway. "Love the Pradas, by the way."

His lips purse into a smirk. He wiggles his manicured toes.

"Just two more years," I say. Toby's going to be a Junior. "Can you believe it's been 18 years that I've been out here?"

"Oh my God! Stop that," Ben says, covering his ears with his hands. "We can't possibly be that old."

"It's just a number," I laugh.

"Easy for you to say, Miss Perpetually Young Asian Girl."

Just then, my neighbor, Jenna appears at her front door. She's a root-dyeing redhead with a high-pitched voice. Her son Stevie is the same age as Alex, and even though Alex now attends private school, they're friendly through Toby. Jenna bears an oversized purse larger than a diaper bag. Most women's handbags get incrementally small-er as their children grow older. Jenna is the rare exception; as if to compensate for her son's growing independence, her purses increase proportionately, matching the size—and bearing the weight—of her gossip. Last year, she was the one I called during the William incident. I was grateful, but then the day after, Toby said everyone at his school heard about what happened. Toby doesn't go to the same school any-more, but he attends the same sports programs, so I knew it had to be Jenna.

Jenna heads toward the Volvo parked in the street, but instead of getting into the car, she starts across toward us.

"Toby asked if he could join us," I tell Ben.

Ben's brows lift with surprise.

"I *know*—major strangeness lately." Since Jenna is now upon us, I switch the subject: "How're the bathrooms going?"

"What strangeness?" Jenna asks, sitting in the chair between us. "You talking about that hockey dad from Crestwood who's having an affair with the guy at the flower shop?"

"Ben, Jenna," I introduce. "Jenna, Ben."

"We were speaking about my bathrooms," Ben says. "What a remodeling nightmare."

"Contractors," she says, digging through her bag. "They're the worst."

I'm just about to ask Ben if he went with the white marble tile with the bluish veins or the brown ceramic planks that look like wood, but Jenna adds, "Connie Williams is renovating her kitchen and bathrooms, isn't she?"

Connie is Toby's girlfriend's mother. "Is she?" I ask.

"That's what I heard." Jenna removes her wallet and continues digging through the bowels of her bag. "Is it true the cancer came back?"

Something lodges in my throat. I'm not close with Connie, but we're friendly enough, given the kids' year-long relationship, and Connie most certainly hasn't mentioned *this*. Neither has Toby, though it is the kind of thing he usually shares with me.

"Amy was just telling me about Toby," Ben says, noticing my discomfort and attempting to switch the subject again.

"Toby?" she says, her ears perking up.

"Right, Toby," I say, cautiously. I describe the behavior—oversleeping, lethargy, moodiness. "He sees Amanda, but only if she comes over. I haven't seen him with other friends in a while. Like today? It's beautiful out and he's in his room."

"Oh, that," Jenna says, waving off my concern. "Stevie's like that. Isn't Alex?"

"Maybe Alex was born a teenager," I say wearily.

"Well," Ben says. "It's a major transition when an older sibling goes off to college. After my sister left for Wesleyan? I must have been the loneliest, most heartbroken person on the planet."

"That's true for moms, too," Jenna says, a hand over her heart. "I remember the first day of Kindergarten. And suddenly, my baby's leaving me. He's going off to college!"

"All I can say is *finally*," I blurt, rolling my eyes. Maybe my voice carries a little too loudly; the entire street seems to go silent. "Alex's bags are packed and waiting by the door."

She chuckles and punches me softly on the arm. "You don't mean that."

I cross my arms. "Uh, yeah, I do."

Jenna shifts uncomfortably. "I better go. I'm meeting Gwen at Bloomingdale's."

I wave her off and watch her cross back to the car and can only imagine the judgements she might be holding: *"And then she said"* ... *"Can you believe she'd be like that?"* ... *"What kind of mother would..."*

Ben smirks and shakes his head at me. "Bad mommy."

"At least I'm honest."

From around the street corner, a young woman appears. She's pale-skinned with light blue eyes and has dark brown hair that's almost black. It's a striking contrast. She also stands out because she's at least 5'8 and lanky thin. "That's Toby's girlfriend."

"Beautiful dog," Ben says, noticing the silvery little Shi Tzu accompanying her off leash.

"The parents gave it to her at Christmas the year Connie got diagnosed. She's the woman Jenna was talking about."

"Cancer?"

"Breast," I nod.

The dog notices us on the porch and runs straight to me on its stumpy legs. I pick her up. "Hi, Santa." She licks my cheek. "Thank you, I love you, too."

Amanda steps onto the porch. "Something tells me Toby's got better things to do now than come out with us old farts," I say.

"Hi, Ms. Wong," Amanda says, blushing.

"He's upstairs. Go on up."

Ben and I head toward the driveway to his car as Amanda lets herself into the house. Barely a minute later, just as we're pulling into the street, Toby races from the house and runs toward us.

"Wait," he yells. "Wait!"

Ben breaks suddenly. My neck cranes forward and back. I open the door and jump out. "What is it? What's wrong?"

"You can't leave," he says.

"You want me to bring you back some matzo ball soup?"

He glances up the street, then down, nervously.

"Toby," I say, my hands at his shoulders. He's crying. He's actually crying.

"You said you'd wait—" he says.

"Okay, I'm sorry," I say, trying to hug him. "I just thought—"

He opens the back passenger door, jumps inside, and shuts the door.

What the fuck is going on? Ben shoots me a bug-eyed look affirming that Toby's behavior is definitely *strange*. Could he be doing drugs? I glance at Amanda, who appears from the house now. Her face is tomato red and shrouded with confusion. She seems ruffled, too, as if Toby knocked her over to get outside. Did the two of them have a fight yesterday? I've never seen Toby treat anyone rudely, never mind like this. Whatever this is, it's way out of my depth. Inside the house, the little dog starts yapping.

"Toby?" I say, leaning into the car. "Amanda came to see *you*."

"I know. She can come if she wants," he stutters.

"Well, um, would you like to ask her?"

Toby rolls down his window. "We're going to breakfast, wanna come?"

"Where are you going?" she asks, the dog in her arms now.

"Village diner," I say, getting back into the car and buckling myself into the seat.

"I have Santa," she says.

"We can drop her off at your house," I say, turning to Ben. "That okay?"

Ben nods. She picks up Santa and gets into the car. Ben points out the front door is ajar, so I release the safety belt and get out. As I walk toward the house, I decide Toby's going into therapy whether he wants to or not. He's asked me to adopt him; as his mother, I'm not giving him a choice. I don't have money for therapy, but maybe Jeff can help. Ever since the divorce, he's been paying me a "salary." It was the only way I could take over the responsibility of Alex's care—taking him to and from appointments, keeping track of and re-ordering medications and therapy devices, scheduling appointments—when Jeff needed to get back to work. What I get from him isn't much, but it pays the bills, gives me mornings to work on designs or go for a long run, and, of course, spend time with Alex. Now that Alex is leaving for college, however, I get a new start.

I draw the front door shut and slide the key into the lock. *If.* As the key turns, there's a metallic snap of the bolt latching. *If everything works out okay.* The car idles in the driveway, beckoning me to hurry.

That night, Alex arrives home just before dinner. He's playing Minecraft on his phone. Without as much as a hello, he makes his way like a zombie to the living room sofa. He sits. Toby's been there all afternoon with Amanda and has to shift positions to avoid getting sat upon. As soon as Alex is beside Toby, Toby gets equally transfixed by the game. I'm setting the table—cheeseburgers with french fries and dill pickles—when I hear Amanda say, "Call me."

"Five minutes and it's dinner," I announce, hurrying onto the patio after her. "Amanda? Everything okay between you and, um—" I nod over my shoulder at the house. "I mean, Toby has a lot going on right now."

"I know." She stares down at the ground. Fidgets with a loose strand of hair.

Shit, I've put her on the spot.

"Toby tells me you're leaving for summer school," I say. "That's so exciting."

She shrugs. "I told Toby to do it too so we could be together, but…"

"Oh, the cost might have had something to do with it."

"No, his Dad was going to give him money, but Toby didn't want it."

"Dad?" There's a restraining order against William. "When did he see his Dad?"

Amanda cringes and backs away. "I, uh, I mean, well, I better go, now, Ms. Wong. My mother's going to kill me if dinner gets cold." She rushes off, her long legs carrying her swiftly down the street. William. Of course.

Toby appears at the front door. His eyes dart one way, then the other. He's like a soldier on watch for an ambush. "What are you doing out here?" he asks. "Let's, eat, okay?"

"When did you speak with your father?" I ask.

He stiffens. "Who—" His gaze freezes on Amanda as she disappears around the corner.

"Don't blame her," I say. "I made her tell me."

Toby storms back into the house, slamming the door in my face.

"Hey! I'm talking to you."

He turns, his arms crossed in front of him. "It wasn't anything."

"Just tell her," Alex says from the couch.

"Tell me what?" I ask.

"There's nothing to tell," Toby says, enunciating each word, and glaring at Alex. "It was just a couple minutes."

"A couple actually means 'two,' you know," Alex mutters.

"That's it," I say, marching toward the house phone. "I'm calling Child Protective Services."

"Don't, wait!" Toby says, blocking my way. "Mom, please."

"Has he threatened you?" I try to dodge around him. "I'm not letting him terrorize you any more."

"He's not," Toby says, clasping his hands together. "I swear."

Alex shakes his head, just slightly, just enough that I catch it peripherally.

"Where did you see him?" I cross my arms and plant my feet firmly on the floor. "What did he say to you?"

"Nothing." Toby's gaze falls to the floor.

"Toby, I need—"

"I said nothing, all right?" he yells, kicking the leg of the coffee table. "He didn't say *anything*." He marches to the dinner table and plops himself in his seat. "Can we eat now?"

I turn to Alex for an explanation, but his mouth pinches. He's sworn to secrecy. He shoves his phone into his pocket, and together, we move to the table. Toby's pale, sweating so profusely that translucent beads shimmer over his nose.

"Maybe I overreacted," he says.

"To what?" I ask, sitting beside him. Then it dawns on me. He's talking about the fight last spring. Toby told William he wanted to live with me after the divorce. William beat him up for it.

"He didn't mean it," Toby says, now.

"Oh, man," Alex says, stuffing a fry into his mouth. "You're calling that an accident?"

"Yes," Toby states, and he's trembling. "It was an accident."

"He broke your fucking rib," Alex says.

"So?"

"So? You know what it takes to break a rib? Shit, man, the velocity of the punch had to have been the equivalent of a minor car crash."

Toby's jaw clenches. He stares down at his plate. "He's my dad."

"He's an asshole," Alex says.

"Alex," I snap.

Toby jumps to his feet. "Like your dad's so much better?"

"Toby!"

"Yeah, actually he is," Alex states, getting up from his seat. "He doesn't need to beat up a kid to feel like a real man."

"Stop it, both of you!" I yell. "Both your dads are flawed, each in his own particular way, okay? Happy now?"

"Not really," Alex says.

"Well you should be! And you—" I say, jabbing a finger in Toby's face. "No one has the right to hurt you, understand? Not your father or anyone else."

Toby opens his mouth, but nothing comes out except short, throaty sounds. Finally, he rasps, "I miss him."

We sit there a moment, no one uttering a word, the greasy burgers going cold and congealing on the plates. How is it that in a single moment, a situation can flip around and be the exact opposite of what one initially believed? All this time, I've badmouthed and demonized William without stopping to consider that for better or for worse, William is his father.

"Would you rather not proceed with the adoption?" I ask, the smell of burgers making my stomach turn.

He starts to cry. "Yes."

The moment stretches out. Vast, empty, cold. "It's okay, Toby," I start to say, but Alex grabs Toby by the collar of the shirt. "That's not you saying it and you know it."

Toby shoves Alex away. "You know everything, right? You have everything, right? Well, you don't know nothing."

Then they're brawling. Plates knock into each other. Dishes slide. Glasses teeter.

"Boys!" I yell, trying to get between them. "Stop it, stop it right now!"

But they're both bigger than me, and stronger. They hold on, their faces distorted with rage, punching and shoving as if to kill one another. Glasses tip. Plates fall. Food splatters over the carpet. Then Alex loses his footing. He slips backward. They careen toward the floor,

Toby falling on top of Alex. Shit! The plate in his skull! Time slows, and yet everything happens faster than I can stop it.

Then I'm screaming. The back of Alex's head strikes the carpeted floor, making a sickening thud.

Toby quickly shifts off Alex. Alex immediately sits up to show he's okay. Still, I can't stop. The sound gushes from my throat. Every ounce of terror I've held onto over the years roars out of me. When it finally subsides and there isn't an ounce of energy left inside me, I collapse to my knees. "I'm sorry, Mom," Toby pleads, trying to hold me.

"It's okay," Alex says, touching and showing me his head. "I'm okay."

"Everything's okay, Mom," Toby says.

Spilled grape juice drains onto the carpet. It's reddish purple, thin and anemic. The boys help me to my room.

Nearly two weeks later, the night before Alex leaves for college, I find Toby at 2 AM, huddled in the corner of the living room sofa. He's clutching his phone to his chest. Who can he possibly be calling at this time of night? "What's going on?" I ask.

"Nothing," he says. Maybe it's the moonlight, but he seems sickly pale.

"Everything okay with Amanda? You have a fight or something?"

"No."

I sit beside him on the sofa. "Sandwich? I was thinking about grilled cheese and ham."

He shrugs.

"Or cookies—I got the chocolate-covered Oreos you like."

His eyes swell with tears.

"Oh, Toby," I say, putting an arm around him. "It's okay, sweetheart. It really is."

"No, it's not." Warm tears bleed through my nightshirt onto my shoulder. "It'll never be okay."

I want to tell him he's wrong. Everything changes no matter how bad or bleak the situation may seem. But I know that feeling he's describing. I've felt it before. It's real. It deserves to be acknowledged.

He starts to sob. Dark crescent moons pouch beneath his eyes. When he's done, he lies limp against my shoulder.

"I know I've been upset lately," I say.

"It's all my fault."

"No, it's not. I love you like a son and you love me like a mom. The adoption thing doesn't change that. We don't need a piece of paper to prove that."

He looks at me, his eyes half closed, and blinks as if the weight of his eyelids is a burden. He seems decades older than his age.

"It's time for bed," I say. "You're exhausted."

"Can I sleep in your room?"

I fix the day bed in my bedroom. It's against the window overlooking the garage. Toby gets under the comforter and winds it around himself.

"Have I ever told you about my father?" I ask. "He left when I was about your age."

"You told me about this bed."

"Oh, yeah." In fact, he's lying on the opium bed my grandfather created. After Dad left us, Ma said she'd cleaved and fried it in the backyard barbecue. Only it turned up years later when Ma closed up her storage space. "Ma could be vindictive, but I guess it's kind of funny when I think about it now," I say.

"Your dad deserved it," Toby says. "From what you've told us, he's kind of a dick."

"Maybe," I laugh. "Look, I don't mean to compare my father with yours—"

"Don't," Toby says, cringing.

"They're nothing alike, actually."

"You can say that again," Toby says, ghostly pale and recoiling into the comforter.

"What I'm trying to say is—" My mind comes up empty. Finally, I say, "It's like my closet. There're all these clothes and shoes, you know? If I don't wear them, they sit there and sit there. So then when I *do* wear them, there's dust all over. No one else can see it, but it's there like this invisible cloak around me. With me so far?"

He shakes his head. No. Absolutely not.

I sigh. "All this with your father? It just brings up all that dust, you know? From what happened with my own father. That's all I'm trying to say."

He sneaks a hand out of the comforter and takes mine, hugging it to his cheek.

"I don't know why my father left. I always felt that maybe it was my fault somehow. Or, partly, anyway. Who knows. I'll probably never know. But what I do know is this: I don't want to go through the rest of my life living in all that dust from my father. It's behind me now. It's over. And I'm moving on."

"I want to move on, too," he says.

"You can," I say. "You will."

"No, it never changes," he says, shaking his head. "And it's my fault for making you sad."

"It's just dust, Toby. As sad as I am that you're leaving, I get it, I really do. I know what it feels like to miss your father. I know what it feels like to want to be with him."

There's a loud metal bang outside my bedroom window. Toby throws off the comforter and peers through the curtains. "Where's my phone?" he rasps, his eyes bulging. "I need my phone!"

"It's just a raccoon," I say, pointing at the garbage can lying on its side. A small creature rummages through the trash. As if it senses that we are watching, he turns and looks directly up at us, his shiny eyes marked by his distinctive black mask. "See?"

Toby's as pale as the moon. I have never seen him so terrified.

"What's going on with you?" I ask. "Toby, please tell me."

Toby shakes his head. "My Dad hates you."

"It's hard for him not to have control over others," I explain. "That's all it is."

"I hate him sometimes."

"That's normal," I say. "You have a very complicated relationship, but that doesn't mean you shouldn't feel like you should be with him. Because you're right. He is your father. And he deserves a chance to be one. I can't stand in the way of that."

Toby starts to sob again.

"I may not love your father anymore, but I'll always love you, Toby. If I had to go through all of that craziness with him again, just so that I could be your mom for a few years, I would do it again in a heartbeat."

He looks at me with big eyes.

"So, thank you," I say. "Truth is I love Alex but I just never loved being a mom. Maybe I didn't know how, you know? And you, when you came along, well, you made me feel like a good mom. It's not so hard to love something once you feel good at it." I kiss his head and hug him tightly, not letting up on the pressure until the tension drains from his body. Finally, he's asleep.

It's the big day. A three hour trip to Cambridge. I'll drive solo—not a great combination when you're feeling exhausted. Alex is going with Jeff via limo. Toby's supposed to come with me, but he wakes feeling sick. I touch his forehead again and find it cool. "I'm just tired," he says, rolling away from me.

"You want to stay home?"

He doesn't respond.

"Um, okay." Way things have been going, I half expect him to come chasing after me as soon I hit the bottom landing of the steps. When he doesn't, I gather sketches I've started in anticipation of school. Technically, they seem fine, yet, something doesn't feel right. At least I'll have time to think about them during the ride. Upstairs, it's quiet. I don't want to baby Toby, and yet, I don't feel good about leaving him home alone. Just as I'm headed into the garage, I get an idea. "Toby?"

He moans.

"Why don't you stop by Amanda's later? I'll call Connie. Maybe you can have lunch there?"

"No, don't," he says. "I'm fine, okay? I just want to sleep. I'll text Amanda later."

"Call me, then, okay?" The University's parent lounge and resources fair—whatever *that* is—starts at 1 PM, and the official "Welcome" is set for three. If I get back on the road right away, I can be home by dinner. I get into the car and spread my sketches on the passenger seat beside me. The idea I want to develop in school is a high-end line of clothes specifically geared toward older women. The target audience would be between the ages of 50 and 70. Modern. Classy. Clean, elegant lines. With special emphasis on material—sweat-wicking "silk" for the Spring/Summer Collection; thermal itch-free "wool" for the Fall/Winter—and spectacularly sexy fit, with firm, Spanx-like support built into each particular garment, and tailored to each specific individual. Flat abs. A shapely waistline. A generous lift at both the bosom and buttocks.

No more sucking in. No more turkey waddle nor hiding behind layers.

Finally 50. The New Modern Woman.

If only I could figure out why the drawings aren't working. Einstein got solutions in the shower. Maybe I'll get some on I 95. It's start and stop traffic, though the kind that makes a sleepy person sleepier. I glance at the sketches. They are each on a cheat sheet, obtained from the internet—a vertical line down the middle of the page with horizontal lines for nine sections of the body, each separated by the length of one head.

There are also red dotted lines, further delineating the neck, elbows, wrists and hands. I've drawn in the head and neck, torso, lower trunk, legs and feet. Four and a half sections are leg, starting with the hip.

The first is a dress with a corset top. It's made with sweat-wicking material and pressurized foam that's sturdy, yet form fitting. Technically, everything fits. So, then what's *wrong* with it? Nothing comes to me. Nothing at all.

Outside Stamford, I stop for gas and a large Diet Coke. There's a slight hissing sound from beneath the hood. I ignore it and get back on the road. Half an hour later, the orange engine light flashes on.

Suddenly, the engine dies.

Steam funnels out from the vents in the hood. Heat rises off the pavement in waves. "Please, please, don't do this to me. Not now. Please." I twist the key counterclockwise toward me, pause a moment, then start the car again. Then, again. Nothing.

There's the smell of gas. I've flooded the engine. I slam my fists against the wheel. "Shit, shit, shit." I hit the hazard button. Click, click...click, click... Despite the emergency lights, more honking from behind. I dig the cellphone from my purse, call AAA, then Jeff.

"It's going to be a while," I say, explaining about the car. "You guys go ahead. I'll be there as soon as I can."

"Is that Mom?" I hear Alex say.

"Don't be silly," Jeff tells me. "Leave the car. I'll call a tow."

"I've already called AAA—"

"Where exactly are you?" Jeff asks.

"What happened?" I hear Alex yelp. "Where's mom? Why isn't she coming?"

"Alex!" Jeff snaps. "Just give me a minute. I can't hear what she's saying!"

"I'm on 95," I say. "Just outside New Haven."

"Did you get off the exit?"

"Unfortunately, I'm dead center in the middle of the highway."

His voice muffles as he speaks with his driver. "We'll be there in fifteen," he finally says.

"No, Jeff, I—" But, Jeff hangs up.

Whatever. I glance behind me. My car is causing major bottle necking. And the heat. Sweat streaks down my scalp onto my face. It pools at the dip between my breasts and under my arms, soaking through my dress. I call Toby but go straight to voice mail. He's probably with Amanda, watching TV. So why do I feel so uneasy?

In the distance, I see the twirling yellow lights of the tow truck, trying to make its way through, if only traffic would allow him to get by. It isn't until a police car appears on the scene that traffic divides, the truck following immediately behind. The cop parks directly behind me. He motions for the tow truck to pull into the right lane, directing traffic so that it now funnels into a single lane. The tow driver pulls on his gloves. He says for safety reasons to wait in his truck.

Jeff's limo pulls up just as the tow hook draws the front of the car off the ground. Jeff steps out. I think he's coming to speak with me, but he goes to the driver side of the car. "I called and settled with the office," Jeff says, "so, take the car to the station and we'll call tonight with further instructions." The driver radios the station.

"That's sweet of you, Jeff," I say, "but—"

"Come on, let's go," he says, glancing at his watch.

The dispatcher confirms that the tow charge for the vehicle has been paid and tells the driver to hurry back. There's another accident at the last exit. He's instructed to drop my car at the garage and get to the next vehicle as soon as possible.

I step down from the truck with purse, bag, and sketches, and reluctantly follow Jeff to the limo. Alex games with his headphones on. I sit directly across from him, my arms crossed tightly over my chest as the limo continues on its way. "Something wrong?" Jeff asks.

"I appreciate the fact that you paid the towing fee. I'll pay you back."

"You don't need to."

I roll my eyes. As efficient and capable as he is, he never supported me when I truly needed it. What makes him think I need it now? "I don't want to be saved, okay?"

"Uh, yeah, Ma, you do," Alex says, matter of factly. "The parent fair starts in two hours."

"The only parent resources I need right now are a bottle of Advil and a soy latte with a double shot of expresso."

"I forgot your mother's humor," Jeff says.

"I'm not joking," I say, because nothing can possibly make a person pissier than her car dying on I-95 on a sweltering August afternoon. "Just like I'm not joking when I tell people to fuck off when they suggest I read *The Parent's Survival Guide to Freshman Year of College* or *Letting Go: A Parent's Guide to Understanding the College Years.*"

Jeff opens the compartment that separates his seat from Alex's to reveal a copy of *The Parent's Survival Guide to Freshman Year of College.*

"You got the wrong one," I say. "You need 'letting go'."

Jeff actually laughs. I tell them about my neighbor Jenna, whose son leaves for Emory in the morning. "She counted down the days like he was a death row inmate."

Alex bursts out laughing. "Oh, man," he says.

"And they called me a helicopter mom." I shake my head. "What a bunch of helicopter nitwits."

"Hey, I may be a helicopter but I'm no nitwit." Jeff's alluding to the seven-figure charitable donation he made to Harvard, as well as the fact that he checked the "Caucasian" box on the application, which read: "Alex Jones," son of "Jeff Jones" and "Amy Jones." Jeff had spoken with a top College Education Advisor who'd explained that more than 21% of the student population at Harvard is Asian. When I questioned him about obfuscating the fact that Alex was at least in part Asian, he responded: "There's a quota, you know, or didn't you realize?"

"Now, if you two don't mind," Jeff says, "I haven't slept the past couple of days. I need to rest my eyes."

Alex is already back to his gaming. Jeff's napping doesn't seem the least bit unusual to him. For me, however, it's a first. During our marriage, "rest" was never a part of Jeff's vocabulary. Logically, however, it makes sense. He's in his 70s now, and slowing down. And yet, who would believe Superman ages? He's supposed to be immortal, goddammit.

Jeff's head lulls to the side. He snores.

There's a strange tug inside me. As much as I've wanted to blame him for everything, he's human, as human as the rest of us.

Jeff's head rests against the window. The snoring stops. His breath grows silent. Sleep shadows the lower lid of his eyes. His chest slowly rises, then falls. He slips deeper into sleep.

From my purse, I withdraw the sketch with the corset top dress. Looking at it now with fresh eyes, it occurs to me that the bottom of the corset comes up too high. It should, I realize, fall as low as the top of the bikini line. This would cover the belly one often acquires with age or after pregnancy, or both, and which, if left untucked, tends to buckle outward like a roll of fat.

Swiftly, I erase and pencil in the new lines.

"Ma," Alex says. "You going home tonight?"

"Oh, god. Thanks for reminding me," I say, digging the cellphone from my purse. I call the insurance company, then an auto rental service. Due to high demand over the back to school weekend, no vehicles are available. I try another auto rental and receive the same response.

"The driver's going back tonight," Alex says, pausing his game. "Just go home with him."

"That's a great idea." I assumed that since Jeff was staying a few days—he likes to be certain that Alex is safely settled—the driver would stay with him in Cambridge. But Jeff may not have the same comfort level with the new driver as he had with the last, who'd worked for him for almost twenty years. "You think Dad will mind if I leave right after the 'welcome' speech?"

"Definitely not," Alex says, "Maybe you could also take him with you?"

"Oh, Alex." The accident had given Jeff a chance to truly connect and love; and he'd taken it, finally dropping all the bullshit—the women, the sexing, the drugging—to put his heart into caring for his child. Only Jeff took it to the extreme. When Alex started sleep away camp, Jeff insisted on vacationing at a resort close by, "dropping in" on occasion, which grew quantum times more suffocating and mortifying for Alex with each passing year. I assumed it was an issue of control. But now, I'm not so sure. Ever since Toby said not to follow through with the adoption, I struggle with a desperate feeling of abandonment and loss. Had Alex's accident triggered a similar response in Jeff? "Be patient with your father," I say softly.

"Please, Ma. Just talk to him."

I watch Jeff sleep. He seems unassuming, vulnerable. I'm suddenly overcome by a sense of compassion. "Okay," I say. "But no promises. You know how strong-willed your father can be."

Alex brightens.

I glance through the sequence of sketches and it hits me: I've drawn the "model's body." That's it! My target audience is not 6 feet tall and 110 lbs, and while I love the high heel, the woman buying my clothes shouldn't have to rely on it to look good.

From my purse, I take out the circles and ovals templates, along with the metal ruler. I open my artist's book and sketch freestyle, segmenting the body using my own dimensions. Before I know it, the sketches are coming alive; they are apprearing to me in 3-D. I'm so engrossed that I'm not sure what happens first.

"Asshole," Jeff yells. He throws punches at Alex. "I'll kill you!"

Alex deftly dives across the limo, landing on my lap. The sketches crumple. Jeff punches the back of the seat. Then, as quickly as it started, it's over. Whatever "it" is. Jeff's asleep, again, his head lolling toward the window.

"What—" I gulp "— was *that*?"

"He won't talk about it," Alex whispers into my shoulder.

"This has happened before?" I say, shifting away.

"Sometimes a couple times a night."

Just as I'm thinking it's not possible—Alex must be mistaken—it happens again. Jeff screams and beats the specter in the empty seat beside him. His eyes are open like he's awake or sleepwalking. "I'll kill you!" he repeats, vehemently.

I push Alex off my lap and onto the seat beside me. "Jeff!" I yell.

Jeff's fist pounds and pounds.

"Jeff!"

"Dad!" Alex screams.

Jeff startles and wakes. He blinks the sleep from his eyes. He glances from me to Alex, then back to me again.

"You okay?" I ask.

"It was just a nightmare." Jeff straightens his jacket by the cuffs, but he seems lost and disoriented.

Nightmare? Jesus Christ. That's no nightmare.

Alex crosses his legs on the seat, hugs his arms around his knees, and stares out the window. The road sign says, "Massachusetts Welcomes You." The limo crosses the imaginary line into a different state.

Harvard. Stately, red-brick buildings. Cathedral ceilings. Cast iron gates. Sprawling quad. The Charles River. It's the moment Alex has worked harder than anyone else for, and yet, now, even when Jeff promises he can have his car on campus by January if he keeps up the grades, Alex barely breaks a smile. None of us does. We unpack Alex into his room, meeting his squash-playing, hair-gel obsessed roommate from Philly, and then walk through the campus to the chapel. Jeff moves slowly, attributing the stiffness in his legs to the long walk he took in Central Park yesterday.

The Dean's "Welcome" is arranged in such a way that students face the Dean whereas the parents sit behind him. There's no mention of famous alumni—former U.S. Presidents, politicians, business magnets, entrepreneurs, or actors—which I find surprising, given that every person I've ever met who went to Harvard makes it known he went there within the first five minutes of meeting. The actual content of the Dean's message slips by as I start to fret. What happened with Jeff in the car? How will Alex fare on his own without all the supports from me and Jeff? Who will take care of him if a bad migraine comes on? Why hasn't Toby called or texted?

Finally, when the Dean arrives at the juncture of his speech when parents are asked to leave, Jeff and I walk the quad together. He remarks about the architecture. I ask about getting a ride home with the driver today and suggest that Jeff return to New York also. "Alex will be fine," I say.

"I know." Jeff stands, arms akimbo. His pride and love for Alex radiates off him. Charisma, I realize, is like sunlight. Everyone leans toward it. Even now. Even me. It's Jeff Jones, the man I met at the party all those years ago, the man I fell in love with on the beach at Cape Cod.

"And we do have matters to discuss," he says.

"Yeah," I say. "Yeah, we really do."

In the limo on the way home, he gets straight to the point. "What occurred earlier is a result of a condition referred to as RBD—REM Behavior Disorder," he says. "It's not so bad in it of itself, but, unfortunately, for many people, myself included, it's a precursor for LBD—Lewy Body dementia."

"Dementia?" I say. "You?"

"More specifically, it's an umbrella term for two related conditions—dementia with Lewy bodies and Parkinson's."

I stare, mouth agape.

He starts to go on about plans he'd like to make with Alex over the next couple of years. Trips to Vietnam and Thailand. A safari in Africa. The summer at The Cape. Over the years, he's gotten closer with one of his daughters. Now, he'd like to try again with the other; forge a relationship, if possible. He talks about stepping down as CEO of his company, moving the buyer from his SoHo store to his design team, and possibly having me take over her position. "Would you like that?" he asks.

Parkinson's. How is it possible? The words don't match up with the man in front of me.

"You've had a second opinion?" I ask, which is stupid because this is *Jeff.* "Well, maybe you should get a third." I reach for my purse. "I'll call Georgie—"

"Amy."

I rummage through my purse, taking out the folder of sketches, wallet, keys, pencil case, makeup bag, the tangled earbuds, gum. Where is the damn phone?

"Amy Wong."

Something pinches inside my chest. How can Jeff do this to me? Now that Alex is gone, I finally get to move on. Finally I get to stop caring. So then why do I care so much?

"Time out," he says, making a T with his hands. "I'm not demented *yet.*"

It's not the least bit funny, but we both crack up laughing. When we finally settle down, he says, "Look, I know I can't change the past, but at JJ NYC, you'll get tons of experience while getting to know our customer, so in a year or two—"

Oh, my god. After all these years, Jeff finally *sees* me. For a moment, I'm that girl again—the one trying on her wedding dress. Hopeful, brilliant, youthfully naive.

"Actually, I start FIT next week," I say, returning the contents of my purse back where it belongs.

He nods at the folder I'm stuffing into my purse. "So that's what the sketches are about."

"It's a new start."

"You don't need another start. You and I will work very closely together, and with all the doctor's appointments—"

Doctor's appointments?

"There's this promising experimental trial," he continues.

So *that's* what this is about. Maybe he can feel the change of barometric pressure because he adds, "But, I suppose if you want to go part-time, it's possible to flex your hours in the store."

"You don't need a buyer, Jeff. You need a personal assistant. Or better yet, a nurse." I expect him to criticize and say how "cold" I am, how selfish.

"No, I've deliberated a great deal about this, and what I *need* is a wife."

"Well, it's a little late for that." I'm not sure if it's revulsion or pity, but nausea rolls over me like a wave. It's possible I may just vomit on him.

The phone rings, and I see that it's Toby. "Where have you been?" I ask.

"Sleeping—but don't worry. I feel better. I'm at Amanda's. Is it okay if I have dinner here?"

"Sure." I glance at my watch. "Good. Just hang out there. I'll be home in a couple hours."

Jeff waits expectantly. "Toby," I say by way of explanation.

"Yes, Alex told me what happened," Jeff says.

My face prickles with shame. Why would Alex tell Jeff that Toby no longer wants me to file for adoption? Doesn't he realize how badly I feel about it?

"I always thought that guy was bad news," Jeff adds.

I feel myself relax. Jeff is referring to William and his abuse toward Toby.

"In fact, I never could figure out why you married that guy," he says.

"Well, it's simple. He was there."

Jeff squints his eyes, unable to comprehend the logic in what I said. Frustration balloons inside me, and then I'm sitting in a bath of resentment, which I know isn't fair. Jeff is Jeff. He's a narcissist—vain-glorious, self-centered. So much so that he doesn't realize that, while he isn't overtly abusive, nor obviously controlling like William, he has those exact attributes.

"Let's see, now," I say. "After the divorce, I was homeless, in debt, and jobless. As soon as I got my foot in at Monarch, when I finally turned things around—with no help from you, by the way—you told me it was my turn to 'step up' with Alex so you could get back to work."

"The company was in terrible shape," he defends.

"No, *I* was in terrible shape, Jeff. Didn't you realize I borrowed money from Georgie so I could take the internship, hoping it would lead to a job? And my mom co-signed a loan on the car."

"Of course I realized. That's why I give you money every month."

"You *give* me money? I was a budding designer when I married you, but if you remember correctly, you felt it was more important for me to raise Alex. Like I could always get back to work later. And then when I finally do it—and I go into debt to make it happen—you declare it's my turn to care for Alex."

"I always said you could take classes or find something during the day—"

"Really?" I say, glaring at him. "Really?!" I feel myself about to cry and have to turn to the window. It was a mistake to ride back together; how stupid to think I'd come away unscathed.

"You gave up," Jeff finally says, sighing. I'm about to ream him with a litany of expletives, when he adds: "For that, I'm sorry. I truly am."

"Sorry for what?" It's the first time he has ever apologized.

"For taking away your wins," he says.

I'm stunned. "Are you in *therapy?*"

"As a matter of fact," he says.

"Wow."

"I know," he grins, and laughing at himself, adds, "The great Jeff Jones."

"The great Jeff Jones," I say. Like magic, or maybe god, we connect just as we are disconnecting.

"Look, just consider the position. You don't need to be my nurse. Or my wife. It's not a part of the job description."

My phone rings again. It's my neighbor. "What's up, Jenna?" I answer.

"I was just packing up the car," she says, cracking her gum. "And, well, Toby's outside your house right now—"

"No, he's at Amanda's," I say, checking the time on the phone. "I just spoke with him about an hour ago."

"Uh, he's at the end of your driveway. I can see him right here from my living room, and your ex-husband's there, too."

It's happening again.

I swallow. "What's going on?"

"It looks like Toby is trying to block him from getting close to the house."

"William wants to get close to the house?" I ask. "Why?"

"Oh, goodness," Jenna utters, and suddenly, she yelps.

"Call 911, Jenna!" I check highway signage outside. We're just passing Milford, Connecticut. It's at least an hour away. "Jenna, hang up," I say, my hands shaking. "911! Now, call right now."

When our connection goes dead, I hang up and count backwards from 60. I don't want to risk disrupting Jenna's call to the police station. 58, 57, 56... Jeff moves to the facing seats to speak with the driver. "We have an emergency," he tells the driver. "We need to get to her house as quickly as possible." 50, 49, 48...

The limo starts to pick up speed. On my phone, I search for the local number for the police station. I ring them, clarifying who I am, that my neighbor must have just called because my son's in danger, and that I'm en-route from Connecticut about half an hour away from home. I say my neighbor indicated my ex-husband and son are in my driveway, and that there must have been some kind of confrontation; I explain that my ex has a restraining order against him and is not permitted near Toby.

The officer tells me a car has already been dispatched to the scene. Just then, another cop radios into the dispatcher. "Man down," he says.

"Code 3, possibly 10-9," the dispatcher radios back, allowing me to listen to their conversation. "There's a restraining order against the father."

"Stand by," the officer radios. "No sign of assailant."

"Copy that," the dispatcher says. "Advise if an ambulance is needed."

"We've got a young Caucasian male, not conscious."

I start to cry. Time stands still. I glance at Jeff, feeling terrified, helpless. First Alex. Now Toby. Why am I always away from my boys the moment they need me most?

"He's breathing," the officer radios in. "11-41, copy that?"

"Copy," she says, pausing. Then: "Ambulance on the way."

"10-39," the cop says, coming back on the line. "Suspicious activity in the backyard. We need backup."

"10-4," the dispatcher says.

"Copy that, 10-17," another officer, a woman, radios in. "We're en route."

The cop radios in again: "Dispatcher, notify the fire department. There's smoke. Do you read?"

"Copy," the dispatcher says. He's silent for a minute, then says, "Engine 229 on the way."

"10-4," the officer responds. "Ambulance is on the scene."

"Dispatcher, 10-23, we're here," the female officer states. "We'll investigate the back of the house."

"10-4," the dispatcher says.

"Hello? Dispatcher?" I yell into the phone. "Is he okay? My son?"

"Just hang in there, Ma'am," he says. "They're doing what they can."

"Victim is now conscious," the officer radios in. "He's conscious."

"10-4," the dispatcher says. Then: "Copy that, Ms. Wong?"

"Thank you," I say.

"We've got a fire over here," the female officer radios in. "What's the timing on 229? It's looking like arson. Standby, 229 may need backup."

"Patient being taken via ambulance to the hospital," the officer reports now.

"10-4," the dispatcher says. Then: "Did you hear that Mommy? You can meet the ambulance at the hospital."

"Yes, thank you," I manage to say. I dial CPS. They take the information and tell me to contact the social worker directly, so I try her next, leaving a message when I get her voice mail.

At the hospital, we pull up behind the police car. Jeff follows me into the ER waiting room. He goes straight to the window to speak with the nurses, and almost immediately, I'm being rushed into the ER. "I'll be right out here," Jeff says, and I nod, grateful he cares enough to stick around. Just then, Jenna calls again. "I'm at the hospital," I say.

"Good," she says. "I wanted to be sure you knew."

"Thank you, Jenna." I swear to God I'll never think a bad thought about her again.

"The fire department came," she says.

"I heard."

"Everything's fine." She sniffles. "There was a little fire in the back of the house, but they put it out. It's nothing."

"And William?"

"Cuffed and in the back of the patrol car."

I lose reception as the nurse takes me into the emergency room. We pass an officer in the hallway writing out a report, and then pause outside a curtained room. I step inside. The second officer is in the room with Toby, asking questions. Toby's lying in bed. He has a pack of ice behind his head and one at his temple. What is it with the head injuries? I wonder. The doctor's flashing light into Toby's eyes. "I was so worried," I whisper, getting on the bed and hugging him to my body.

"It's okay, Mom," he says.

I lift the ice pack at the side of his head, revealing a large lump the size of an egg. "Oh, my god. He did this to you?"

"It's over," he says. "We can move on, now."

"What—what's going on, Toby?"

"Just dust."

"What dust?" I ask.

Toby retches, and I quickly lean him against me so that when he vomits, he won't aspirate. It seeps through my blouse and bra.

"Concussed, not speaking cohesively," the doctor says, ordering an X-ray. The nurse grabs a bunch of paper towels and hands them to me.

"What happened?" I ask the officer, brushing at the muck on my chest.

"From what I gather, his father struck him with a blow torch."

"Blow torch?" I turn to Toby. "What?"

"He thought you were inside," Toby says, holding his head in his hands. "I told him you were sleeping, you took a pill."

None of this makes any sense.

"He said if you went through with the adoption—" Toby utters, squinting from the light. "He had a plan." The doctor switches off the light, which seems to make it easier for Toby to see. He looks at me. In his eyes, I see a sadness so deep and raw, it's crushing. I glance at the officer by the door, taking notes.

"What did he say, Toby? You can tell me."

Toby pushes away from me to vomit on the floor on the other side of the bed. The effort or force of the endeavor makes him groan and clasp his head harder.

"Sweetheart," I say when he finally quiets. "If I went through with the adoption? What about it?"

Toby bursts out crying. "He said he'd rather see you dead."

"You mean he was going to burn down the house with me inside it?"

"Ow, ow, ow," Toby sobs, the gasping motion so painful that his entire body clenches between breaths. The doctor instructs the nurse to add a pain medication via IV, explaining it is both to avoid Toby vomiting up the medication and to keep him from getting dehydrated. He leaves, making room for the officer to move closer. Toby convulses, he's crying so hard. "He said he'd tie you up in the basement, douse you with oil, and set you on fire."

"Oh, baby," I say, pressing him to me. "He was just trying to scare you."

"I didn't believe him, either," Toby says, "but I snuck into his house a few weeks ago to get something, and I saw this picture he taped on the kitchen wall, and he meant it. He really meant it."

"What was this picture?" the officer asks.

"It was this Chinese monk or something, just sitting there on fire."

My body shudders. While it was obvious to me that William was emotionally troubled and abusive, and for this reason, to be feared, especially after the divorce and the breakup with his girlfriend when he lost any sense of control, I had no idea of the depth of his mental illness. Toby's describing the famous photo taken during the early 60s. A Vietnamese monk self-immolated himself on a busy Saigon inter-section in protest of the government. Likely, the officer has the same photograph in mind because he swallows as if he's gulping down an egg, whole. The nurse locates a vein on the inside of Toby's elbow and starts the IV, attaching it to a pole.

The officer asks if there was an altercation between him and his father, and Toby replies yes.

"What was the actual cause of the altercation?" the officer asks.

Snot drips from Toby's nostrils. "He was trying to get inside the house, but I couldn't let him."

"He would have realized I wasn't home?" I suggest.

Toby nods, the slight movement causing him to clutch his head at his temples. "Yeah, it wouldn't have worked if he'd realized you weren't home."

"Setting the fire?" the officer asks.

"Yeah," Toby says. "I called him and said Mom was asleep so if he wanted to talk with me, I could come outside …"

"You mean you set him up?" I ask.

"He got really pissed I 'accidentally' locked myself out of the house."

Gently, I touch the bump at the back of Toby's head. He knew his father so well; he saw so clearly the full extent of William's illness.

"I just needed it to be behind me," Toby says. "To move on."

"Oh, Toby." He's using my words.

"I couldn't live like that, anymore," Toby says. "Just waiting, you know?"

Paranoia. Moodiness. Exhaustion. It all made sense, now. Toby's strange behavior didn't seem so strange anymore. He must have been up every night, patrolling from the living room sofa, ready to call for help if necessary. "I'm so sorry," I say, holding him. "Mommy's so, so sorry."

Transport arrives with a wheelchair. The nurse clamps the tubing and disconnects the IV. I move off the bed and help Toby into the chair. Toby holds one of the ice packs to his head.

I walk beside Toby as transport pushes him to X-ray. It's all too familiar. Feels like déjà vu. Only this time, my son reaches for *my* hand. I take it. This boy, my child, risked his life to save mine. The wheelchair rolls down the corridor, past patients and buzzing machines, one after another after another, and it's like leaving the dust of former lifetimes, and very possibly, I think, even this one.

A Closet Into Eternity

The casket. It's sparkly copper with a silver trim. The top's open, revealing a shiny, off white interior. Over the bottom half rests a spray of white lilies. Wreaths of white chrysanthemums, tulips, and mums—each on a self-standing easel and red sash naming the family it's from—line the four walls. From where I stand at the back entrance of the room, behind the rows of folding chairs, there's no view of the body at all. The wake doesn't start for another hour, and yet the room is already occupied with at least forty people, mostly older, either seated in the guest area, milling about, or talking in hushed tones. Maybe it's the jet lag, but everyone seems distant and muted. Their shapes seem almost fuzzy, as if I'm looking through a dense fog.

The Wife. Which one is she? I've never met her or The Son, nor have I seen photos. Ma once said she wasn't pretty, just young—only a year or two older than Georgie—but I never believed her. For Dad to leave, either the woman had to be spectacularly beautiful or Dad had to have hated us that much.

And The Son. He's here, too, somewhere.

"You're late!" Ma says in a low voice, appearing from the muddle. She's wearing the black, pleated Jeff Jones skirt I got from work. It was my birthday gift to her last year.

"I didn't make the earlier flight," I say. "I couldn't leave until after the presentation."

"New designs?" She's thrilled about my recent promotion to Executive Creative Director. She smooths her fingers over her skirt.

"No, numbers," I say. "Corporate wants to cut back again. That looks good on you."

"Pretty, uh?"

The people closest to us turn to stare. I have never seen any of these people before, and yet I get the feeling they all know who I am.

I eye a 60-ish-year-old woman with heavy makeup, blown-out hair, and long, immaculate lash extensions. She's decked out in Akris; a double-faced, leather-inset sheath dress. She's older than I, but not by much. Maybe five or six years. Could it be her?

"Quick," Ma orders. "Go see your father. We're starting soon."

"Wait." I notice Georgie, in the far corner of the room, deep in conversation with a slender, six-foot Chinese gentleman. He hands her a pen and tome of papers, points to the page as if indicating where he'd like her to sign. Attorney? No, can't be. Even from where I'm standing, I can tell he's wearing a handsome suit, not conservative enough on one hand, and much too lovely on the other, for the typical attorney. Then, again, this is Hong Kong. Ma always says people here take better care in how they dress. "Who's that hot—" I start to ask.

But Ma's attention is elsewhere; something over my shoulder. Nearsightedness forces her to squint. I glance around to see an older man with thinning hair. He waves. Her cheeks flush. She returns the gesture.

"Who's *he*?" I ask.

"Uncle."

"Uncle as in blood relative?" I smirk, "or Uncle as in one of Dad's friends and you're actually *flirting* at his funeral?"

"Zen me le?" What happened? Ma tsks. "A person shouldn't have manners?"

"No, really, Ma," I laugh. "Who are all these people?"

Ma surveys the gathering. "Family."

"Family!" I've yearned for family for how many years, and she's telling me now that all these people I never knew about were part of it?

"Ah yah—" Ma utters, shaking her head. "Ta de," *hers*. Ma search-es the room, and not finding her, says, "You know who."

"I thought this thing wasn't starting for another hour."

"For outside people." Ma rolls my carry-on suitcase, then nudges me toward the front of the room. "Now, go."

I pause. In my mind, I've had this idea about the moment I first see Dad. There's the possibility that I'll come to some kind of realiza-tion about my life, or his, or perhaps the one we shared and then not shared. I might sob in front of everyone. On one hand, crying is proof I care. It is a declaration that love existed; that I matter. And yet I don't want a spectacle, not in front of strangers, and especially not in front of *her* and The *Son*. There's the part of me that doesn't want to give them the benefit of knowing I care at all. And as much love and com-passion as I've tried to cultivate as a newfound Buddhist, it doesn't ac-tually extend to them. I hate them. I've never hated anyone more. The Buddha taught that holding onto anger is like drinking poison and expecting the other person to die, and yet, I gulp it down like nectar.

Ma brushes something from my forehead.

"What?" I ask, self-consciously touching my face. Do I have a piece of lint stuck to my forehead? Is my makeup smudged?

"You look terrible," she acknowledges. "I've never seen anyone wearing Chanel look so terrible."

I smile. "An 18-hour flight will do that to a person."

"You didn't sleep?"

"You kidding? Ambien the whole way."

"Ambine," Ma nods. "Ambine ding hao," the best. After all these years, it's here at Dad's wake—over small talk about sleeping pills—that Ma's letting me in. She never admits it, but she blames me for what hap-pened. The first time Dad left, she literally dragged him back from China, practically on a leash. But Dad had ongoing business in Shanghai, and because of me, Ma couldn't jet set off with him. That woman had a boy; Ma got stuck with me. Heat floods the backs of my eyes.

"Don't," Ma says.

"I know." Don't cry. Whatever you do, don't cry.

I scan the faces that fill the room.

"They're not here right now," Ma says, squinting, her gaze shifting with mine.

"You sure?"

"I know. You think I don't know?" she whispers. "Maybe they went to pay. I show you later. Now I'm going outside." She gesticulates with a pointer and middle finger. She's going for a smoke.

"Georgie told me you quit," I say.

"Ay, that was last year." She grips the handle of my carry-on suitcase and heads for the hallway. "I'll put this away for you."

I step toward the casket. Then, without drama or emotion, I'm standing in front of it. In front of him. Dad looks older than I expected. His hair is thinner, a mottled mix of white and grey dust. He's shorter than I remember—he must have shrunk at least a couple inches—and even with a sports jacket, he seems frail. Intellectually, I know he's got to be close to ninety, but emotionally I'm stuck on the Dad from when I was 16. The two don't match up. What's more, the make-up artist used too much powder. It's meant to cut the plastic-looking sheen over the skin. Noticing it makes me uneasy; the body has already gone through the embalming process.

"Let him go," the woman had said. "He deserves a few years of happiness."

"Were you really that unhappy?" I ask, silently. "Because we loved you, Daddy. I loved you."

The map in my mind automatically reverts to the same place. If only I had better grades like Georgie. Was smarter. Worked harder. I should have been more Chinese. More beautiful. A boy.

Loneliness is a vacuum inside me. It's buried beneath my smile, invisible, and yet as dense as stone.

"Didn't you love me anymore?" I ask. "Didn't I mean anything to you?"

All of a sudden, I smell him. Dad. It's as if I'm five, curled up and asleep on his lap. The closeness I feel is startling. He's here. Daddy's here.

Behind me, an elderly man with a cane waits patiently for a moment with Dad. I indicate with a finger that I'll just be another minute.

"I'm sorry you never got to know my boys, Daddy," I say. "They're my everything."

Then, nodding at the gentleman behind me, I step aside. The old man shuffles to the coffin, and I leave to go find Ma. In the long corridor outside Dad's room, I pass a Buddhist procession. There's a resonant sound of men chanting. A six-foot statue of Buddha sits at the front of the room, an altar filled with at least a dozen smaller Buddhas, flowers, lit candles and incense. To the side, there's a framed photo of the deceased and the urn containing the body. On the dais sit three monks clad in brownish gold robes, cross legged, eyes closed. The drone of their voices lulls the room full of kneeling guests.

While I consider myself Buddhist, these rituals seem foreign and strange. If my paternal grandmother hadn't been converted by the Catholics who went to Shanghai, this would be the ceremony Dad would be having, too. His body would be cremated. Housed in an urn; the vessel holds the ashes, the body holds the soul.

A moment. A memory. That's all we are.

The funeral home has a glass entrance that looks out over Causeway Bay. I can see Georgie with Ma outside in the intensely bright, Hong Kong heat. With the elegant black skirt, the up-do and large black sunglasses, Ma looks like a Chinese Audrey Hepburn. It's hard to believe she turns 75 later this year. She doesn't look a day over 50.

The attorney I saw with Georgie appears from the restroom. There's confidence in his stride, a debonair and gentlemanly quality that is striking. He's not a "guy." He is the kind of man who takes the time to dress and style his hair. He's wearing a two-piece suit. Definitely Italian. A Kiton? No, it couldn't possibly be. Oh, my god, it is. Black, wool, and by the looks of it, 12 or 14 micron. Two-button jacket with flap panels, notch lapel, basted sleeves. Single-pleat trousers. Look at that cut. Meticulous. And, oh, the hand stitching. Flawless.

He asks me something in Mandarin. He speaks a little too quickly for my ability. When he sees I don't comprehend, he says it in English. British English, not American. "May I help you?" he asks.

"I don't know who you are," I say, "but I'm simply in awe of your suit."

"Not so bad yourself," he says. His looks and accent would make any girl swoon. He holds my gaze. Draws closer.

"Peter," he says, pronouncing it "Pe-ta." He leans to kiss me on one cheek, then the other. I'm not expecting the second kiss, and as a result, his lips brush against mine.

"Oops," I say, heat rushing to my face.

He smiles. "And you are?"

"Amy," I say. "Amy Wong."

A shadow passes over his face. He steps back. It hits me. It's him. The Son.

I leap away. Shock. Horror. Confusion. It's a total mind fuck. I'm 55; he's 39. Emotionally, I'm stuck at 16; I'm expecting the little boy who stole my father.

"No," I say, shaking my head.

He nods. "Yes."

"You look older than I expected," I say.

"That's fine then," he says. "Because you look younger than I expected."

"Isn't that funny."

"Yes. Isn't it."

We laugh nervously.

"If you don't mind my saying," he says, "you and your sister are quite different."

"Yeah?" Georgie steps inside with Ma. She has short cropped, peppered hair and no makeup. In the past few years, she has gained more weight. The black top and slacks fit well but the jacket's too snug. It needs letting out at the arms and waist. She's wearing a pair of Prada loafers, as if the name can cover up the fact that she has given up on beauty and love. It's hard for me to look at her. One of my meditation teachers says the world is but a reflection of you. If this is so, Georgie shows the side of me I resist most. She's aging and alone. She has resigned herself to this fate.

"Xiao di," Ma says uncertainly. "You met my younger daughter."

"Yes, Aunty, we've met," he says, and there's a kindness, a deference toward her that makes him instantly likable, despite everything I've felt toward him all these years. "Thank you for coming."

"Of course," Ma says.

Someone steps out of Dad's room and waves Peter over.

"You'll have to excuse me," he says, glancing at his watch. "The family will be starting in ten minutes and guests should be arriving in half an hour for the service."

"We'll be there in a moment," I say.

He rushes back to the room. Once he's inside, Georgie says, "He seems nice enough."

"All I can say is his mom must be gorgeous," I say.

"Ha," Ma huffs. "You kidding?"

"Not as gorgeous as you, of course," I quickly add.

"That's right," Ma says. "You obviously haven't met her. She's old and fat."

"Excuse me?" Georgie says pointedly, tugging at the lapels of her jacket. "I take offense to that."

"Why? You old and fat?"

"In fact, I am."

"Xia jiang!" Ma says. "Foolish talk. Take it back."

Georgie fixes her glasses. "No."

"My meaning is Xiao Di looks like Daddy," she snips. "Not *her*."

"Really?" I say.

"If you had seen your father when he was young," Ma sighs. "So debonair and handsome. So many women. A real—how you say?—'player,' yes?"

Georgie and I start laughing. When I notice Ma's sadness, I take her hand. "I'm sorry, Ma."

"Don't be. Maybe I'm the lucky one."

"What do you mean by that?"

"Your daddy could be very difficult."

"Excuse me?" Georgie says. "Daddy was not difficult."

"Was he?" I ask.

"Oh, you don't remember," Ma tsks. "Very bad temper. Some days he's not happy. Then whatever you do, nothing is right. Nothing is good. Yelling, yelling."

Maybe Georgie remembers something because she goes quiet.

"You're right, I don't remember that," I say.

"Ai, after Daddy left, all you remember is the good things. Now come." She takes our hands and leads us back to the room. Inside, everyone is forming a line that circles three quarters of the room. Ma walks us straight to the front of it. Peter checks a typed list, and from it starts rearranging people accordingly. "All the cousins," Ma explains. "Everyone has to be in the right order."

"Exactly what order?" Georgie asks.

"First cousin, second cousin," Ma says. "Very important."

"For whom?" Georgie asks, seemingly perplexed. "Dad's dead."

I can't help but laugh. For someone so smart, she can be so dense. Sometimes, she really can be such a robot.

"Chan jie," Ma says, jabbing me with an elbow and introducing me as Dad's younger daughter. Dad's wife has short-cropped, over-dyed black hair, and drawn-in eyebrows. She's tall, possibly 5'5". There's something weathered and broken about her. She's heavy set, and when she takes a step toward me, it's obvious she has arthritis in the knees. Her skin is dove white, almost doughy. Maybe she douses herself in Shiseido every night. Still, from the low bridge of her nose, wrinkles spread across her face like roots.

I offer a hand. "Hi."

"Hello, Aunty," Ma corrects. The expression on Ma's face vacillates between embarrassment and smugness.

"Ga haw ke," so good looking, she says, speaking in Shanghainese. "Gen Mommy yi yang," Just like your mommy.

"Na li, na li," Ma says, politely. Not at all, not at all.

Ma had said she might be the lucky one. Now, I get why. Chan Jie is twenty years younger than Ma, and yet Ma's right—she's ancient and fat. *He deserves a few years of happiness.* Chan Jie had given Dad her best years. Had she been successful in making him happy?

It's possible that losing Dad was the best thing to have ever happened to Ma, and from the smirk on Ma's face, there's no doubt this possibility crossed her mind. Chan Jie got Dad, all right. In the end, she got what was coming to her.

Karma. Wow.

Peter goes to the front of the line. His mother follows immediately behind. Then, Ma. Georgie sandwiches herself between Ma and me. Silently, the line circles the casket. Peter leans into it and kisses Dad on the forehead.

Then, Chan Jie.

I shrink back. Is this what we're *all* supposed to do? Dad's face looks fake, as if the embalming process drained away what was real and left behind a mask.

Ma follows Peter's and Chan Jie's lead, pecking him on the cheek.

"Well, this certainly is an arcane ritual if I've ever seen one," I hear Georgie mutter.

"Don't do it," I instruct. There is absolutely no way I'm going to touch, never mind kiss, a corpse, even if the body used to be my father.

But Georgie bends to the casket, and as if in tune to some kind of melody, kisses Dad on the forehead.

Then it's my turn.

Ma shoots me a stern look that says, He's your *father*.

He's dead. "Expired," as Georgie had put it. But even as I'm thinking this, the rest of me moves in rhythm to this strange, soundless music. With my heart beating in my ears, I reach closer and closer to the mask that resembles Dad's face until my lips touch his clammy, cool forehead.

Death. The cold moves through me. My entire body shudders and I recoil. Then I'm back in line, towed along with everyone else, and maybe I'm going to be sick. My lips feel soiled. I want to spit. Wash my mouth, both inside and out. I want to cry.

Peter leads us to the open area facing the coffin. The visitor seating area has been pushed back. On the floor are flat yellow pillows, the kind I've seen used in meditation centers. He moves to the pillow furthest left in the front row. With a great deal of difficulty and a stifled groan, Chan Jie kneels at the pillow beside him. Ma settles next to her. Like dominoes, the rest of us follow, until we are three rows deep on our knees.

The casket. Sparkly copper with a silver trim and a silky soft interior. A closet into eternity.

A man appears with a microphone.

"Who's that?" I ask Georgie.

"They said they got an emcee."

"A *what*?"

"To host," Georgie says. "I suppose."

"Everyone ready," the emcee says, in Cantonese. "Bow!"

The entire family kowtows to the floor. After a pause, we rise back to our knees.

"Everybody ready," he repeats. "Bow." On cue, we all do as instructed.

And then, for a third and final time, we all move in unison. We are one.

Peter sniffles, and I see he's crying. Everyone is, including, I realize, myself. The tide of movements has washed away my revulsion, and in its place is the possibility of a brother and the comfort of being with all these people, many of whom I've never met before, and whom I will now know, maybe only for this one singular moment, as family.

Lost and Found

Come Monday morning, every team is in the office by 7:30 AM. The strategy meetings start at 8:30 AM. We're accountable to the new CEO—Jeff stepped down last year—for soft sales three weeks in a row. I examine the numbers, take some quick notes. I sip my latte. It's still hot when the buyer for Men's Apparel appears at my desk. "We've got a problem," he says.

"Welcome to the witching hour," I say, setting down my latte.

The buyer shows me the invoice from a new manufacturer making a line of men's blazers. He points out cost inconsistencies. Contractually, we agreed to a price five dollars and 15 cents cheaper than they are now charging. "I had a bad feeling about this manufacturer," I sigh, handing back the loose pages. "Oh well. What'd they say?"

"Take it or leave it."

"Fine." I sign off on it, which means we'll take a major loss. While we would win this conflict in a court of law, we are contractually just as obligated to our retailers who are expecting the blazers in just five days. The last manufacturer who did this kind of detailed work for us shut down. "Just make sure to black them from our lists," I say.

"Already done," he says.

"Run the numbers and get back to me. We may need to take this up with the lawyer."

He's barely out the door when the buyer for Women's Apparel sticks her head in the door. "Got a minute?" she asks.

"Did you get out of the jumpsuits?" I ask.

"First thing I did." She tells me she's getting estimates from a couple other manufacturers for the slip dresses, which were the best selling items for two weekends in a row. The current manufacturer cannot go beyond commitment if we need more. "There's just a slight problem with the couture line," she says.

"Oh, no."

"The maxi dress," she nods. "Apparently, one of the shipments is 'lost'."

I gasp. During a recession, if it isn't design theft, it's this off-the-back-of-the-truck thievery that can put a company out of business. "Did you track it?" I ask.

"The box arrived," she says. "But the dresses did not."

I rub my temples. "Contact the manufacturer for more supply."

"Already done."

"Call insurance," I say.

One of the marketers interrupts by knocking at the door. I tell the women's buyer to check in with me later with status. When she leaves, the marketer takes a seat at my desk. I hold up a finger so she'll wait, giving me a moment to gulp down the rest of the latte. It's cold, but still yummy. "Okay, shoot," I say, once the cup's empty.

"Neiman Marcus Houston just called," she says. "The buyer insists we modify the decoute on the print midi and the hemlines on the sheath dresses."

"So speak with design," I say, getting annoyed. Retail *always* asks for something "special" that's specific just to them. Especially Neiman's.

"I have," she says, cautiously.

"But?" I say, impatient now. "Out with it, already, Ms.—"

"The manufacturer finished ahead of schedule. They shipped yesterday."

It takes a moment for me to comprehend what is happening. In a world where nothing is ever ahead of schedule, our dresses are not only way ahead, but already shipped to retailers, one of which is insisting on alterations to two of the designs. I ask about dates. "Are you telling me that you okayed the design with the manufacturer before the retailer came back with approval?"

"No, they loved the pre-collection presentation," she says. "And the modifications we already made for them."

"Who's the buyer again? Randy, right?" I say, fully comprehending now why Jeff insisted I work a few years in marketing. I travelled to Houston at least twice a year. "This doesn't sound like her."

"It's not," she says. "There's a new buyer. Randy moved to Saks."

My phone dings. I have it set so that it sounds when Jeff texts. 1PM appt w/ Dr. P.

"Hold on a second," I tell the marketer.

"I'll meet you there," I text Jeff. "Oyster rolls!"

After Jeff meets with the doctor, a "movement disorders specialist," we always have sushi at the Japanese restaurant across the street. It happens to be one of the best in the city.

"How was sales?" he writes. Then, a moment later: "Strategy!"

"Oh, shit," I say, jumping up from the desk and grabbing my iPad and notes. "The meeting! We're late!"

The marketer races with me to the conference room. I tell her to arrange a call to the new buyer at Neimans this afternoon and conference me in. I suggest she speak with Marco, Jeff's favorite designer, to come up with a dress for our fall line, which will be sold only in JJ boutiques and Neimans.

The team is seated around the conference table with the CEO at the head. He's got an Ivy League haircut and dons a Brooks Brothers pin-striped suit that's slightly too long in the jacket. Anyone at this table would say it needs to be taken in more at the arms. It's a statement, a reminder that there's a division between the business side and the fashion side. I sit in the open seat beside the CEO. The tension is palpable, though the meeting has yet to start. Marco refuses to look at me, though I can see he is flustered. He doodles on a pad. He uncrosses his legs and re-crosses them the other way. I wonder what, if anything, has already been said.

"Sorry, I'm late," I say.

"I was just commenting on the numbers," the CEO mentions.

Jayne, the buyer for Women's Apparel, shoots me an exasperated look. "I was mentioning some of our more recession-proof ideas," she says.

"Spring line," I say. Creative has been developing this idea for months now.

She nods. "Marco's Punk Oriental." The Met is having a retrospective of the China exhibition "Through the Looking Glass" from over a decade ago. Marco's designing a line of dresses and jackets using technology to create lace similar to the one Jeff used for my wedding dress. Retro meets history … meets *fire*. Marco's line is timed to come out the week of the Gala opening, an event which is sure to have an impact on the season for most couture designers.

"I just want to be sure the numbers are substantial enough considering the market," the CEO says.

Jayne and I exchange glances. "The only thing not substantial enough is his dick," she likes to say.

I try not to smirk as she and Marco present their drawings and samples. Research provides graphs and diagrams. The CEO takes notes as the team gives their presentation.

When they are finally done, the room falls silent as the CEO continues to scribble and make calculations. When he finally looks up, he asks Jayne, the marketer, and the research team to provide more specific figures regarding latest trends and breakdowns. He wants them by the next morning. "I need proof that this 'Oriental' line will succeed," the CEO says.

"Punk Oriental," Marco corrects. "And it will."

"You're sure about that?"

"I know." Marco crosses his arms in front of him.

The CEO laughs. Is that a hint of derision in his voice? He flips through the handout. He circles some numbers, makes a calculation, then tosses the pages so that they slide across the glass table. "Perhaps you should reconsider the expense of manufacturing a fabric when you could be using machine-made lace at 1/4 the cost?" he says.

"This is couture!" Marco insists, his eyes bulging from the sockets. He looks around the room, an expression of incredulity and disgust across his face. "This man has no business in couture."

Everyone shuffles uncomfortably in their seats. The CEO looks unruffled, but there's a vein pulsing at his temple.

"What Marco means—" I start to say.

"What does it matter what he means," the CEO says, cutting me off. "Because Marco's redundant as far as I'm concerned. There are younger designers who need far less pay and can work more demanding hours."

Marco leaps to his feet and announces he can't be fired because he's quitting.

"Dime a dozen," the CEO states.

"Wait," I say, standing so quickly that my seat falls back, thudding against the floor. "Stop!" Everyone freezes. "Everyone sit down. No one's going anywhere. Marco, that includes you."

Marco returns to his seat. I'm about to talk about how we need to work together, but the CEO cuts me off again. "It's plain and simple, there's not enough research to support the line."

"Enough?" I say, and this time, I stare him down. He thinks that his job is to rip everything to shreds. In fact, he takes pride in it. But what he doesn't see yet is that he's destroying what we are creating faster than we can actually create it. He may "win" this game he's playing, but in so doing, he will also destroy the company, us, as well as himself. "Sometimes knowing *is* enough," I state. "It's all we've got."

"That's sweet, Ms. Wong," he says, "but can we get down to business for a moment?"

I'm at a loss for words. Can he really be patronizing me? After all, I'm the Executive Creative Director. Everyone at this company reports to me.

"If Jeff was here—" I say.

Again, he cuts me off. "He's not, Ms. Wong."

My entire body goes rigid. I've never heard anyone ever dismiss Jeff in such a manner. "My married name was Jones. That might be confusing since I look Chinese."

He opens his mouth to speak and I say, "Even if corporate were the brains of this operation, this company is nothing without its creative heart." I circle a finger around the table. "This here? This is Jeff Jones."

The CEO looks at me, clearly amused by my pronouncement.

If Ma could see me, now. *Who you think you are?*

For the first time since Jeff "retired," the impermanence of it all becomes palpable. Empires rise and fall. People are born and then they die.

Outside the glass walls, the Men's Attire team convenes for their 9:30 meeting. Seeing them, Women's Attire automatically concludes and files out of the conference room. I watch them leave.

My resentment gives way to sadness. I think about Jeff, who, until recently, groomed himself impeccably, dressing only in the finest button-up shirts and jackets. Jeff was part of a clinical trial for new medication. That, along with a battery of daily supplements, exercise, memory games, and a host of other therapies, successfully kept the LBD at bay for the past ten years. Recently, however, there's a stiffness about the way he moves—especially the legs—and the nurse tells me he needs her help to get dressed.

Giving up. I feel like I'm letting Jeff down just by thinking it, but maybe it's time. Jeff Jones. Maybe it's the end of the legacy.

I arrive at the neurologist's office just as the nurse appears to call Jeff into the room. Jeff's personal day nurse hangs back in the waiting area so I can go in with him. She's blonde, and young, and Jeff insists she wear normal clothes instead of nursing scrubs. Jeff doesn't want people to know he needs a nurse; he'd rather people think he's with a twenty-something year old. In the room, he sits on the examining table. The paper crinkles. I sit in a plastic chair by the wall and set my purse in the chair next to mine. Jeff gets up from the table and moves to sit beside me. I pull my purse to my lap.

"You look like you got raked over the coals," he says, smirking.

"Yeah, well." When it comes to the company, I usually tell him as much as possible about the positive things going on and as little as possible about the negative. His health depends on it. Today, after a series of Not-Substantial-Enough meetings, I'm too spent to hide my resignation. "There's been some friction between Creative and Corporate."

"Oh." He waves it off. "Tell me something new."

"It's a real problem, Jeff."

"One that every company has experienced since the beginning of time."

"Morale is pretty low."

"Well, now you know why I've got you there," he says, "where you are."

Executive Creative Director. Isn't it supposed to be someone strong and confident about her abilities? I gaze into his eyes. "*Why* am I there?"

"Because you're my man." He brushes a hand up my thigh. "Woman."

"Stop teasing," I say, smacking his hand away.

Jeff laughs. "Come on," he says, nuzzling my neck.

"Jeff! This isn't a joke."

He sits back. Rolls his eyes, exaggerating his boredom. "Go on, then."

"I understand the financial responsibility the company has to the shareholders, I really do," I say.

"But?" He picks off a piece of lint from his slacks.

"It's the CEO. No one likes him."

"Is that what people call him? He doesn't even get a name?"

"Actually, to some people, he's 'Not Substantial Enough'."

"Which 'some people' would that be?"

"Jayne, for one," I say.

"Hmmm…" Jeff sits back in the hard plastic seat.

"She's about to jump ship," I say. "So is Marco."

"Marco?" he says, stunned. His lips purse. "That's not good. That's not good at all."

"We need something new, something spectacular, but… Every team pitches, and every team fails."

Jeff glances out the window. From the angle where we sit, there's bare grey sky. He looks back at me. "You're saying Jeff Jones needs a new CEO."

I'd thought of it, but it never seemed a real possibility to consider. "Actually, um, yes," I say. "I guess I am."

"I'll bring this up at the next board meeting."

"Didn't you just have one?" Typically, it convenes every six months. The board consists of six people.

"I'll call an emergency for Thursday afternoon," he says. "Alex will be back that morning, yes?"

I nod. Alex is returning from skiing in Switzerland with his wife and 8-month-old, Kathryn. Jeff brought Alex onto the board before stepping down as CEO. Nepotism aside, Alex had by then established himself in his own right: he'd sold a start-up for 100.3 million dollars. *BrainHeal* focuses on innovative 3-D technological games and programs that treat brain rehabilitation and disorders ranging from Parkinson's to Depression and ADHD.

"I'll speak with Alex and Ben," I say. Over the years, Ben established himself as a fashion writer for *The New York Times*, *Vogue*, *Y* and *GQ*. Jeff offered him the position of Editor of *Y*, which Ben accepted, then asked him to join the Board the year I joined the company.

"I'll speak with Rain Bow and Jim." Rain Bow is senior CPA at Ernst & Young and Jim Thompson is a Partner at a boutique law firm for Creatives called DREAM.

"What should I say?" I ask.

"We're voting on the new CEO!"

"But who do you have in mind?"

Jeff smiles. "Alex."

"Alex?" Granted Alex is a dot.com genius; and he certainly thinks out of the box. "But he doesn't know a thing about fashion."

"Oh, yes, he does," Jeff scoffs. "He couldn't have escaped us if he tried."

Just then, the doctor steps into the room. We've been waiting now an hour. He's the young medical version of Jeff, his costume a long, white coat. Beautiful, charismatic. Full of himself. He examines Jeff, asking him to walk from one side of the room to the other. He tests reflexes, and asks Jeff to hold his hands straight out in from of him. It's only then that I notice the tremor. The doc takes notes. He asks Jeff if there have been any new developments.

"Some stiffness, perhaps," Jeff says, rubbing his knees.

"Not some," I say. "Sometimes, he has difficulty standing up when he's been seated."

Jeff quiets.

"Sleep?" the doc asks. "From one to ten, ten being the best, how's the sleep?"

"Two," Jeff states. "Or, one."

"That's a noticeable decline from your last appointment," the doc says.

"I'm out of the Ambien."

"I'll call in more," he says, typing the prescription into the computer. Then he rolls his chair so that he's facing Jeff again. "You've had a great run of things—"

"Thirteen years," Jeff says. He's been committed to a daily regimen of cognitive and physical therapies, a battery of supplements, and is always seeing different energy healers.

"You've obviously defeated the odds. Many patients would be progressively more symptomatic," the doctor says.

"And without meds!" Jeff states, proudly.

The doctor presses his lips together. "It might be that time," he says. Jeff allows the mask to take over and doesn't respond.

"Just consider it," the doctor says. "I would start you on something called Levodopa, coupled with Carbidopa, a peripheral decarboxylase inhibitor."

"Are there side effects?" I ask.

"Initially, there may be some anxiety, but that often tapers off. Dizziness. Hand tremors—"

"Will the medication make it worse?"

"That's hard to say. It may. It may exacerbate the insomnia as well, I can't say until we try."

The light around Jeff seems to dim.

"It's possible there may be minimal side effects. Every person responds differently. And likely, it may even help to extend the positive streak with your health."

I'm touched by the doctor's sensitivity, which I've never seen before. "Anyone in your family with LBD?" I ask.

"Parkinson's," he says. "My grandfather."

"Is that why you went into this field?"

"I was already in neurology," he says, "but, yes, it influenced my direction. Especially in terms of research."

"How meaningful—" I start to say.

"Thank you, doctor," Jeff says, standing abruptly. The force of him pushing off the back of the chair causes it to bang against the wall.

"Oh," I say. Jeff shakes hands and in three evenly-paced steps is out the door. I get to my feet, fix the strap of my purse at my shoulder, and thank the doctor. "See you soon," I say.

"Talk to him," he says.

I nod and hurry after Jeff, catching up to him only in the waiting room. "You sure they got the diagnoses right?" I ask. "Cause I can't keep up with you."

Jeff instructs the nurse to pick up the prescription from the pharmacy and to meet him at home. Then he turns to me. "Oyster rolls," he says, offering an arm to grab onto.

I slip my arm through.

We're enjoying our deep fried yet ungreasy Agedashi tofu and Tatsuda age appetizers when Jeff says, "As soon as Alex gets back, we need a meeting."

"I agree. It's a good idea taking it to the board."

Jeff seems confused.

"You think Alex can handle it?" I ask. "I mean, he's so *young*."

He looks at me, stoney faced, and says, "He's as young as I was when I started the company."

"True."

"But there is the issue of whether he'd want to step in as CEO."

"Exactly," I say. "I don't want to spring it on him. He may already have something going on. You know how he is. In fact, wow, how lucky are we that he's with Beth?"

"She's a lovely girl," he says.

"That, too," I say. "I'm just grateful she puts up with him."

"Genius comes with its petty quirks."

"You can say that again," I laugh.

The waiter arrives to clear the plates.

"And the little one," Jeff says, once the waiter's gone. "She's gifted, also."

"Uh, she's eight months," I say. "You can already tell she's Einstein?"

"Just you wait. She's going to be the queen of fashion." He swallows. "Like her Pops."

"You can tell this from the way she lies on her mat and stares up at her toys?"

"I know these things," he says. "Am I not always right?"

I smile. It's true. He is.

The sushi arrives. All the pieces for each roll line up perfectly.

"Seriously, though," Jeff says. "When I said 'meeting,' I meant a family meeting. So, board meeting Thursday," he says. "The three of us can meet for lunch Friday. Does that work?"

"It can wait until next week," I say. "There's no need to rush things."

"Why wait?" he insists. "You never know. I could get hit by a truck tomorrow. Then, what?"

"Don't talk like that. You've done incredibly so far. The doc even said so. Keep up the good work and you've got another thirteen, fifteen years. At least."

"I'm merely saying we should take care of business," he says. "But since we're on the subject, if anything ever happens—"

"—Nothing's going to happen."

He pauses.

"Stop it, stop this craziness right now."

"Though it may seem rather morbid, I have a typed out list in my desk with the lawyer in charge of my will, the financial advisor in charge of my investments, the passwords for all my accounts—"

I cover my ears. "La, la, la, la—can't hear you, can't hear a word you're saying—"

"Amy Wong," he says, with his no nonsense voice.

"La, la, la—" I push my plate away and wave for the waiter. "Check, please?"

After lunch, Jeff insists on giving me a lift to the office. I tell him, No, I'll take a cab. He can't force me to listen to his crazy shit.

"All right," he says. The limo pulls away. It's cool out and starting to drizzle, yet damp with the kind of humidity that makes one perspire. There's congestion, but traffic is moving. A couple yellow taxis go by, but both are taken. How is it there are cabs all over but none when you really need one? The sidewalk feels uncomfortably crowded. The subway is only a block away, but the thought of even more people jammed together in a sardine can—with their umbrellas, no less—is more overwhelming than I can handle right now. I check the CityCar app on my phone to see if there's one within a few blocks.

But my phone rings, interrupting the app. It's Jeff. I don't answer. What can I possibly say that he will actually hear? It's his life, right? He can do whatever the fuck he wants with it.

The app indicates there's a CityCar only a block away. I'm just about to order it when the phone sounds. It's Jeff, again. I refuse his call, but by then the CityCar is three blocks going the opposite direction. Great, just great.

Just then, Jeff's limo pulls up. He swings the door open. "We're late for Creative," he says. He's lit up again. He has the intense, open look that he gets when inspiration strikes. With his rigid schedule, requiring all the different therapies for the maintenance of his health, it's hard to believe Jeff's actually visiting the office. And yet, here he is.

"Talk," he says. "Tell me about your spectacular company-saving idea, Ms. Executive Creative Director."

As annoyed as I am, I get in the car. The team hasn't seen him much since his departure last year. This surprise is exactly what they need. Jeff Jones. An infusion of his energy, drive, charisma—and leadership. "Not immediately," Jeff likes to say, "Eventually."

"Okay—" I pause.

"Ben mentioned you have a new line," he says.

"Sort of," I gulp. It's now or never: "Remember those sketches?

The designs I was working on when we took Alex up to school?"

He nods. "Go on."

We discuss my new line—target audience, sales pitch, marketing strategy.

Jeff asks the driver to make a stop at my apartment. I race upstairs, grab the portfolio, and jump back in the limo. We leave for the office. I show him the drawings, the boards, sample fabrics, and my estimated sales projections.

My stomach flutters. "Think it will be 'substantial enough'?"

"That's up to the Executive Creative Director to decide."

Me. Oh, my god. This is it. The moment I've been waiting for all my life.

I glance out the window at the blur of people crossing the street in front of us. The rain comes down like a steady mist. I can hardly sit still, I'm so excited and happy, but nervous at the same time.

Jeff gazes at me.

I feel it before I actually look at him. "What?"

"I know we've had our ups and downs, but I've never stopped loving you."

"That's it," I say, my hand on the door handle. "Let me out of here."

"Wait," he says. "Just hear me out."

"Hear you out?" I gasp, tearing from rage and disgust. "You, you, you. You've always been such a fucking narcissist, Jeff. You know that? Everything's always gotta be about you. It's just criminal."

"Look at me," he says softly.

I make the mistake of looking. It's Jeff. Not Jeff the man, but Jeff the boy who shared a lollipop with me on a beach at Cape Cod; he'd told me about his mother, a woman on her deathbed who told him he would be nothing without her; that he would fail.

"Don't do this," I say. "Whatever you're planning, just don't."

"You've seen what LBD does to people."

"It's not so bad," I say, even though I've seen crushing videos on

YouTube. One man kept seeing "bugs" on the floor even though his daughter pointed out none actually existed. And there was a video of a woman who said she always felt someone was behind her, almost an ominous feeling, and it made her paranoid, which is why she always felt compelled to look around and check. Another man became aggressive and menacing. He went after his wife and daughter, attempting to punch them with his fists.

"That's not me," he says. "I don't feel comfortable in this straight-jacket."

"You have time. The doctor said—"

"He said it's time to consider medication. You know how that goes. Side effects. More meds to take care of those side effects. Then more meds on top of that. And, for what?"

"For what?" I say, raising my voice. "How can you actually ask that?"

He watches as I continue my tirade. "You can't take away your son's father. Or your granddaughter's Pop-Pop—"

"Darling," he says, softly. "It's exactly that which I intend to preserve."

We arrive at the office. The driver comes around to help us. I step out first. Jeff hands me the portfolio. This time, the driver has to move into the car to help Jeff up from the seat. For the first time, Jeff allows me to see his struggle. He puts an arm over the driver's shoulders, and the driver practically has to haul him from the car. Jeff fixes his jacket. He pulls at the cuffs of his shirt sleeves so that they are just barely showing. The sheer effort up to this point is so great that perspiration dots his brow. Even then, he's looking around and checking that no one else—especially from the company—has seen him get out of the car.

"You okay?" I ask.

"As okay as I'm going to get," he says, reaching for the portfolio. "Ready to do this?"

I hand him the black case. Together, we enter the building.

As soon as we step off the elevator at our floor, the receptionist, a woman who has worked for the company close to twenty-five years, runs out from behind the desk to greet Jeff. It's as if he's risen from the dead. I realize that while people may not know what he's battling against, they've known all along it's something serious. "Mr. Jones," she says. "It's so wonderful to see you."

"The pleasure is all mine, Rose," he says. "How's your grand-daughter?"

"I have two now," she says.

"They must adore you."

"I spoil them," she says, nodding. "May I get you some coffee?"

"Believe it or not, Rose, I cut out coffee when I got on this health kick."

"No!"

Jeff leans over to give her a kiss on the cheek. She blushes.

We make our way through the office. He stops to greet each employee who comes up to him in the same manner he greeted Rose. If he doesn't remember the person's name, he manages to recall something about the person, or at the very least, says something humorous or charming. Buzz and a general sense of excitement and hope spreads through the building. Upon entering Studio One, Jeff is actually greeted with a full-blown standing ovation.

"Thank you," Jeff says, clearly touched by it all. "Thank you."

Finally, everyone settles down. "It's so wonderful to be back, surrounded by all my favorite—" he pauses for emphasis "—mannequins."

Deadpan. Everyone laughs. Jeff catches my gaze. He has proved that the Parkinson "mask" is good for *something*. A feeling of awe moves through me.

"No, really," Jeff says. "Look around."

We look at one another. Then everyone glances about as Jeff points out the design samples and story boards, the industrial half- and full-body mannequins, both men's and women's, many of which are dressed or pinned. Floating at the back of the room are racks of the season's latest sample garments from Everyday wear to Couture. Against the wall are shelves overflowing with fabrics and textile samples, including the usual cotton twills, printed linens, cotton voile, silk crepe de Chine, and floral brocades. Nothing is new. Nothing particularly special.

"It all starts here," he says. "This—"

Tears swell to Marco's eyes.

"You," Jeff says, "are Jeff Jones."

"Yes," Marco agrees. "But the problem—"

Jeff holds up his hands to stop him from saying more. "I hear we have some Not Substantial Enough business to talk over," he says, unzipping the portfolio. "But, first, I'd like the honor of introducing a truly spectacular line, something that has taken years in the making, and in many ways it's a culmination of a life's work and experience. "This," he says, "is Amy's new and latest brainchild—"

He pulls out a sketch. The corset-top dress from my second thesis portfolio.

"This line will be geared toward the more mature, modern woman," he says.

Jayne gives my hand a soft squeeze.

"Finally 50," Jeff says. "These are the comeback women, the ones who were beautiful in their 20s and 30s but never seemed to know it on the inside. We all know one or two of these women, now, don't we?" He glances at me. At Jayne. The other's nod, yes, yes.

"Well, now they've come into themselves. They're more confident, more spiritual. They are 50, 55, 60. They realize exactly how beautiful they are. They walk down the street and it's 'Yes, look, this is the real me and I love it.'"

Jayne claps, and others follow suit.

Jeff hints at the fact that the board will meet to discuss returns being Not Substantial Enough. He suggests that there's going to be a new talent, someone he's asking us to train in this business and "raise" up. "Do it the way I have for you," he says now. "I'm counting on you, okay?"

By the end of the meeting, Jeff has slipped his left hand into his jacket pocket, and I realize there must be a tremor. He's tired; it has been a long day, especially since he wakes at 6 AM to start all his physical and cognitive therapies. Several employees want to stick around and have a word with Jeff, but I cap it after Jayne and Marco. I hook my arm through his, and we take the elevator down to the lobby. In the car, Jeff tells the driver to drop me off at my apartment before going home.

"No, I'll come back with you," I say, interlacing my fingers with his. I can feel the tremor, now. I thought it was in his hand, but it seems to come from somewhere deeper.

Jeff sighs. "Congratulations."

Warmth rises from my chest to the backs of my eyes. "Thank you," I say.

"I meant every word."

All the years flutter through my heart. Yearning, desire, addiction. Frustration. Depression. Wanting to be with him. Wanting to be free of him. Friends. Lovers. Disconnecting. Reconnecting.

Yet, here we are now. Love lost. Now found.

"Jeff," I whisper, because a dark hole opens inside my chest, and then everything's about to get sucked inside. "You can't leave me," I say.

"Either way, baby, I'm going. You know that."

His hand trembles over my cheek. I press mine over his.

"This is me," he says, kissing me, now.

"Yes," I say. "Yes."

Black Lace and Blue Secrets

"**Y**ou like?" I say, as my one and only grandchild, Kathryn, joins me in the living room to inspect my latest creation: a lace-up, 3-inch ankle boot. The quarters are made of a gunmetal-sequined fabric, the front vamp a black suede, the laces a thick satin.

"Ohhh," Kathryn says, holding the right boot. She settles on the red opium bed, which I doubled up with sofa-thick padding, and examines my workmanship. "They turned out beautifully."

"Très couture, don't you think?"

"Def. I'd ask for a pair, but I've already got something else in mind."

"Pray, tell, mademoiselle." I return the boot back to the top shelf with its partner. My apartment is unusual in that my bookshelves are filled with shoes and boots instead of books, and except for the first real pair of boots I ever purchased—a black-lace knee high stiletto—all were crafted since I retired ten years ago. They include Kathryn's first pair of shoes, hot pink Mary Janes, ballet flats, and lace-up riding boots. After a long and frightful Doc Marten stage during her high school years, elegance and beauty finally came back into vogue. Kathryn took to placing shoe orders with me, expressing ideas to add her own unique twist to things. "Your wish is my command," I say.

"I've got something I need to tell you first," she says, beating me to the punch. The purpose of calling her here is to discuss the company. Alex is in his 50s now; he isn't young anymore. It's time she learned the business.

Kathryn giggles. Whatever she has to say, it must be serious. I haven't heard her giggle since she was a teenager prone to crushes. She pats the seat beside her. "Come, Grandma. Sit with me."

I get this unsettling feeling that I'm being lowered into a lion's den. Kathryn is following in her Pop-Pop's footsteps. She's a star at FIT and already noticed in the industry. Her work at school was picked up by CoutureCulture; the Spring line received rave reviews. The buzz got her into some trendy New York boutiques, and then one of her A-line dresses appeared in *Vogue*. Is she planning a new line? I wonder. Does she need capital?

"I'm not so keen on surprises," I say.

"Just sit, Grandma." She smiles, teeth clenched with excitement. The red bed is up against the window with a view of the Hudson.

I sit turned toward her. She takes my hands in hers, and that's when I notice. A ring. 2 carat. Emerald cut. Platinum. Pavé frame.

"But—" All the disappointments in my life flash in front of me like a massive karmic flipbook, and in one single stroke, my hopes and expectations for Kathryn are suddenly dashed. How can this be? She is 21, the same age Jeff was when he first got noticed. Suddenly, the glare from outside hurts my eyes.

"I'm engaged!" she chirps, wiggling her fingers out in front of her. The diamond catches the light and sparks rainbows across the walls and ceiling. I feel as if I got sucker-punched. There's an ache in my heart, and yet I'm strangely numb to it. Kathryn, however, chatters on: "Vanessa invited friends over for her birthday, and when I asked who brought the Tiffany, she said she didn't know, she'd have to open it. So she did, and I was like wow, what the hell, and before I knew it, she was on her knee proposing, and at first, I had no idea what was even going on—" Kathryn laughs. "And then she says it's her birthday and there's nothing she'd love more than for me to be her wife!"

My darling Kathryn. All that potential. Lost. She could follow in her grandfather's footsteps or mine, and now I see she is choosing mine.

Kathryn continues on about the wedding—something about a tent affair—and the dress she's going to make, gesticulating with her arms as she describes the bodice. "It's going to be strapless with a silk corset on top, sort of like a mini with layers of feathery lingerie chiffon up to the mid thigh. So *lots* of leg. And then this awesome feathery train, you know?"

I nod as if I'm listening. On clear sunny days, the Hudson appears liquid silver. Sunlight glints off the river. With the help of a new, experimental treatment, Jeff defied the odds and remained stage 3 of the condition for the next ten years, finally passing as a result of pneumonia brought on by an upper respiratory infection. He left a quarter of his assets to each of his three children, and the last fourth to me. With it, I bought this apartment.

"You'll design a pair of boots for the wedding?" she asks.

"Hm?"

"Boots." She extends her long legs. "Short, maybe ankle? And lace. Definitely lace."

"Floral or mesh?"

"Floral. No mesh. I don't know."

"Three inch?"

"Four?"

"Platform?"

"Yes," she nods. "Oh, and black. The dress is black."

"As long as it's not black and blue." I mean it jokingly, yet as soon as the words leave my mouth, I feel the ache expanding in my chest. My life; hers. Repeating patterns. Karma. Is there a lesson to be learned from this? A way to change this in consciousness?

"What's wrong, Grandma?" she asks, taking my hand.

"Nothing."

"You sure? Because you don't look very happy. I thought you would be happy for me."

"Of course I am, sweetheart." But even as I say it, a voice inside says, There's no fucking way; who do you think you are? "It's just—" I sandwich her hand in mine. "Isn't marriage a little outdated these days? I mean the notion itself?"

"Oh, Grandma."

"Half of them fail." I don't need to mention her parents. Her mother remains bitter and alone while Alex has remarried and started a new life with a woman half his age. Kathryn frowns at me. I shrug. "I'm just saying."

"Looks like you've got some interesting beliefs about marriage," she says, crossing her arms and trying to sound as if she were me.

"I should know," I say. "I've done it twice."

"So, no more," she says. "That right?"

"Exactly."

She glances outside, then back at me, and point blank, says, "So is that what happened with Cameron?"

Cameron is the man I've just broken things off with; we'd been seeing each other for the past three years. We initially met through the Masters Class but got to know one another better at a Buddhist meditation retreat. Marriage—the idea of it—must be in the air. "I'm 78 years old. I'm too old for that business," I say.

"And I'm too young, right?"

"Uh, actually, yes, you are."

She shakes her head. "I never thought I'd hear you say you were too old for anything."

"Well, there's always a first time."

She sighs. "For what it's worth. I really liked Cameron."

I cross my arms. "He's a good man."

"What's that supposed to mean?"

"Are you looking for a hidden agenda here? Because this would be where you back off. As much as I love you."

"No, Grandma. I'm simply asking what it means. You're the one who tells me all the time to question my beliefs and ask if they serve me. It would be a shame if one stood in the way of you experiencing the true love of your life."

"So you have determined he's the true love of my life, now, have you?" I feel my blood pressure spike.

"Isn't he?"

"If you really need to know, Cameron doesn't believe in Viagra," I say.

Katheryn's eyes bulge. "TMI," she says, making a T with her hands.

"You asked."

She fidgets with the ring.

"Do you actually think people stop fucking when they get older? Or is it that you think orgasm is reserved only for the young?"

"I don't know. Sort of. I guess." Kathryn blushes. She catches my gaze and all of a sudden we're laughing until tears are flowing from our eyes. It takes a few minutes to gather myself. "No, seriously, Kathryn. You're doing so *well*. What's all the rush?"

She smiles. There's an earnestness about it that feels deadly. "We want to start a family."

My heart—everything—stops. What is wrong with this younger generation? They have freedom to choose who and what they want to be. What they want to do. Where they want to go. Everything my generation of women fought against, they embrace like shit got turned to diamonds.

"What about your career?" I ask.

"What about it?"

"Your father and I think it's time you joined JJ."

"Why would I do that?" she says. "I want to have my own line."

"The two are not mutually exclusive," I say. "The company could use your creative talent."

"I don't know, Grandma."

"Think about it, Kathryn. Your father's not getting any younger. In five or ten years, he'll be handing the reins over to you."

"What if I don't want it?"

"Not want it?" I yell. "This is Grandfather's legacy."

"Okay, I'll think about it."

"Think long and hard. The decisions you make now can impact your entire career. Your life."

"Oh, Grandma. Career and family aren't mutually exclusive either."

"Do you really think it's so easy to juggle kids with a career? Just like that?"

"Of course not."

"Have you given any thought—any thought at all—to who will take care of the kids while you are working?"

"Vanessa will help," she says. Vanessa is an academic with two published books—one about the politics of beauty and the other about feminism and fashion—who teaches in the women's studies department at Columbia. I thought her feminism, intelligence, and prudence would eventually butt up against Kathryn's unwavering impracticality and unbridled creative passion. If Kathryn gets an idea to do something—it could be designing a dress made from safety pins—everything else gets dropped until she successfully completes, or totally fails at, the task. From my viewpoint, what makes them such an incredible couple is how driven they both are to succeed in their careers, and I assumed, wrongly, I now realize, that the success of both their careers took priority over all else. Wouldn't it be possible for Kathryn to succeed as a fashion icon in her own right before squelching her energy and attention by focusing on marriage and children? At her age, I had assumed I could have it all, too, and look where it got me. A few golden years before retirement, and even that only because of Jeff. I was lucky.

"You don't really like her, do you?" Kathryn says.

"That's not true and you know it. She's one of the most comfortable people to be around. And, I love her brains."

"Well, I love her heart," she says, and maybe it's the way she says it, but I can actually feel the depth of her connection to Vanessa. Kathryn has my eyes, and with the lash extensions, her beauty can be overwhelming. But she's a third generation Master, and having been given the tools as a child, moves fearlessly through life without the resistance older people tend to have. At the workshop, we are reminded that we are source beings. Kathryn doesn't need reminding. She already *is*. Even now, I can feel her using one of the techniques to calm me down. Despite her own emotions, there is no judgement or anger or even frustration. Only light and compassion. And her attention, her appreciation for the struggle I am creating, shifts me out of the upset and fills me with warmth and love.

"God damn it," I say. "It's infuriating that you're using the techniques against me."

She smiles. "You're happy for me, aren't you?"

"Yes, sweetheart, I am." I brush the hair from Kathryn's face, and even though my heart is breaking, I can appreciate her both fully and deeply. Here is the most beautiful creation in my life.

Then I see her. I see myself.

A week later, Toby stops by my apartment to say hello. He has just returned from a healing workshop in Las Vegas. In his first lifetime, Toby was a grant writer and fundraiser for organizations like NAAS-CA, The National Association of Adult Survivors of Child Abuse, and NCADV, The National Coalition Against Domestic Violence. Now, he's laid that gauntlet down and practices as a vortex energy healer and speaker. Toby has a sixth sense, a survival skill he developed as a result of his experience with his father and me, and has a way of appearing when I'm at my worst.

Looking for inspiration for Kathryn's booties, I spent the past two days combing through fabric stores. Many specialize in Chantilly lace, yet none of them stand out to me. The quality of some varieties seems shoddy. Others seem too delicate. Shoemaking requires some stretching of the leather or fabric, and anything substandard or too delicate might tear. Upon returning home empty handed, I've sketched, scoured magazines and the Web, searching for ideas, and yet nothing comes to me. I'm as empty as the years during my first marriage. With each successive attempt, I feel a deeper sense of foreboding about the wedding, which fills me with dread and guilt.

Toby kisses me on the cheek. He's wearing a black henley, blue jeans, and black leather loafers that I made for him last year.

"They look great," I say. We enter the living area of my apartment. He glances quizzically at the magazine photos I've taped up on the walls and the numerous drawings, all pencil, strewn across the living room table, sofa, and floor. "A lot's happened in the last week."

"Ah," he says, his head tipping back slightly.

"She told you?" I shouldn't be surprised. As a child, Kathryn gravitated toward her godfather. She was in high school during her parents' contentious divorce, and it was Toby she confided in, often refusing to stay with Alex on his allotted days, and instead, coming to stay with me so Uncle Toby could take her to the movies or dinner or for a walk through Central Park. With me, she poured her heart into every creative outlet she could find, and later at FIT, she transformed all the pain into her creations, blossoming as an artist and developing a distinct fashion style.

"She was afraid she'd disappoint you," Toby says.

"Well," I say, stacking the papers and tossing them all aside and sitting down. "How was your workshop?"

"Successful." He nods. "Lots of meditation. Lots of gambling. What more could you want?"

"How those even go together in the same sentence is beyond me."

"It's all energy, you know that. I need to be certain I'm moving it correctly. As a healer, I mean. The craps table let me see how I was moving it. The dice gave me just the validation I needed." He grins. "I made a good three bucks."

"Wow."

"Not bad for a wedding present."

I bite my lip. Try to keep the hurt from leaking out.

"Come. Let's go for a float," he says, getting to his feet. He's told me about them before. Sensory deprivation tanks can induce a relaxed, meditative state. Sometimes euphoria. He stands with his back to the window. The sun hangs low in the sky behind him.

"You have an appointment?" I ask, squinting.

"In less than an hour." He stands up from the sofa. He offers to give me his appointment if the other float tank is not available when we arrive. I consider it because it's Monday, meditation night. I'd like to avoid Cameron. This will give me something to do instead.

"I don't know. What if I go crazy in there?" I wave a hand at all the drawings and pin ups. "I've got plenty to do."

"How can you create when you're sitting in upset and discouragement?"

I glance at the mess. "Literally."

"Don't worry, Mom." He extends an arm to me. "I'll be there with you."

I take my son's hand.

The float is a lime-tiled room within a room. Almost like an enclosed bath. The owner and I stand in the outer room while Toby hovers in the doorway. The owner, a gangly man in his 70s, tells me it has been in existence since the 60s. He explains that the water is kept at skin temperature, 94.5 degrees, and is saturated with epsom salts so that the body "floats" rather than sinks to the bottom. He points at the u-shaped pillow in the corner, indicating that it may be best to use it to keep from straining my neck. Finally, he insists that everyone must shower before entering.

"What's going to happen in there?" I ask Toby, once he's gone.

"Something," he says. "Or nothing. Whatever occurs, you're going to love it."

"I don't feel comfortable taking your float," I say, hedging now. Upon arriving, we learned the other tank would be occupied. Toby insisted on giving his session to me.

"They already fit me in for tomorrow at 11AM," he says. "I'm meeting Kathryn for lunch afterwards if you'd like to join us."

"Mm. Possibly."

He quiets. "May I ask you something? What is it *really* that's upsetting you so much?"

"I don't believe in marriage. You of all people should know that."

"You didn't react this way with Alex."

"So now I'm sexist? That's not fair and you know it."

"I do?"

"Look, I love all of you, each in your own way. But your brother is different. As brilliant as he was, he had no motivation outside of those video games. I figured he was content to live off his father's fortune."

"And you were right about him?"

Leave it to Toby to serve up the humble pie. What I had labelled as "destructive," Alex had used to create the possibility of healing and hope for millions of individuals suffering from ADHD and other neurocognitive disorders. He got to the underlying issues at the root of the problem.

"He's achieved infinitely more than I could ever have dreamed."

"Kathryn's not doing so badly either, if you ask me."

"It's not the money. Money doesn't mean anything. Jeff and I had money. But I still dropped everything to take care of Alex."

"And then me."

"Yes," I sigh. "Kathryn has talent. She has that special something that other people don't have. She's special. Okay? There, I said it."

"You're afraid she's going to make the same mistakes you did. End up with someone like my dad. Have regrets."

"Something like that."

"In essence, you'd like her to live out your dreams for you."

"That's not what I said."

"Isn't it?"

"No."

"So then what's really eating you?"

It's a valid question, and one that maybe only Toby has the ability to ask in a way that I can actually tolerate. "Go on," I snap, shoving him out the door. "Let's get on with this already."

"I'll be waiting out here—"

I shut the door on him. Set my purse on the folding seat. Then I peel away my clothes. Hang up my blouse. Fold my skirt. Remove my bra and undies. I take a rubber band to my hair, then blast the shower. Soaked, I shut it off and slide open the float chamber door. I step inside. The water feels lukewarm and comes up to the knee. It's thick, almost slimy and already not enjoyable. Now I have to lie down in it?

Fuck it. I kneel down and lay back, locating the pillow to scoot behind my head. The owner is right. Even with a floating device around my head, I can feel the tension in my neck. With my right hand, I set my fingers against the right side of the chamber, and with my left, I tap the light switch. My body rises through the murk. The water feels thick, almost gelatinous.

The room goes pitch dark. If a hand were to appear in front of my face, I would never see it. Maybe it's the city girl in me but this kind of darkness reminds me of horror movies just before someone gets violently murdered.

Why am I thinking about this right now? I wonder. My heart races and because the room is devoid of sound, the beats sound louder and faster than I've ever noticed before. Maybe I'm going to have a heart attack? Then what? Will someone find me here, naked and with my eyes bulging? I panic. But just as I start to flail around, my foot sweeps the bottom of the tank, and I feel downright foolish. I lay back again, and this time, focus on my breath the way I do every Monday night. I know the meditation by heart.

"Breathing in, I follow my in breath from the beginning to the end," Thich Nhat Hanh recites, "breathing out, I follow my out breath from the beginning to the end." There's the ring of the prayer bowl, low and deep, resonating through my body even as I think about it. I feel my body relax. Let go.

"Breathing in, I see that my in breath has become deeper; breathing out, I see that my out breath has become slower." My neck releases.

"Breathing in deeper, breathing out, slower." Tension drains from my body. The bell sounds again. *What belief is causing upset over Kathryn's marriage?* "Breathing in," Thich Nhat Hanh says, drawing me back. "I feel well when I'm breathing in…"

My body slips away. For a moment. For a lifetime. My life dissolves and only then does it show itself to me. There's the time I discover how to touch my own body, there in my princess bed, rubbing with my fingers, terrified someone might find out. *What belief?*

And Jeff. Our last visit to the bay beach, sharing a rainbow lollipop and watching the sun set over the ocean.

There's the moment when Alex is in surgery and I make a deal with God to give up my career, give up everything, so long as Alex survives.

There is Dad's wake, a train of people circling his casket, the entire room of relatives kowtowing—once, twice, then three times. *What belief?*

And Ma. The sudden onset of chest pain and shortness of breath less than two weeks after Dad's funeral, as if they'd been a close, elderly couple, walking hand in hand together for decades.

There's Kathryn's birth, her blanketed little body in my arms.

It's then, in the emptiness, and devoid of body and mind, when only memories and moments exist, that it's revealed to me. *She's going to be the queen of fashion.*

There it is: my queen, my hope, my promise.

My body buoys at the surface. I become aware of my beating heart, the coolness of my chest, my sagging nipples and toes just above the water. Then, all at once, I'm flying. I'm at the end of that shooting pain, a long red cord that extends outward. On one end, I'm attached to a body floating in a tank of water, and on the other, I'm a soul flying in space. Off to the left, in my peripheral line of vision is the Buddha, a statue-like image lit from behind. Each time I try to look at it directly, it shifts, remaining always in the periphery.

I'm flying. Making figure eights through the universe.

The light switches on. It shines through my eyelids. It brings me back to the moment at the back of the shoe store when I'm 16. The black lace boots. Only now, I'm floating on water. I sweep my hands over my body. Crotch, belly, breasts. I've found myself. Dry salt coats the dip between my breasts.

"Everything okay in there?" Toby calls from outside.

"Yes," I say, my eyes crusty from dry tears. "Oh, yes."

Upon returning home, I examine the black lace boots. Intricate floral lace with paisley drops. Nude interfacing to hold the shape of the boot.

Perfect. I measure the length of the fabric, and when I'm certain there's more than enough material to make booties, I take an X-acto knife to it, carefully separating the lace from the trim. Once that's done, I set it aside and get started with the rest of the boot, not leaving my apartment for an entire week. Kathryn and Toby stop by, separately, and when I don't allow either of them inside, I get an email from my daughter-in-law, Beth, who, despite being divorced from Alex, continues to be a close confident. "Would you like to meet for lunch?" she asks. Even Alex calls from Turks and Caicos where he is vacationing.

"What is it with you all?" I say, and I tell him what I told the others: "I'm busy."

The only person I don't hear from is Georgie, and that's likely because at 82, she's going deaf and doesn't answer the phone.

I sketch and re-sketch the boot until I "find" the right design. Booties sculpted just above the ankle bone. Black lace upper with a black suede trim. Peep toe and lace-up vamp. 4-inch, suede-covered stiletto heels.

To begin, I drape the last with masking tape, then rub it down with the back of the scissors. With a pencil, I draw in the featheredge, the center front line and center back line. I measure and mark the counter and vamp points. Next, I transfer the design of the boot onto the last, and with an OLFA knife, cut down the center, removing the tape from the last. I take this formé pattern and flatten it onto manila cardboard. I cut it out, then window and bridge the style lines.

Inside quarter. Outside quarter. Vamp. I trace the shapes onto the lace and cut them out. Day shifts to night. Night shifts to day. I work and work. The sole, insole, heel. The inner vamp. I sew. Cut. Sew more. I check the cut, the stitching, the heel. The sun sets over a deep, lavender Hudson. I feel my entire life in each singular moment. I'm alive.

Finally, the booties are done. When Kathryn calls again, I invite her over. In my bedroom, I have a full length mirror. I move it to the living room. Situate it so that it faces the sofa. As soon as she arrives, she finds the boots on the living room table top.

"Oh Grandma," she sighs. She picks one up, holds the toe in one hand and the heel with the other. "Where did you find this lace? It looks just like—" she stops, glances at the empty shelf where my former boots had been displayed. "Oh, Grandma—" Emotion swells to her face.

"It's going to be a perfect wedding," I say, "for a perfect couple."

"I'll cherish them forever."

"You better. Now, try them on."

She's wearing a pair of Louboutins and a mini dress to show off her legs. She steps out of the pumps. I kneel before her and slip them on. Right foot. Left.

"A perfect fit," I say.

"I feel like a princess," she says.

"That's because you are. Now walk for me."

She models them, taking my apartment hallway like it's the runway, and I can already see her long bold strides coming down the church aisle, my son at her side as she steps into this new stage of her life, the strapless corset dress with a layered chiffon mini, and trailing behind, a long and feathery train. All leg and vintage-lace boot.

Delicate. Resilient.

"There," I say. "Just beautiful."

Acknowledgments

Special thanks… Cliff Yu. All that you do makes it possible for me to be a happy mother, writer, (and shoemaker!). James & Tyler Yu. You give me hope. So proud of you. Charles Salzberg. You've been an incredible friend and teacher all these years. When I'm down, you pick me up. I cherish movie day. Please always be an elevator ride away. Jayne Bayer. When I moved to the city, I wanted to be close to friends. One floor down is pretty close. You are my family. Jolie Chylack. You are proof that God exists in people. The golden thread in my life. Marie Lee. For all your help and always getting my back. You are an inspiration. Michael Cunningham. Then at the beginning and now at a new one—you've always been there. Milda DeVoe. For getting me on my feet and back to work. Building the Pen Parentis community with you has been so rewarding in every way. Melanie Locay. Giving me a real space to work made this book possible. Mon Kammerman. You are a writer's block lifesaver. Vivian Conan. Your editorial feedback is invaluable. Amazed by you. Kristine Tenace, et al. in the M/Th workshops. Your incredible feedback makes a difference. Lucille Kaye. For believing in my future. Rebecca Masson. For clueing me in to the business aspects of fashion. Mat Johnson. You are a gem. Next time, speak up. Emily Putterman, Paula Gold, Lorraine Klagsbrun, Julie Dam, Ria Osborne, Veena Mosur, Rebecca Reisman, Kevin Silva, et al. from shoemaking. There's no one I'd rather skive or laugh with. Arlene Katz. Showing up has made all the difference. Marguerite Bouvard. For believing in my ability even when I don't. Ross Klavan. Talks with you kept me sane. Miriam Cohen. This one's for you. Val Dejean. Back on track because of you. Frank Gomez. Being around you is like standing in sunlight. Sheila Pleasants. Thanks for lifting me up and dusting me off. Mignon Chiu & Janinne Milazzo. For fighting the good fight. Terry Biaggi, Tina Fanelli, Karen Guttman, Patty

Lang, et al. from knitting. For being there through the worst of it. The only thing better than knitting that coat is the friendships we knit together. Kathryn Herrington, Pam & Bill Berger. For listening. The Cape with you will always be some of my fondest memories. Maxine Hong Kingston, Lan Samantha Chang, Cari Luna, David Ebenbach, Helen Benedict, Elissa Schappell, Jean Kwok, Helen Schulman, Sergio Troncoso, Sharon Gurwitz for swooping in to save the day. You have my appreciation forever. Andrew Gifford. For not just believing there is a need, but doing something about it. Gish Jen. For choosing *Beauty* and seeing its soul. Allen Gee. You are the editor I've been searching for. So happy I found you.

Thank you Virginia Center for the Creative Arts, Hedgebrook, U Cross, and The Ragdale Foundation for believing in me and other artists who need a moment of paradise to create. The time and space to work and rest made it possible for me to keep plugging along. I'm here for you always.

Love to Ayana Matthews and Anne Fontaine for making one of the best moments of my life so utterly beautiful.

Much appreciation also goes to Columbia University School of the Arts, Bates College, the New York Public Library and the Wertheim Room, The New York Writers Workshop, The Marlene Meyerson JCC Manhattan, The Asian American Arts Alliance, The Asian American Writers' Workshop, *Poets & Writers*, Pen Parentis, Prison Writes and Youth Writes.